Lisa B. Kamps

A York Bombers Hockey Novel, Book 5

LISA B. KAMPS

Lisa B. Kamps

PLAYING IT SAFE

For Cindy and Joel
A match made in heaven!

Playing It Safe
Copyright © 2018 by Elizabeth Belbot Kamps

All rights reserved. Except for use in any review, the reproduction or utilization of this work in whole or in part in any form by any electronic, mechanical or other means, now known or hereafter invented, including xerography, photocopying and recording, or in any information storage or retrieval system, is forbidden without the express written permission of the author.

The York Bombers™ is a fictional semi-professional ice hockey team, its name and logo created for the sole use of the author and covered under protection of trademark.

All characters in this book have no existence outside the imagination of the author and have no relation to anyone bearing the same name or names, living or dead. This book is a work of fiction and any resemblance to any individual, place, business, or event is purely coincidental.

Cover and logo design by Jay Aheer of Simply Defined Art
http://www.simplydefinedart.com/

Photographer: CJC Photography
http://www.cjc-photography.com

Cover Model: Gideon Connelly
https://www.instagram.com/gideoncon/

Proofreading by Cat Parisi of Cat's Eye Proofing and Promos
https://www.facebook.com/catseyeproofingpromos/

All rights reserved.
ISBN: 1985726785
ISBN-13: 978-1985726789

CONTENTS

Title Page iii
Dedication v
Copyright vi
Other titles by this author ix

CHAPTER ONE 13
CHAPTER TWO 24
CHAPTER THREE 32
CHAPTER FOUR 45
CHAPTER FIVE 54
CHAPTER SIX 63
CHAPTER SEVEN 72
CHAPTER EIGHT 81
CHAPTER NINE 94
CHAPTER TEN 102
CHAPTER ELEVEN 109
CHAPTER TWELVE 115
CHAPTER THIRTEEN 123
CHAPTER FOURTEEN 130
CHAPTER FIFTEEN 137
CHAPTER SIXTEEN 143
CHAPTER SEVENTEEN 153
CHAPTER EIGHTEEN 160

CHAPTER NINETEEN	168
CHAPTER TWENTY	178
CHAPTER TWENTY-ONE	186
CHAPTER TWENTY-TWO	193
CHAPTER TWENTY-THREE	202
CHAPTER TWENTY-FOUR	212
CHAPTER TWENTY-FIVE	217
CHAPTER TWENTY-SIX	224
CHAPTER TWENTY-SEVEN	236
CHAPTER TWENTY-EIGHT	243
CHAPTER TWENTY-NINE	250
CHAPTER THIRTY	257
EPILOGUE	264
About the Author	269
CROSSING THE LINE preview	271
WINNING HARD preview	277

Other titles by this author

THE BALTIMORE BANNERS

Crossing The Line, Book 1
Game Over, Book 2
Blue Ribbon Summer, Book 3
Body Check, Book 4
Break Away, Book 5
Playmaker (A Baltimore Banners Intermission novella)
Delay of Game, Book 6
Shoot Out, Book 7
The Baltimore Banners 1st Period Trilogy (Books 1-3)
The Baltimore Banners 2nd Period Trilogy (Books 4-6)
On Thin Ice, Book 8
Coach's Challenge (A Baltimore Banners Intermission Novella)
One-Timer, Book 9
Face Off, Book 10
First Shot At Love (A Baltimore Banners Warm-up Story)
Game Misconduct, Book 11
Fighting To Score, Book 12
Matching Penalties, Book 13

THE YORK BOMBERS

Playing The Game, Book 1
Playing To Win, Book 2
Playing For Keeps, Book 3
Playing It Up, Book 4
Playing It Safe, Book 5
Playing For Love, Book 6
Playing His Part, Book 7

Lisa B. Kamps

THE CHESAPEAKE BLADES

Winning Hard, Book 1
Loving Hard, Book 2
Playing Hard, Book 3
Trying Hard, Book 4
Falling Hard, Book 5

FIREHOUSE FOURTEEN

Once Burned, Book 1
Playing With Fire, Book 2
Breaking Protocol, Book 3
Into The Flames, Book 4
Second Alarm, Book 5

STAND-ALONE TITLES

Emeralds and Gold: A Treasury of Irish Short Stories
(anthology)
Finding Dr. Right, Silhouette Special Edition
Time To Heal
Dangerous Passion

CHAPTER ONE

"I hate you! I wish you were dead!"

Aaron Malone schooled his face into an expressionless mask, refusing to let his daughter see how much the words hurt. It didn't matter because Brooke spun on her heels and ran into the house, sliding the patio door behind her with such force, he was surprised it didn't come off the track.

A small hand gripped his, the flesh of the trembling fingers cool against his callused palm. He looked down and saw Isabelle staring up at him with wide eyes that were already filling with tears.

"Daddy?" Isabelle's soft voice shook with uncertainty and a hint of fear. Aaron swallowed back his own hurt and kneeled next to his youngest daughter. He hid the pain the movement caused behind a forced smile and ran his hand through Isabelle's long hair.

"It's okay, Sweet Pea. Brookie's mad at me, not you." No, she was mad at the world and had been since that awful night four months ago when her mother died. But Aaron couldn't say that out loud, not to Isabelle. Not when the ten-year-old had gone through the same nightmare as her sister. Their worlds had been turned upside down, their safe existence shattered when Aaron's ex-wife had been killed in a car crash.

Had they heard the rumors? Did they know it was because she'd been out partying with her latest boyfriend? That they had both had too much to drink, but he decided to drive anyway?

The accident had taken both their lives, leaving behind so much more than the remnants of charred, shattered wreckage. Aaron wondered again if he had done the right thing, moving his daughters back here to live with him in Pennsylvania, uprooting them and taking them away from everything they had known for the last four years.

Forcing them to live with a father they had only seen a week at a time for those same years.

He shoved the doubts from his mind. Yes, of course he'd done the right thing. They were his daughters. His flesh and blood. No way was he going to leave them with his ex-wife's parents a thousand miles away, no matter how many arguments and obstacles they had thrown in his path.

It was the right decision, no matter how often he questioned it.

No matter how many times Brooke fought against it.

Aaron pressed a quick kiss on the top of his youngest daughter's head then pushed to his feet, grimacing at the pain shooting through his knee. "Why don't you go in and grab the plates and bring them outside while I finish cooking?"

Isabelle hesitated, that heart-wrenching expression of sadness and uncertainty still on her face as she stared up at him. Then her face cleared, the sadness replaced by a small smile that made his heart lurch in his chest.

"Okay, Daddy." Isabelle tugged her hand from his then skipped across the patio and into the house. He watched as she slid open the door, watched as she carefully closed it behind her.

So different from her sister.

Aaron sighed, the sound weary even to his jaded ears, then turned back to the grill to check on the chicken breasts. Six of them lined the grate, thick and plump and dripping with barbecue sauce. What the hell had he been thinking, putting so many on? He wasn't cooking for a few of his teammates—he was cooking for himself and his two daughters.

Sure, he'd eat two with no problem. Isabelle might eat half of one. And Brooke...well, he doubted Brooke would even come out of her room to join them for dinner.

He sighed again, squinting against the gentle smoke coming from the grill as he turned each breast. Four months. Shouldn't he have learned how to cook for his own daughters in that time?

Yes, he should have. But there was so much to learn, too many mistakes just waiting to be made. And too many mistakes to be made up for.

Motion from the corner of his eye caught his attention and he looked over, surprised to see Savannah Weber walking toward him, two bottles hanging from her long fingers.

"Looked like you could use one." She held out one bottle, a small grin curling the corners of her full mouth. Aaron hesitated then accepted the beer with a small grunt of thanks. He twisted off the cap and lifted the bottle to his mouth, watching the woman standing next to him as he drank the beer.

Savannah had moved in next door a year ago, and they often ran into each other if they were outside. Not hard to do, considering their houses were barely twenty feet apart and no fence separated their yards. And he'd grown accustomed to their chats, to the time they spent together and the way she made him feel: grounded, relaxed. At ease.

She was friendly, with an easy, open smile that sparkled in her hazel eyes. Light brown hair framed her oval face, the blunt ends gently curled under just below her chin. He had no idea what the style was called but it suited her: crisp and sharp and somehow easy-going at the same time. She did something in marketing, he had no idea what, and worked a lot from home.

He'd thought about asking her out once, but never did. What would a professional woman like Savannah ever see in a beat-up, worn-down, past-his-prime hockey player like him? Nothing. She was funny and bright and striking and probably had lots of men asking her out. She sure as hell could find better.

Not that it mattered, not anymore. He had his daughters to worry about now.

Aaron pulled his gaze from hers, surprised at the heat filling his face and hoping like hell she hadn't been able to see what he was thinking. He sat the bottle next to the grill and reached for the tongs, more for something to do. "I guess Brooke was a little loud."

Savannah shrugged, that small smile still playing around the corners of her mouth as she leaned against the picnic table. "I take it things didn't go well today?"

"You could say that." Aaron flipped the breasts one last time then reached for the beer. He'd taken both girls to register them for school today, to make sure all the paperwork was done and their records transferred before the school year started in a few weeks. Isabelle had been quiet and a little curious, just as he'd expected. And Brooke—

Well, Brooke had gone in full of attitude, all of it negative as she found fault with everything, from the layout of the middle school to its proximity to the elementary school to the classes she'd be taking.

Just as he'd expected.

Savannah's smile turned sympathetic. Her gaze drifted to the house, then slowly back to his. "Give her time. She's still adjusting."

"I know." Aaron looked away from those clear hazel eyes that seemed to see so much more than he was willing to show. He cleared his throat then pulled the chicken from the grill, wondering again why he'd put on so many. The leftovers would go into the refrigerator, where they'd be forgotten until he tossed them later in the week. Unless…

He didn't stop to think, didn't even question the sudden impulse. "Did you, uh, feel like staying for dinner? I made too much and the girls will never eat it all so there's plenty to go around. If you want, I mean."

Savannah's laughter caught him off-guard. Breathy and light, it wrapped around him, warming him in ways he hadn't felt in years. It wasn't just her laughter, either—it was the way she was looking at him, with her head tilted to the side so the ends of her hair brushed against the gentle slope of her bare shoulder. Her full mouth curled into a charming smile.

"How could I resist such an irresistible invitation?"

Damn, there it was again, that annoying heat that filled his face. Too late, he realized how he had phrased the invite and he looked away, wondering if she noticed the blush creeping across his cheeks. He opened his mouth, tried to stammer out an apology, and was saved from saying anything by the sound of the back door sliding opening then closing again.

Isabelle's face was scrunched up in concentration as she made her way across the patio, her hands filled with plates and silverware. Three glasses—the real kind, not plastic—wobbled from their perch on top of the plates. Aaron tossed the tongs down, his breath held as his gaze locked on those wobbling glasses, knowing they were seconds away from crashing to the patio.

He started to move but Savannah was quicker, her long, slim legs reaching Isabelle in three quick strides. She leaned over and rescued the glasses just as they started to topple, catching them before they could hit the pavers and splinter into a thousand shards that would have sliced Isabelle's thin legs.

"Looks like you've got your hands full, kiddo. Let me help."

His daughter looked up at Savannah, a shy smile of gratitude on her face. "Thank you."

Aaron released the breath he'd been holding then turned back to the grill and reached for the tongs. Heat seared his thumb and he quickly dropped them, swallowing back the curse that wanted to tumble from his mouth. He glanced at his thumb then brought it to his mouth, sucking on the small burn across the fleshy pad as he called himself an idiot for not paying closer attention.

"You okay?"

He glanced over, surprised to see Savannah by his side, amusement dancing in her hazel eyes as she stared at his hand.

No, not at his hand—at his thumb, which was still in his mouth like he was some stupid baby. He yanked his hand away, rubbed it against the leg of his gym shorts, then reached for the tongs again, this time making sure his hands stayed safely away from the grill.

"Yeah, fine. Wasn't paying attention."

Savannah laughed, the sound light and carefree, then turned back to Isabelle. "Did you need help setting the table?"

"Yes, please."

A lump settled in Aaron's chest, one that wouldn't disappear no matter how many times he swallowed. How stupid was it to read so much into the fact that Savannah had asked if she could help, instead of just taking over? Yeah, that was pretty damn stupid.

He turned off the grill and grabbed the platter of breasts then stood there, watching as Savannah helped Isabelle set the table. Three plates. Three glasses. Three forks and three knives. Three napkins.

Three.

"Isabelle, Savannah's going to join us for dinner so we need one more place setting."

Surprise flashed in his daughter's eyes, quickly replaced with excitement when she looked over at Savannah. Aaron's gut twisted at the sight. Was it simply because Isabelle happened to like their neighbor, or was there something more to it? Was Isabelle craving a mother's presence more than he realized? Or was it just a woman's presence that she needed?

Doubt threaded its way through his mind once again. Not for the first time, he wondered if he had done the right thing by bringing the girls to live with him. Yes, he was their father, but they barely knew him. And he knew nothing about raising girls.

He knew nothing about raising kids, period.

He pushed the doubts away, shoving them into a corner of his mind and ruthlessly slamming a mental door on them. He was their father. Bringing them here was the right thing to do. No, it hadn't been an easy four months, and they still had a lot of bumps ahead of them, but they were *his* daughters. They belonged with him.

Savannah and Isabelle disappeared into the house, returning a few minutes later carrying a pitcher of iced tea and the tray holding the salad he had tossed earlier along with the tub of coleslaw—

And no additional place setting.

Savannah must have seen his questioning look because she caught his eye and quickly shook her head as Isabelle put the tray on the table.

"Brooke said she wasn't coming out to eat. And..." Isabelle hesitated, then leaned closer and lowered her voice to a loud whisper. "And she called Miss Savannah a bad word."

Anger mingled with embarrassment coursed through Aaron and he darted a glance at Savannah. "She *what*?"

"It's okay, she's just going—"

"No, it's not okay. She can be mad at me all she wants, but that's no excuse to talk to you that way."

Savannah stepped closer and placed her hand on his arm, the touch gentle and reassuring. "Aaron, really, it's okay. I'll just go home—"

"It's not okay. And you don't need to go home. I invited you for dinner." Aaron stepped away from her, felt the late-summer breeze brush against his skin where her hand had just been. Odd, how chilled that breeze felt compared to the warmth of her touch. He gave himself a mental shake then motioned to the bench across from him. "Sit. The chicken's getting cold."

"Aaron, it's not—"

"I said sit." He realized how gruff he sounded, like he was barking orders. Savannah's brows shot up, a small smile teasing the corners of her mouth. Heat filled his face again as he cleared his throat. "Uh, I mean, please."

"But Brooke—"

"Needs to learn she's not going to get away with this kind of behavior. She can join us if she gets hungry." Aaron slid onto the bench and stabbed a chicken breast with his fork. He dropped it onto Savannah's plate then stabbed a second one for Isabelle and cut it in half, watching Savannah from the corner of his eye, his breath held as he waited to see what she would do.

The small smile on her face bloomed into a grin as she finally took a seat across from him. An answering grin curled his own lips as he spooned coleslaw onto Isabelle's plate then passed the tub to Savannah.

"I feel bad, thinking that Brooke is missing out on dinner because of me."

"It has nothing to do with you. It's her choice, and she needs to learn choices have consequences." Aaron finished helping Isabelle cut her chicken, then filled his own plate.

"She's—what? Thirteen?"

"Yeah." *Thirteen, going on thirty.* He didn't say the words out loud; Savannah's sympathetic smile let him know he didn't have to.

"That's a tough age. And with everything else going on…" Savannah tossed a glance at Isabelle then offered Aaron a shrug. "It'll get better."

"That's what I keep hoping."

"It will. Just give it time."

"Yeah, but how much? Training camp starts next month. Then the regular season. Road games. I was hoping—" Aaron stopped, swallowing back the words with a bite of chicken. He'd been hoping for a miracle, but he couldn't say that out loud, not without sounding ridiculous.

Savannah popped a slice of cucumber into her mouth then chewed and swallowed. "Have you figured out how you're going to juggle the schedule?"

"For the most part. My mom's going to be helping out as much as she can, coming to stay when we're on the road. And on the nights we're playing home, if she can't watch them, I'll bring them to the games with me. Harland's wife said she could watch them." No, it wasn't the best arrangement, but it would work. At least until he could think of something better.

"I like Miss Courtney." Isabelle wiped the barbecue sauce from her mouth, completely missing the smear on her cheek, and gave Savanna a big smile. "She has a little boy and she lets me help watch him sometimes."

"Yeah? Sounds cool."

Isabelle bobbed her head up and down with an enthusiastic smile. "It is."

Savannah smiled at Isabelle then looked at Aaron, her hazel eyes steady on his. "If you find yourself in a pinch, you can always call me."

"Thanks, but I couldn't impose—"

"You wouldn't be imposing. I offered, remember?"

Aaron opened his mouth to tell her no, then snapped it shut again. No, he wouldn't take advantage of Savannah like that, it didn't matter if she offered or not. But it was better to keep his options open, just in case something unexpected came up. "Thank you."

"Not a problem. Besides, I think it would be fun. What do you think, Isabelle?"

"I think it would be fun, too! But I don't think Brooke would like it."

Aaron stared at his daughter in surprise. "Isabelle—"

"But she wouldn't, Daddy. Brooke doesn't like anything anymore. Not even me."

Aaron clenched his jaw, anger and sorrow filling him at the way Isabelle's lips trembled on those last words. He reached over and ruffled her hair, then pulled her in for a quick side hug. His gaze darted to the windows upstairs. The curtain in Brooke's room swayed just a little, like someone had been watching and quickly stepped back, afraid of being seen.

Was she up there now, watching? Was she sorry she wasn't down here with everyone else? Or was she still angry, spiting herself just to make a point?

Probably both. And Aaron had no idea what to do about it, no idea how to bridge the distance that kept growing between them.

CHAPTER TWO

Savannah sat at the patio table, the glass of water held halfway to her mouth totally forgotten as she tried to pry her tongue loose. Thank God she was wearing sunglasses, because she was certain that her eyes were bugging out at the sight next door.

Aaron Malone had just returned from his run, his skin flushed and damp with sweat. The muscles of his arms, thick and well-defined, moved and bulged as he grabbed the hose and turned on the spigot. He leaned over, bent at the waist, and doused his hair with the stream of water, then drank greedily from the hose. She let her hidden gaze drift across his body, from the muscles working in his strong throat with each swallow, to the damp tank shirt clinging to his broad chest, to the loose gym shorts hanging low on lean hips. And his thighs…God in heaven, those thighs. They were like tree trunks, thick with muscle, powerfully built from all the years spent on the ice.

How many times had she stared at him, just like this, over the last year? Too many, to the point of being pathetic. But her neighbor was such a fine specimen of manhood that it would be criminal *not* to watch—and enjoy herself doing it.

And the man was completely clueless. He had no idea how good-looking he was, no idea how just seeing him made her heart race and made sweat break out on her palms. It didn't matter if he was returning from a run, all hot and sweaty like he was now, or leaving for a game, dressed in one of his immaculate suits. And dear God, the first time she had seen him in a suit had nearly made her faint in appreciation. The way the expensive material had draped his rugged body was sinful.

So deliciously sinful.

Savannah sighed, a breathy sound of desire mingled with regret. Yes, she had the hots for her neighbor. Had fantasized about running her palms all over that rugged, chiseled body, had wondered how his skin would feel against hers. Had dreamt about the sensation of his large, callused hands skimming along her own heated flesh.

But that's all it was: a fantasy. And that's all it ever would be. Not only was Aaron completely oblivious to his effect on her, she truly doubted if he saw her as anything more than his next-door neighbor. A casual acquaintance, nothing more. And now that his daughters were living with him…

Savannah sighed again. Oh well. At least she could still fantasize.

"Are you sure you don't want to just run over and jump him? Get him out of your system?"

Savannah reluctantly dragged her gaze from Aaron's body and resettled it on her best friend, Tessa Franklin. She took a sip of her water then placed the glass on the table next to her with a small shake of her head. "I don't know if that's even possible."

"What? Jumping him? Or getting him out of your

system?"

"Both. But especially the first one. The man is totally oblivious."

Tessa lowered her sunglasses to the tip of her nose then shifted in her chair, turning to study Aaron. Her head tilted from one side to the other then she turned back to Savannah and shook her head. "Nope. Don't see it."

"Don't see what?"

"The attraction. Or maybe I should say *obsession*. Because that's what you are, you know: obsessed. And I honestly don't get it."

"How can you even say that? I mean, God, just look at him!"

"I am. I did. And I still don't get it. I mean, okay, fine. Sure. Yes, he's built like a freaking tree. But there's just something about him. He's what my aunt would call an 'old soul'. And there always seems to be this heavy sadness around him. In fact, I don't think I've ever seen him smile."

"You've never even met him. And he does so smile." Savannah immediately jumped to his defense, which told her more than anything else that maybe Tessa had a point. Maybe she *was* obsessed. "He's just going through a lot right now, especially now that his daughters are living with him."

"That's another thing. His daughters. Plural. Seriously? Why would you even think about getting involved with someone who had all that baggage with him? Especially you. How many times have I heard you swear off family?"

"That's not the point."

"It's exactly the point. You don't want a family, Van. How many times have you told me that? You're happy by yourself, living life on your own terms."

"Good grief, Tessa. I'm talking about having sex, not doing a reboot of the Brady Bunch."

"Uh-huh. Sure. Except your neighbor isn't the kind of man you just have sex with, and you know it." Tessa tucked a long strand of sleek blonde hair behind her ear and re-crossed her long legs. She glanced over her shoulder then turned back to Savannah. "That man has way too much baggage. Do yourself a favor, stay away."

"He doesn't have 'baggage'—he has two daughters. That's not exactly the same thing."

Tessa reached for her glass, making a small humming sound as she raised it to her mouth. Savannah leaned back in her chair and stared at her friend. "What's that supposed to mean?"

"What?"

"That little sound."

"Nothing."

"Why don't I believe that?"

"Probably because you know me too well." Tessa laughed and leaned forward. "Listen, Van. I know you like him. But do you really want to get involved with a man who has a ready-made family? One that he's still trying to figure out himself? You said yourself that he was struggling with the whole parenting thing. And that his oldest daughter was trouble waiting to happen."

"That doesn't mean—"

"Think about it. His *oldest* daughter. A teenager. Rebellious. Headstrong. Hates her father. Why would you even want to go there?" Tessa sat back and shook her head. "That way lies insanity. Do yourself a favor, find someone you have more in common with.

Someone not quite so old."

"Aaron is not *old*."

"He has a teenage daughter! How old do you think that makes him?"

"For your information, he's only thirty-four. Just a few years older than you and I."

Tessa's brows shot up. She glanced over her shoulder again, a frown settling on her face. She shook her head then turned back to Savannah. "Well, he looks older. Just do yourself a favor and get over it already."

Now it was Savannah's turn to utter a noncommittal hum. She ignored Tessa's knowing glance and pretended to study the laptop in front of her. Not that she actually saw anything on the screen. It didn't matter because she wasn't fooling Tessa and she knew it.

Maybe her friend was right. Maybe she had let her tiny crush bloom into this odd obsession that was blinding her to reality. Aaron had his hands full with his daughters, with trying to figure out how to be a father. Isabelle was a sweet kid but Brooke…yes, he was definitely going to have his hands full with that one. And she had sworn off ever having family of her own. Growing up as an only child in a dysfunctional, divorced household had taken care of that urge. Besides, she enjoyed her freedom too much, enjoyed being her own boss and not having to answer to anyone, professionally or personally. She had worked hard to get where she was and liked her life just the way it was, thank you very much.

It was just such a shame, because she really, really liked him.

She lifted her head, ready to ask Tessa if she wanted to go out later and do something—anything to get her mind off her neighbor—and jumped in surprise. Aaron was walking toward them, his gait strong despite the small limp as he favored his right leg.

She straightened in the chair, resisting the urge to do something stupid, like toss her hair or lick her lips or reach down to undo another button on her shirt. "Aaron. Hi. Went out jogging, I see."

And oh God, did she sound as lame as she thought she did? Judging by the look Tessa gave her, yes. She couldn't see her friend's eyes behind the dark lenses of her sunglasses but she didn't need to—she could *feel* Tessa's eye-roll.

"Yeah. Trying to get a head start on training camp." He shifted his weight from one foot to the other, tossing a curious glance at Tessa. Savannah mentally smacked herself then made a quick introduction. Aaron shook Tessa's hand then stood back, looking uncomfortable and out of place.

"Where are the girls? I haven't seen them outside today."

"Shopping for school clothes with their grandmother. I was told I'd cramp their style if I went."

Savannah laughed at the expression on Aaron's face, like he couldn't quite understand how he would cramp anyone's style. She choked the laughter back and quickly looked away. "You probably wouldn't have enjoyed it."

"No, I guess not." He ran a hand through his damp hair, pushing it back off his forehead, then cleared his throat. "I just stopped by to let you know we're having a cookout Saturday. Some of the guys are coming over and all. You're more than welcome to stop by if you want."

"Oh. Um, yeah, sure. Maybe." She took a deep

breath and looked away. She should say no, tell him she had other plans. Not that he'd actually invited her or anything but still…this would be the perfect time to start weaning herself from her obsession. "I think I have plans though."

Tessa kicked her under the table. "You don't have any plans."

"Yes, I do."

"No, you don't."

Savannah narrowed her eyes at Tessa. "I do. I have that thing."

"What thing?"

"You know. That *thing*. The thing we were just talking about? That you said I needed to get over and finish?"

Tessa elbowed her then turned to Aaron with a bright smile. "She doesn't have a thing. She'll be there."

"Tessa!" Savannah hissed her name, then slid down in the chair and lowered her head to hide the blush heating her face—but not before she saw the confusion crossing Aaron's face.

"Okay. Great. You're more than welcome to join us, too."

"Sounds like fun."

Savannah watched as Aaron turned to leave, her breath held until he was safely out of earshot. Then she leaned forward and smacked Tessa on the arm. "What are you doing? Are you insane?"

"No, why?"

"Weren't you the one who just sat there, not two minutes ago, and told me to get over it already?"

"I changed my mind."

"Changed your mind about what?"

"About him. That man has the saddest eyes I've

ever seen. He needs some happiness in his life. Of the horizontal kind."

"And what does that have to do with me?"

"Everything." Tessa lowered her sunglasses down her nose and fixed Savannah with a steady gaze that was both determined and amused. "You need to have sex with that man. Lots of sex. Hot, steamy, sweaty, mind-blowing sex."

"Tessa—"

"Because if you don't, I will."

CHAPTER THREE

The day was bright and clear, an almost perfect day, if not for the humidity. But it was mid-August, and the humidity was to be expected. At least it was tolerable. Mostly. And Savannah had dressed for it, in a loose pair of bright blue linen shorts and a crisp blue-and-white striped sleeveless shirt with tiny buttons marching down the front. Her brightly-colored toenails, their color almost perfectly matching her shorts, peeked out from the open weave of the wedge sandals on her feet. She looked cool, comfortable, and poised...

And completely out of place.

She shifted on the overstuffed patio chair and glanced around at the small crowd dressed in loose t-shirts and gym shorts or cargo shorts. When Aaron had said 'the guys', he hadn't been kidding. Only a few other women were there—three, to be exact, and they were obviously the wives or girlfriends of some of the players. Aaron had smiled when she walked over—without Tessa, who had backed out at the last minute, the traitor—and motioned for her to join him. He had made quick introductions and she was only able to catch half the names, not that it mattered because it didn't seem like anyone else was really paying attention. Then Aaron had been distracted by something else and he walked away, disappearing into the house.

Savannah had stood there for a full minute, feeling like an outsider. Then she mentally shrugged and headed to the cooler, helping herself to a wine cooler before moving over here to the patio.

Where'd she been sitting by herself for the last fifteen minutes.

She wiped the condensation from the bottle then took a small sip, her gaze still wandering. Tessa would die when she found out what she was missing. A dozen men, their athletic bodies on clear display, mingled amongst themselves, laughing and joking. And every single one of them was drop-dead gorgeous.

Served Tessa right, she thought.

One of the women walked over, her dark blonde hair pulled back in a messy bun, a young boy in tow. The boy was maybe three or four, his face scrunched in a comical expression of stubborn anger. The woman pointed to one of the empty seats, her fingers moving in rapid sequence as she spoke.

"You know better, young man. Now sit. You have a time-out."

The boy made a loud huffing sound and crossed his skinny arms in front of his chest, pointedly looking away from the woman. She stepped in front of him and leaned down, her fingers moving again. "Noah Robert Day, don't even try that with me. Now sit."

The boy hesitated, obviously on the verge of mutiny, then reluctantly climbed into the chair with another odd-sounding sigh. His legs swung back and forth, his lower lip pushed out in a classic pout. His gaze darted to hers, looked away, then shyly darted back as a tiny smile curled his pink mouth.

Savannah bit down on the inside of her cheek and looked away from the little charmer.

The woman—obviously the boy's mother—rolled her eyes then tapped the boy on the shoulder and made a few more signs with her fingers before dropping into the seat beside him with a loud sigh.

She looked over at Savannah and smiled. "He's entirely too much like his father."

Savannah smiled and nodded, not knowing what to say. Since she had no idea who the boy's father was, she couldn't really comment. But she could at least make an attempt at conversation. "How old is he?"

"He just turned three in April. And he's definitely learning to push his boundaries." The woman's laugh was gentle, like she had expected nothing different from the cute boy next to her. Savannah felt a small pang in her chest when she saw the pure adoration and love in the woman's eyes as she glanced at her son. What was it like, to feel that much love for your child? What was it like, to be totally responsible for the life and well-being of someone so young?

She had no idea, and nothing in her life had even given her a small taste of experience she could draw on. Her own parents had loved her—in their own way. But they'd been so caught up in their professional lives, bouncing her back and forth between them, that she sometimes felt as if she had been nothing more than an after-thought. She certainly didn't remember ever seeing either one of them look at her the way this woman was looking at her son.

The woman turned her gaze to Savannah then leaned forward, one slender hand held out. "I'm Courtney Day. Harland's wife."

Savannah accepted the woman's hand. "Savannah Weber. And I don't know anyone here, so I have no idea who that is."

Courtney laughed and sat back in the cushioned seat, shifting to tuck one slender leg under her. She nodded to the boy next to her. "Well, this little guy here is Noah. And Harland is the one standing over there next to the cooler."

Savannah looked over her shoulder, her gaze resting on the three men standing where Courtney had pointed. All three were a little taller than average. One of the men had dark blonde hair, shorter in the back and a little longer in front, so it fell across his forehead and into his eyes. The second man had thick black hair and the most startling pale blue eyes she had ever seen. The third man looked more serious than the other two, brooding and somehow dangerous. Or maybe it was just the assortment of tattoos covering his arms that gave her that impression. Yes, that must be it, because the man's face lit up in a devastatingly sexy smile when a lithe woman with gorgeous red hair walked up to him and pressed a quick kiss against his cheek.

"That's Haley, Zach Mummert's girlfriend. The guy with the pale eyes is Jason Emory. And the one with the crooked smile looking this way is my husband."

Savannah turned back around, her gaze shooting to the young boy who was starting to squirm in the chair.

"Yes, he looks exactly like his father. Doesn't seem fair, since I did all the work." A sweet smile lit Courtney's face as she ran her hand over the boy's head. Then she focused her curious gaze on Savannah. "How long have you and Aaron been dating?"

Savannah nearly choked on the wine cooler. She dabbed her mouth with the back of her hand and quickly looked around, hoping nobody—particularly Aaron—had heard the question. "Um, we're not. I'm just the neighbor."

"Oh. I'm sorry. I just thought—well, that's what I get for being nosey, isn't it?"

Savannah waved off the woman's apology, chalking it up to a natural assumption. That's all it was, right? Yes, of course. There was no reason to think that maybe Aaron had said something to this woman to make her think that they were dating, so there was no reason for her heart to be skipping in her chest the way it was.

What was the word Tessa had used? *Obsessed*. Savannah still thought that description was a bit excessive, but she was starting to wonder if maybe her crush wasn't getting a little out of control.

Except she was twenty-nine—entirely too old to have a crush. What she had was a bad case of pent-up sexual frustration. Yes, that was definitely it, because she could feel her face heating from simply thinking about it.

"So how long have you known Aaron?"

"Hm?" Savannah pushed the heated thoughts from her mind and forced her attention back to the other woman. "About a year, I guess. Since I moved in."

It looked like Courtney was ready to say something else but she was interrupted by a cheerful squeal as Isabelle came running toward them. Or rather, toward Noah. She skidded to a stop and dropped to her knees, her thin arms wrapping around the little boy in a big hug. "Noah!"

The little boy uttered a strangled squeal of his own, hugging Isabelle back. Then the smile abruptly died on his face, replaced by the saddest frown Savannah had ever seen. He shook his head, his tiny fingers moving as he stared at his mother.

"No, you can't get up yet. You have another minute left in your time-out."

Isabelle's disappointment mirrored the little boy's and Savannah had to choke back a laugh when she dropped into the seat next to Noah and patted him on the head. "Poor Noah. It's no fun getting punished, is it?"

"Like you would know. You get away with everything."

The comment was filled with bitter resentment that matched the expression on Brooke's face. The teenager stepped around them and plopped onto the wicker loveseat, slouching down so far that she was in danger of falling off. She crossed her arms in front of her and shot her sister a dirty look.

"I do not!"

"Do so. And you're a little snitch, too. It's all your fault I'm in trouble."

"Don't blame your sister, Brooke. She's not the one who was trying to sneak out last night." Aaron's voice came from behind Savannah. She turned, surprised to see him standing so close, his hand resting on the back of the chair right behind her shoulder. He glanced down at her, offered her a weary smile, then looked back at his daughter.

Savannah studied the two girls through the thick tension hovering over the small group. She wouldn't have thought to look, to note the differences and similarities, if not for the conversation she'd had with

Courtney.

Isabelle favored Aaron, from the shade of her black hair to the shape of her chin and jaw, the squareness not nearly as rugged as her father's and softened by her full mouth. Her eyes were the same brown as Aaron's, fringed with thick, dark lashes.

Brooke had those same dark lashes but that's where the resemblance stopped. Her hair was thick like his, with soft waves that Savannah would pay a ton of money for. Her hair wasn't black but a deep blonde that would glow even more golden in the coming years. Her face was more heart-shaped, her upper lip just a little fuller than the bottom, even with the pout she now wore. Her eyes were a different color, dark blue with a hint of green, their shape more exotic. And she was already blooming at thirteen, her body hinting at the curvy beauty she would become as she got older.

Did she resemble her mother? Did Aaron see his ex-wife every time he looked at his older daughter? Or did she resemble someone else, an aunt or a grandmother or a distant cousin?

Her study went unnoticed as Brooke huffed her anger in one impatient breath filled with the attitude that only a teenager could achieve.

"Whatever." Brooke waved her hand in a dismissive gesture then slid down even further, staring at the toes of her flip-flops. She brought one hand to her mouth and absently chewed her thumbnail, acting like she didn't have a care in the world. The expression on her face—a mixture of anger, resentment, and sadness—said otherwise.

"Don't *whatever* me, Brooke. I'm not in the mood for the drama today."

"Fine. Then let me go back to my room instead of

staying out here."

"No, I don't think so. I think making you stay out here is a better punishment. Less for you to get into that way."

"That's not fair!"

"This has nothing to do with being fair, and everything to do with learning about consequences."

Brooke opened her mouth then must have gotten a good look at the stormy expression on her father's face because she snapped it closed again. She rolled her eyes then went back to chewing her thumbnail, effectively dismissing everyone around her by turning to the side.

The tension was finally broken by Isabelle, who asked if Noah's timeout was over. Courtney's nod was followed by a squeal of excitement when Isabelle helped the young boy off the chair then grabbed his hand and tugged him across the patio to the yard, chattering away.

Courtney stared after them, then shook her head with a small laugh. "She does know he can't hear her, right?"

"Yeah, but I don't think she cares."

Savannah stared after the two children, giving herself a mental slap as the pieces fell into place. Courtney's finger movements. The odd grunt and squeal from Noah. He was deaf. Of course. Now it made sense.

Her silent revelation went unnoticed as Courtney pushed to her feet and faced Aaron. "Did you need help bringing anything else out?"

"No, I've got it. You sit down and relax. Better yet, go give the boys a hard time. Tell them if they call me *Pops* one more time, I'll be forced to show them all up."

Aaron and Courtney were already walking away, leaving her sitting there in confusion, wondering what she had missed. *Pops?* Who were they referring to? Certainly not Aaron. She shifted in the chair, her gaze colliding with Brooke's, surprised at the cold curiosity she saw in their depths.

Savannah quickly stood and made her way to the house, not wanting to be subjected to Brooke's negative attitude any more than necessary. No, that didn't make her a coward—it made her smart.

Aaron turned at the sound of the sliding door closing, a tired smile teasing one corner of his mouth. The smile faded too quickly, though, leaving him looking tired and drained.

And lonely.

"I thought you were Brooke and was getting ready to tell you to get back outside."

"No, just me." Savannah moved through the large country kitchen and leaned against the granite-topped island, studying Aaron's profile as he pulled containers from the refrigerator and piled them on the counter.

He really did look tired, she thought. Not physically, like he'd been up for thirty-six hours straight or anything like that. This was more of a…she frowned, searching her mind for the right word.

Weariness, maybe? That was better, but still not quite right. What she saw in him—what she *felt*—went much deeper than weariness. It was like his soul was spiraling deeper and deeper into a dark hole of misery, becoming more lost with each passing day.

And good God, she needed to stop listening to Tessa's stories about her aunt.

She gave herself a mental shake and pasted a bright smile on her face. "So. Who's *Pops?*"

Aaron turned, surprise flashing in his eyes. Another smile teased his mouth, this one staying in place a little longer. "That would be me."

"You? But why?"

"Just the guys being funny." He closed the refrigerator door then leaned against it, crossing his arms in front of him. Savannah forced her gaze away from the defined muscles in his arms—not just his biceps, but his forearms and wrists as well. And since when did wrists even have muscles?

Since when did she even notice?

She ignored the way her heart pounded in her chest, ignored the flush of excitement tingling at the back of her neck. What had they been talking about? Oh, yeah—his teammates being funny.

"Why is that funny?"

"Because I'm old."

"What! You most certainly are not."

Aaron's grin widened just the smallest bit, the scar that ran from the corner of his mouth down to his chin making the grin slightly crooked. "I'm the oldest guy on the team so yeah, I'm old."

"Being the oldest doesn't make you *old*. That's just being ridiculous."

The grin faltered and died as he pushed away from the refrigerator and stepped toward her. No, not toward *her*—toward the stack of plates resting on the island right in front of her. He reached out and fingered the rim of the top plate, his arm so close she could feel the heat of it brushing against her own flesh.

"Yeah, well. Lately I feel ancient, so maybe they have a point."

Sympathy welled deep inside her. "Brooke still giving you a hard time?"

He grunted then leaned his elbows on the counter, the motion bringing him even closer to her. Savannah told herself not to read into it, forced herself to pay attention to what he was saying instead of staring at the contours of his full mouth as he spoke.

"That would be an understatement. I could handle her giving me a hard time. Hell, I could even understand. But this—" He sighed and shook his head. "This is something more. I don't even know what this is."

"I know this isn't any of my business, but have you thought about maybe getting counseling for her? For both of them, really. The past few months can't have been easy."

"I have. I mean, they do. Once a week. But it's not doing any good from what I can see. With Isabelle, yeah. But Brooke?" He shook his head again, agony flashing in his eyes when he looked at her. "I don't think it's helping."

"I'm sorry. I wish there was something I could do to help."

Another sad smile crossed his face. He straightened then turned to lean his hip against the counter. "Thanks, but it's not your problem. I'm starting to wonder if I made a mistake bringing them here, you know? Maybe Brooke would be better off with her grandparents. Hell, maybe both of them would. What the hell do I know about being a father?"

Savannah stepped closer, capturing his gaze with her own, letting him see the truth in her words as she spoke. "You don't mean that, Aaron. From everything I've seen, you're a great father. It'll work out. You just need a little faith."

"Yeah, well, easier said than done."

"Well, *I* believe in you." Savannah rested her hand on his arm, felt the muscles tighten and bunch under her palm. She had only meant it as a comforting touch, a gentle reassurance to reinforce her words. But something shifted, stirring the currents around them, making the air thicker and heavier. Aaron glanced at her hand then looked at her, his eyes deep and fathomless. Her face heated—from embarrassment at what he might see on her face, from the flash of desire that danced across her skin—and she tried to move her hand, ready to mumble an apology and step back.

His hand closed over hers, big and rough but achingly gentle as he held it in place. He shifted, turning toward her, his body so close, his questioning gaze holding her immobile so that not even hurricane-force winds could have dislodged her. And then he dipped his head and brushed his mouth against hers.

Once. Twice. Soft and gentle. Hesitant. Seeking.

Her breath left her in a sigh, breaking whatever restraint had been holding him back. Aaron's hand cupped the back of her head as he deepened the kiss, his tongue sweeping past the seam of her lips and dancing with hers. Slow, tantalizing. Full of promise.

Stars exploded behind her lids as her pulse soared. She had time to wonder if maybe she was going to pass out, then her mind went wonderfully, blissfully blank as she surrendered to the sensations crashing over her.

Savannah curled her hand in his shirt, felt him shift so she was braced between Aaron's hard body and the side of the island counter. And thank God, because there was a very real chance she'd turn into a boneless puddle of need if not for that support.

She dragged her other hand along his arm, her fingers tracing the line of muscles of his biceps and shoulder and chest. Down his side, feeling the ridges of his rib cage and the dip of his abdomen. Her fingers curled around the hem of his t-shirt, her knuckles grazing smooth, heated flesh as she pushed the soft material up. Aaron groaned, the needy sound empowering her, stoking the flames of her own need. She wanted to feel. Touch. Taste—

"Hey, Aaron, where's the—oops." An embarrassed breath, then a deep chuckle. "Way to go, Pops."

Savannah jerked back, the strange voice acting like ice water. She pulled her hand from Aaron's shirt and pushed him away, wondering if it was possible to die from embarrassment and then wishing it was.

"I—I'm sorry." She muttered the apology and hurried toward the door, ignoring the sound of Aaron calling her name, ignoring the curious gaze of the man with the pale blue eyes as she pushed past him and hurried across the yard, back to her house.

CHAPTER FOUR

"For someone of your advanced age and maturity, you sure are stupid."

Aaron narrowed his eyes but otherwise ignored Zach. Let his teammate think the grunt was some kind of response—it wasn't. The grunt was from the strain he felt at lifting the weights.

Mostly.

"Yeah. You should have gone after her at least."

"Really, Emory?" Disbelief and disgust mingled in Zach's voice. "The whole damn thing was your fucking fault."

"What are you talking about? How is any of what happened *my* fault?"

"Because you're an ass. You walk in on someone getting hot and heavy, you don't laugh and say 'Way to go, Pops'. You back out nice and quietly and pretend you didn't see a thing."

"Hey, I was surprised, that's all. Seeing Pops making out like a horny teenager caught me off-guard. It wasn't like I interrupted on purpose."

"Christ. You are beyond hope. Anyone ever tell you that? Megan must be a saint or something to put up with your shit."

The sound of weights crashing against a rack echoed around them. Jason heaved a sigh, wiped his brow with the back of his arm, then jammed his fists on his hips. "What the hell is that supposed to mean?"

"Nothing. Let it go." Zach replaced his own weights then straddled the bench, a towel draped around his neck. Aaron forced himself to ignore the stares of both men, forced himself to concentrate on each rep. Inhale. Curl up. Exhale. Curl down. Again. Over and over until muscles burned and cramped, then one more time with a deep grunt as he pushed through the final rep.

He lowered the weights to the floor then reached for the water bottle, drinking deeply. He capped it, tossed it to the side, then moved toward the chest press machine.

"Aren't you going to say *anything*?"

Aaron glanced at Zach, shaking his head as he adjusted the weight. "Nothing to say."

"Did you at least go talk to her?"

"Did you see me go talk to her?"

"I don't mean during the party. I mean later that night. Or the next day. Or fuck, any day in the past five days since it happened."

Since it happened.

Guilt swept through him again. What the hell had he done? Manhandling Savannah that way, pushing her up against the counter like he had. What the fuck had he been thinking?

He hadn't been thinking, that was the problem. He still wasn't sure why he'd kissed her. She was only being nice, trying to reassure him, offer him comfort in that gentle way she had. But he had looked down and seen her hand on his arm, looked into those clear hazel eyes and thought he saw the same desire he'd been feeling.

He'd obviously misread the entire situation. Yeah, he'd seen desire alright—but it hadn't been hers. It had been nothing more than a reflection of his own. And the way she had pushed him away then run out, like she was mortified over what he'd done and couldn't get away fast enough.

Fuck. Just what he needed on top of everything else going on right now. Savannah had been his one beacon of peace and sanity in the last four months—more than he had realized—and now he didn't even have that.

All because he'd misread things and acted on impulse. He was worse than some of his teammates.

No, he was worse than all of them, because he was old enough to know better.

"Well? Have you?"

He glanced over, saw Zach and Jason watching him. And it wasn't just those two. Ben and Travis had joined them as well, and he could see a few of the other guys throwing curious glances his way.

Everyone except Tyler, who stayed to himself working on his samurai goalie skills. Aaron tried to tell himself it was because Tyler wasn't interested in the gossip, or the fact that the old man had completely embarrassed himself, but he knew better. The reason Tyler was off by himself was the same reason he and Jenny hadn't come to the cookout: because Tyler and Jason still weren't speaking and hadn't been since he ran off with Jason's sister.

Yeah. Wasn't that going to make for a fun season?

Aaron straddled the bench and wrapped his hands around the padded handles of the machine. He closed his eyes, inhaled, and extended his arms.

Only nothing happened.

He dropped his arms and glanced over his shoulder, the muscle in his jaw working when he saw Zach leaning against the weights. "Do you mind?"

"Yeah, actually, I do." Zach straightened and moved closer. "Have you at least talked to her?"

"And tell her what? Sorry for manhandling her? Christ, Mummert—"

"Why do you even think that?"

"Think what? That I was manhandling her?"

"Yeah. From what I hear, it was a kiss—one she was participating in."

"You weren't there."

"No, but I was." Jason grinned and tapped Aaron on the shoulder with his fist. "And she was definitely participating. She damn near had your shirt up around your hairy armpits."

"Fuck, Emory. Do you ever shut up? You need to shut up because you're not helping. Now go away. I mean it." Zach pushed him to the side then waved his hands in a brushing motion at everyone else. "That goes for all of you. Especially you, Banky. You're too innocent for this conversation, even if you are turning into a man-whore."

A blush exploded on Travis Bankard's face. Even the tips of his ears turned beet-red. He stammered for a minute then narrowed his eyes at Zach. "What's that supposed to mean?"

"What? *Man-whore*? Go look it up in the dictionary. Or better yet, ask Ben."

"I know what it means, you ass. I just don't know why you're calling me that."

"Because that's what you've turned into. Do yourself a favor and stay off social media."

"But you—"

"That was before I got smart. Now go away. All of you."

"But—"

"Come on, Banky. Let's leave the kids alone before Zach has a coronary. You too, Jason." Ben Leach tugged on their arms, leading both men away, muttering under his breath about hen-pecked boys.

Aaron felt Zach stiffen and reached out to grab him, pulling him back before he could go after Ben. "Let it go. And stop giving Travis a hard time. You're not making things easier for him."

"Easier? What the fuck is that supposed to mean?"

"Just what I said. He's beating himself up for getting involved with those women last season." Aaron pinned Zach in place with a narrowed gaze. "Which he wouldn't have done if you hadn't egged him on."

"Yeah, well. I didn't think he'd take me seriously."

"He's still young and naïve and on the rebound."

"Young? He's almost twenty-two. Definitely old enough to know better."

"When you get to be my age, that's young."

Zach leaned against the machine and folded his arms across his broad chest, leveling an unreadable gaze at Aaron. "Why do you do that?"

"Do what?"

"Keep calling yourself *old*. You're not, you know. Thirty-four is still prime."

"Not in our line of work, it isn't. I've been playing pro or semi-pro hockey for half my life. Trust me, I'm old."

"Bullshit."

"You just wait—"

"Yeah, whatever. We can save that conversation

for another day. I want to know why you haven't gone to talk to your neighbor at all."

Aaron turned away from Zach, hoping the man would get the message. He didn't. Instead of walking away, he simply moved in front of Aaron.

"Well? Why haven't you?"

"And say what? Sorry for forcing myself on you? Fuck. Shit like that—no, there's nothing I can say to her that would make it better."

"Why are you so fucking convinced you forced yourself on her?"

"I don't know. Maybe because she pushed me away and ran off?"

"When did she push you away?"

"After Jason came in and caught us."

"Okay, number one, he didn't 'catch you'. That implies you were sneaking around like some horny fucking teenager. And number two, did you maybe stop to think she was embarrassed? I mean, fuck. This is Jason we're talking about. You know how he is. He could embarrass the devil himself just by opening his stupid fucking mouth and saying the wrong thing."

Aaron shook his head. He wanted to believe Zach, wanted to believe that he hadn't acted like a total ass and did something wrong…but he couldn't quite convince himself of that. "You didn't see the look on her face—"

"No, but I saw yours."

"What the hell is that supposed to mean?"

Zach ran a hand through his hair and down his face, his breath leaving him in a rush. He glanced around then stepped closer, lowering his voice to just above a whisper. "Remember when that bastard hurt Haley? How fucked up I was? Pissed and angry but beyond that, scared shitless. I was so fucking scared I was a fucking basket case."

Aaron closed his eyes, the memory of that night almost six months ago coming back to him. Haley's ex-boyfriend had broken into her apartment and attacked her, leaving her cut and bloody until Zach found her an hour later. The police had actually arrested Zach, thinking he'd been the one to hurt her. Aaron had picked him up when he was released from jail a few hours later, all charges dropped when the police realized he'd had nothing to do with it.

Zach had been a shell of himself, pale and empty and so shaken that he'd been violently ill. Aaron had taken him to his condo and forced him into the shower so he could wash Haley's blood from his skin before taking him to the hospital. It had been a living nightmare for all of them, but especially for Zach.

One he wouldn't be able to forget for a long time.

Aaron blew out a deep breath. "Yeah, I remember."

"You had a similar look on your face."

"That is such—"

"You did. Not scared shitless, not like that. But you had this panicked look in your eyes, like you'd just lost something you never realized you had."

"That is the most fucking asinine thing I have ever heard you say. Zach, she's my *neighbor*. We're friends. Acquaintances. That's it. We don't even socialize much. Nothing beyond saying hi or chatting or hanging out a little if we're both outside."

Zach's brows shot up in disbelief. "Really? Then what the fuck are you doing kissing her if she's nothing more than an acquaintance?"

"I—" Aaron's mouth snapped shut, his mind

searching for an explanation. There had to be one…he just couldn't find it.

"Yeah. Uh-huh. That's what I thought. If it had been any one of these other guys around here, it'd be no big deal. But that's not how you roll and we both know it."

"That doesn't mean anything."

"Listen, all I'm saying is go talk to her. Apologize if you think you need to. Then ask the woman out."

"I don't think that's a good idea."

"Why? Because she might say no?"

Maybe. And because he was afraid she'd slam the door in his face. But damned if he'd admit that to Zach. "In case you're forgetting, I have two daughters I need to worry about. And right now, they're about all I can handle."

"You're a big boy. Learn to multi-task. They're in school now, right?"

"Yeah, they started yesterday."

"And you said your neighbor worked from home, right?"

"Yeah."

"Then ask her out to lunch. Lunch dates are innocent enough. Piece of cake." Zach swatted Aaron on the leg with his towel then sauntered away, whistling under his breath.

Aaron almost laughed at the irony of the entire situation. Zach Mummert, one of the team's biggest players, giving *him* dating advice.

Except Zach wasn't a player anymore, and hadn't been for a while. And he was totally committed to Haley.

So maybe some of what Zach said had merit.

Maybe.

Except it all hinged on Aaron working up the nerve to go see Savannah. To apologize. And that meant taking a chance on having her slam the door in his face.

He wasn't sure if he could handle that.

CHAPTER FIVE

"You look like you're melting. I have no idea why you're sitting outside in this heat when you could be inside, in the air conditioning. Where it's cool."

Savannah glanced up from the notes she was making on her next presentation and shot Tessa a dirty look. "I am *not* melting."

"Looks like it from here." Tessa leaned forward, the angle of the camera lens comically distorting her face. She tapped on her own screen, the sound traveling through cyberspace and echoing in Savannah's ear as a hollow thud. "Your face is all shiny and sweaty."

Savannah had been reaching for a napkin to blot the sweat from her face. She pulled her hand back at Tessa's words and frowned. "It is not."

"Liar. Tell me again why you're sitting outside when it's two hundred degrees and sweltering."

"You're exaggerating. As usual. And I happen to enjoy the fresh air."

"Uh-huh. I think it's the view you enjoy, not the fresh air. There is no fresh air, not with this humidity."

Savannah ignored the comment about the view, knowing better than to start that discussion with Tessa.

Again. "It's not that bad. I'm in the shade under the canopy, and I have the pedestal fan on so there's a nice breeze."

"Hmm. If you say so." Tessa's face disappeared from the screen as she leaned to the side. Her image reappeared just as she popped a carrot stick into her mouth. "Let me guess: your neighbor is working outside or something and you're just using work as an excuse to ogle him."

"You guessed wrong."

"Why don't I believe that?"

"No idea but look, you can see for yourself." Savannah turned her laptop around, aiming the camera at Aaron's empty yard. She spun it back in time to see the surprise on Tessa's face. "See? Told you."

"I don't think I buy it. If he's not out there now, then you're hoping he will be. That has to be the only reason for you to be sitting outside."

"I told you, I enjoy working outside. And trust me, if I *did* see Aaron, I'd hightail it back inside right away."

"Are you still agonizing over that whole thing?"

"I'm not *agonizing*. I'm just avoiding."

"You're doing both. Admit it."

Savannah thought about denying it but she clamped her mouth closed against the lie. She *was* doing both. She was still too embarrassed. Worse than embarrassed. She was mortified.

"I don't see what the big deal is. You kissed him. That was it."

"Tessa, I was trying to strip him naked."

"Yeah? So? That's what you've been talking about doing for the last year."

"But we were in his kitchen!"

"And?"

"What if someone walked in on us?"

"I thought someone *did* walk in on you?"

"I mean his kids. What if it had been Isabelle or Brooke? Having his teammate catch us was bad enough. I can't even imagine what I would have done if it had been one of the girls."

"I think you're overreacting just a bit."

Was she? Probably. But that didn't lessen the embarrassment.

And it certainly didn't lessen the memory of that intense kiss. She hadn't expected it, at all. Thought about it, yes. Fantasized about it, most definitely. But actually expected it? No way. And it had been toe-curling amazing, too. Feeling Aaron's hard body—and she did mean *hard*, in every way possible—pressed against hers. Feeling his tongue sweep into her mouth. Tasting him, touching his heated flesh. The kiss had unleashed something wild inside her. She had wanted nothing more than to see and touch and taste every inch of him. The desire had been so fierce, she had forgotten where they were.

What embarrassed her even more than being caught was knowing that she wouldn't have stopped if they *hadn't* been, not until she had Aaron naked and deep inside her.

She didn't even want to think what would have happened if someone had walked in on them *then*.

"Ooooo. What are you thinking?"

Savannah's head jerked toward the screen. "What? I'm not thinking about anything."

"Yes, you are. And from the way your face got all red, I'd have to say it was something really good, too. Now out with it."

"No. It was nothing."

"Liar." Tessa leaned forward, a wide grin on her face. "You were thinking about him, weren't you? About that rugged body all hot and sweaty and naked and rubbing against yours, weren't you?"

Savannah choked back an embarrassed laugh. "Tessa!"

"Well damn." Tessa leaned back, waving a hand in front of her face. "I think I need to go see my battery-operated-boyfriend, bring him out for a little playtime."

Savannah laughed again, her face heating a little more because she'd been thinking of doing the same thing. "If only we could replace all men with BOB. Wouldn't that—"

"Hey Savannah."

She jumped at the deep voice calling her name a few feet away. Her mouth opened and closed, her mind completely blank as she stared at Aaron. A shrill squeal echoed from her laptop.

"Oh my God, is that him? Is he there? Did he actually hear you? Girl, if you don't fuck his brains out right now—"

Savannah slammed the laptop closed, cutting Tessa off before she could say anything else. And oh God, had Aaron heard her? Had he heard either one of them?

She wanted to die. To spontaneously combust and disappear in a pile of ash.

Or just run into her house and slam the door behind her and search for a new place to live. Like maybe Antarctica.

But she didn't do any of that because she was frozen in place from embarrassment, and from those deep brown eyes watching her.

"Uh. Aaron. Um. Hi." She glanced at the closed

laptop then back at him. Had he heard any of their conversation? He must have. He'd have to be completely deaf not to. But he didn't *look* like he'd heard—not unless he had the world's best poker face. And if that was the case, the man seriously needed to go to Las Vegas.

She settled back in the chair and crossed her legs, ignoring the damp tenderness and trying not to feel like she'd just been caught playing with herself. "Did you, um—I mean, was there something you needed?"

He stepped closer, moving under the shade of the canopy, his dark gaze darting to the closed laptop before shooting back to hers. "I didn't mean to interrupt. I can come back—"

"No! Um, I mean, you weren't interrupting. Did it sound like you were interrupting? Because you weren't. You didn't. I mean—" Savannah snapped her mouth closed and pasted a bright smile on her face. "Whatever you heard, it didn't mean anything. Just, um, just girl talk and—"

Savannah snapped her mouth closed again as Aaron moved closer, one corner of his mouth kicking up in a sexy grin. He reached out with one hand and for a second, she thought he was going to pull her to her feet and into his arms and kiss her. And she'd be totally fine with that, in absolute agreement with whatever he wanted to do.

Instead of touching her, he curled his finger around the cord dangling from her left ear and gently pulled. The earbud dropped to her chest, just above the swell of her breast. Relief coursed through her and she sagged against the table.

"Oh, thank God."

Aaron chuckled, the sound drifting over her like a

warm breeze. "Do I even want to know?"

"No! No, you definitely don't want to know."

"Fair enough." He shifted his weight from one foot to the other, amusement flashing in his eyes. "Who's Bob?"

"Nobody. He's, uh, he's nobody." Savannah jumped from the chair and gathered the laptop and notes and moved toward the French doors. She was still so flustered that she nearly tripped but Aaron was right there beside her, steadying her with a hand on her elbow.

She offered him a smile—at least, she hoped it was a smile, she was still so flustered she wasn't sure—then walked inside, Aaron following her. She tossed the laptop and her notes on the coffee table. "Did you need something? Would you like something to drink?"

"Actually, I came to apologize."

Savannah stumbled to a stop then spun around, her brows lowered in confusion. "Apologize?"

Aaron shoved his hands into the front pockets of his shorts. His shoulders hunched around his ears as a small blush stained his stubbled cheeks, making him look like an awkward teenager who had just been busted for doing something he shouldn't have. What, she couldn't imagine.

"Yeah. For what happened. I shouldn't have—I didn't mean—" He cleared his throat, the blush deepening a little more.

Savannah's mouth dropped open in shock as she stared at him. Was he really apologizing for the kiss? Oh, dear God, he was. She couldn't believe it. Or maybe she could. This was *Aaron*. The next-door neighbor she'd been fantasizing about for the past year, and not just for his looks. He was quiet, not shy but definitely a bit reserved. Always holding a piece of himself back, like he was afraid to fully jump into life. A gentleman. Maybe that sounded old-fashioned—and how sad was that?—but he was. And while she knew all that, she never in a million years expected him to think he'd done something wrong simply by kissing her.

Unless there was something else he was apologizing for.

She stepped closer, trying to wipe the confused frown from her face. "Are you apologizing for kissing me?"

His face turned even redder as his gaze darted to hers then quickly dropped. "That. And for being rough. I shouldn't have—"

"Don't."

His head snapped up. "*Don't?*"

"Yeah. Don't."

"Don't, what?"

"Don't apologize."

"But I—"

"Aaron, if I hadn't wanted you to kiss me, you would have known it. I would have kicked or punched or pushed you away or—"

"You did."

"I did what?"

"Pushed me away."

Savannah frowned, trying to figure out what he was talking about. Pushed him away? Not even close. She'd been shoving his shirt up his body and would have worked on his shorts next if his teammate hadn't interrupted them.

The memory came back to her and she mentally groaned. She *had* pushed him away—but only because she was so embarrassed at what she might have done that she gave in to the overwhelming desire to run away.

"The only reason I pushed you away was because your teammate walked in on us. I was embarrassed."

Something resembling relief flashed across his face, but only for a second. He shook his head, his brows pulled low over his dark eyes. "I still shouldn't have done what I did. I was out of line."

He was serious! He honestly thought he'd done something wrong. Savannah didn't know whether to laugh or cry or…or…

She stepped closer, so close she had to tilt her head back to look him in the eyes. Heat from his body washed over her, flaming the desire that had been smoldering inside her for the last few months. She watched as awareness flashed in his eyes, as his pupils dilated and his lips parted on a harsh breath.

"Do you know *why* I was embarrassed?"

Aaron shook his head, his voice nothing but a harsh whisper when he spoke. "No."

"I was embarrassed because if that guy had walked in five minutes later, he would have found you on the floor, naked, under me."

And oh, dear God, what had she been thinking, telling him that? She could see the shock on his flushed face, in the way his eyes widened and his breath left in a shocked gasp that she would have never heard if she hadn't been so close.

Her own face was heating from embarrassment. It would be so easy to turn around and run away and hide. Aaron wouldn't follow her, wouldn't ask her what she meant. And then she'd probably never see him again, except for the occasional wave across their yards, because he wouldn't know how to act.

Which meant she had two choices: she could either run away—

Or she could take the lead.

When it came down to it, there was really only one choice.

She curled her hand into his shirt and pulled him closer, pushing up on her bare toes so she could capture his mouth with her own.

CHAPTER SIX

He would have found you on the floor, naked, under me.

Aaron was still trying to wrap his mind around those words when he realized Savannah was kissing him.

Savannah was kissing *him*.

He froze, not knowing what to do. What the fuck? He *knew* what to do. Her mouth was soft and warm against his, the curves of her soft body pressed against him. What he needed to do was wrap his arms around her and pull her even closer, to delve his tongue into the hot recess of her mouth. To hold her and kiss her back.

He didn't move. He couldn't. He was thrown so completely off-guard that he was literally frozen to the spot. This wasn't supposed to happen. Not that he didn't want it to—fuck, he did, more than he'd allowed himself to admit. He'd been thinking of nothing else for the last few months.

No, that wasn't true. He'd been thinking about doing a hell of a lot more than just kissing her. But he never thought he'd actually be doing it.

Only he wasn't *doing* anything, except standing there like some fucking statue, completely out of his mind with shock.

Savannah's mouth left his, the warmth of her kiss replaced by the cold air circulated by the air conditioner. Her lips were wet and swollen, her cheeks flushed, her chest rising and falling with each short breath.

And he still couldn't fucking move.

Her lids fluttered open, revealing hazel eyes glazed with passion. She blinked, a slow up-and-down of her eyelids, and the passion faded away. She released her grip on his shirt then stepped back, her gaze focused on the middle of his chest.

"Guess I read things wrong, huh?" Her voice was pitched just above a whisper, infused with the tiniest bit of humor that seemed just a little forced.

"Savannah—"

"No, it's okay. Not a big deal." She reached out and smoothed his shirt, then let her hand drop to her side.

Aaron wanted to reach for her, to pull her into his arms and tell her it *was* a big deal. To reassure her she hadn't misread anything. But his tongue was suddenly stuck to the roof of his mouth, the words lodged in his throat.

"So." Savannah took another step back, the smile on her face too wide, too bright. "Was that all you came over for? To apologize? Because if it is, I think we're probably even now, huh?"

"I came to ask if you wanted to go to lunch." And *fuck*, that wasn't what he meant to say, not now. Earlier maybe, before she had kissed him, but not now.

"Lunch?" Her brows shot up in surprise as twin patches of red stained her cheeks. "Lunch. Okay then. Um, wow. I really did misread things, didn't I? Maybe

I need to rethink Antarctica. Maybe Siberia would be better."

"What?"

"Nothing. Just me, talking to myself. Lunch, huh? Thanks, but I already ate and—"

"A date. A lunch *date*. Next week." He forced the words from his mouth, inwardly wincing at how awkward they sounded, how uncertain. Savannah glanced at him then quickly looked away. She pushed the hair behind her ear and he noticed that some of the red was fading from her face. That was a good thing, right? It meant she wasn't embarrassed anymore.

Didn't it?

"Next week." She frowned then shook her head. "I can't. I'm meeting with a client in DC next week."

"Oh." Aaron hid his disappointment—maybe a little too well because Savannah peered at him through narrowed eyes. Great, now she probably thought he hadn't been serious. Or maybe she thought he was just humoring her. Or…hell if he knew. He wasn't used to this dating shit, had no idea what the hell he was supposed to do now. He asked her out, she said no. Should he ask again? Because maybe she really did have meetings next week and she wasn't just blowing him off.

She wouldn't have kissed him like that if she was blowing him off.

"What about the following week?"

"For what?"

"For lunch."

"You're serious?"

"Of course, I'm serious."

"About a lunch *date*?"

"Yeah. A lunch *date*."

"You're not just asking because you're feeling sorry for me after the way I threw myself at you?"

"You didn't throw yourself at me."

A small laugh fell from her mouth, the sound filled with an odd mixture of humor and sarcasm. "Aaron, exactly how long have you been out of the dating scene?"

"Probably too long."

"Well, then, you'll have to trust me. I threw myself at you." She offered him a sad smile then started to move past him. "I appreciate the offer but really, you don't need to try to make me feel better. I'm a big girl. I thought you were interested but I misread the situation. You don't—"

Aaron grabbed her arm as she moved past him, spinning her around then catching her when she stumbled against him. She placed her hands against his chest, her touch searing him through the thin cotton of his t-shirt. He held his breath, waiting for her to push him away.

She didn't.

"Savannah, I don't feel sorry for you. And I *am* interested."

Brows lifted above hazel eyes filled with surprise and just a touch of humor. "So, I didn't misread?"

"No."

"Then why were you just standing there?"

Aaron hesitated for the briefest second, wondering what to tell her. He settled for the truth. "You caught me off-guard. And…I wasn't sure—I mean—"

"Aaron?"

He swallowed the jumble of words tangled in his throat, his mind going blank under the searing heat of

Savannah's gaze. "Yeah?"

"Shut up and kiss me."

Whatever hesitation he still had evaporated at her words. He tightened his hold around her waist and dipped his head, his mouth closing over hers with a desperate need that surprised him. She wrapped her arms around his neck and pressed her body against his. Her breasts were soft and firm, the tight peaks of her nipples hard against his chest. He groaned and deepened the kiss, his tongue meeting hers. Hot and wet. Deep and slow. He palmed her round ass and pulled her hips against his, swallowed her sigh as she rubbed against his straining cock.

Shit. Fuck. What was he doing? He had only meant for this to be a kiss, no matter how hard his cock throbbed with need. He groaned and started to pull away but her arms tightened around his neck, holding him in place.

He relaxed, just the tiniest bit, reveling in the feel of Savannah. He dragged his hand along the soft curves of her ass, along the flare of her hips and the damp flesh of her back as he ran his fingers under her shirt. She sighed again, the breathy moan unleashing the last of his hesitancy.

He dragged his mouth from hers, pressed kisses along her jaw, up to the sensitive spot just behind her ear. A tremor went through her and her nails dug into the hard flesh of his biceps. He kissed that soft spot again, playfully nipped it with his teeth, heard her breath rush out in a hiss.

He pulled back, ready to apologize, but her glazed eyes met his and she shook her head. "Don't stop. Please."

The need in her voice matched the same need

coursing through him. Rough. Hot. Desperate. He dipped his head and caught her mouth again, drinking from her, losing himself in the sweet taste of her. He slid his hands along her sides, grabbed the edge of her shirt, and eased it up.

He pulled away, yanked the shirt over her head, then stared down at the rosy flesh of her bared breasts. Full, soft and firm, the hardened nipples tightened into twin peaks of dusky rose.

Aaron swallowed, his cock straining against the zipper of his shorts, threatening to bust free as she reached up and rolled each nipple between her thumb and forefinger before gently pinching.

Fuck. He was going to fucking lose it, right here, right now, if she kept doing that. Did she know? Could she see it in the set of his jaw, in the way he held himself rigid, almost afraid to move?

Yes, dammit, she knew. The knowledge was in her teasing smile, in the way her tongue darted out and swept across her full lower lip. "Do you like that?"

He cleared his throat, forced his gaze to hers. "A little too much."

She smiled again then reached for his hand and he held his breath, waiting. But instead of guiding his hand to her breast, she tugged, leading him through the living room and up the stairs, down a short hallway and into her bedroom.

"Savannah—"

She cut him off with a deep kiss that took his breath away. Then she was leading him to the bed and pushing him down, her hands roaming over his body, her mouth touching and teasing his flesh as she pulled his shirt off. She kissed her way down his body, the tips of her nails gently scoring his ribs, his stomach. She undid his shorts and pushed them down and off, shedding her own shorts at the same time.

And then, fuck, she was straddling him, rubbing her wet heat against the throbbing length of his cock as she kissed his chest. Her lips closed over the flat of his nipple, her teeth gently biting before she pulled it into her mouth and sucked.

He groaned, long and loud, knowing he needed to fight for control, knowing he should roll her to her back and kiss his way down her body. To taste and lick until her hips bucked under his mouth, until her body clamped around his tongue. To pleasure her until she was limp and boneless, until she begged him to stop.

No, what he really wanted to do was grab her hips and hold her in place as he drove his cock into her, hard and deep. But fuck, he couldn't even do that, not with the way she was sliding along his body, driving him to the brink of insanity with each little touch. Each little caress. Each little kiss and flick of her tongue.

And then her mouth closed over his hard length and he nearly lost it right then and there. It had been too fucking long for him, for his body to endure this exquisite torture.

Endure? Who the fuck was he kidding?

He reached down and curled his hand in Savannah's hair, holding the soft strands in a loose fist as her mouth drove him to the brink over and over. He closed his eyes and tilted his head back, his jaw clenched as he struggled for control. Close, so fucking close—

"Savannah." Her name was nothing more than a harsh whisper ripped from his throat. He tugged, gently easing her mouth from his cock, then pulled her along the length of his body until he could claim her mouth with his.

He wanted inside her. Now. No, not want—need. Hot and frantic, clawing at his skin, shredding the last of his restraint. He twisted and rolled, settled himself between her legs, the tip of his cock poised at her wet entrance.

A wisp of sanity returned and he rolled away, his lips clamped over a string of profanity. He inhaled through his nose, his fist curling in the downy softness of the comforter.

"I don't have any condoms." *Fuck*. Of course, he didn't. Because he didn't do this kind of thing. He wasn't like some of his teammates, didn't shove condoms into his wallet and carry them around, replenishing the supply every fucking week.

Fuck. Shit, fuck, damn.

"I do."

Aaron's eyes snapped open and he turned his head, his gaze landing on the pale globes of Savannah's ass as she leaned over the side of the bed and opened the drawer of her nightstand. Then she was kneeling beside him, her slender hands rolling the condom down the throbbing length of his cock as she kissed him.

He wrapped his arms around her and rolled once more, tucking her beneath him before driving into her. She gasped, the sound turning into a long sigh of pleasure as he rocked into her.

Her eyes closed and her head tilted back, her hair fanning across the pillow as he drove into her. She gasped again, louder this time, then bit down on her lower lip as she reached for him. Nails scored his shoulder, his arm, his ass. Their slick bodies moved together, her hips meeting each hungry thrust of his own.

Faster. Harder. Deeper. Over and over until her legs tightened around his waist and her back arched. His name fell from her lips, a desperate cry as she shattered around him.

Aaron clenched his jaw, drove himself deeper. Once. Twice. Again. One final time until his own climax crashed over him and he fell on top of her, oblivious to everything except the tiny sighs of the woman beneath him.

CHAPTER SEVEN

Aaron stretched his arm over his head, a contented smile on his face as Savannah ran her fingers over his body. *Contented?* He almost laughed. That word didn't even come close to what he was feeling.

Contented? Yes. Relaxed. Sated. At ease. Peaceful. But none of them were right. There was a better word out there, he knew it. But right now, his mind was too preoccupied to come up with it.

Savannah had been cataloging the different bumps and scars on his battered body for the last fifteen minutes. She would trace each one with her finger, press a kiss against it, then ask what it was from.

She reached the smooth scar running just above his hip bone, tracing it like she had the others. He held his breath as she dipped her head, the ends of her hair trailing against the bare skin of his inner thigh. Would she—?

No. She pressed her lips against the scar then draped her arm over his stomach and rested her chin on her forearm. The glint of amusement in her eyes told him she knew exactly what he'd been hoping. "What's that one from?"

"Skate blade."

She laughed then leaned down to press another gentle kiss against the scar. "Yeah, right."

"No, seriously, it is."

Horror flashed across her face, followed by disbelief. "You're teasing me."

"No, it really was from a skate blade. Maybe eight or nine years ago, when I was playing in Tampa."

"That's…I can't even imagine. Did it hurt?"

"Not really. I only missed seven minutes of the period while they taped it up."

She pushed up on her elbow, her eyes wide with shock. "You mean you kept playing?"

"Yeah. Why wouldn't I?"

"Because—because—" She sputtered some more then finally shook her head and moved up, stretching out beside him. "That just sounds barbaric."

"It's hockey. It's a tough sport."

"And how long have you been playing?"

"Seventeen years."

"Really? That long?"

"If you only count my time playing pro and semi-pro, yeah. But I started playing when I was four."

Her mouth dropped open then quickly snapped shut. He could see she didn't want to believe him, that she thought he was joking. "Wow. That's—"

"A really long time."

"Yeah, it is. And the Bombers—they're semi-pro or pro?"

"Semi-pro. We're the minor league team for the Banners, down in Baltimore."

"So, do you play for them, too?"

"No. Not unless they get really, really desperate. My time in the pros is over." He shifted, draping his arm around her shoulders as he trailed his fingers along her arm. "Haven't you ever been to a hockey game?"

"Nope. I watched part of one on television once. Some guys in suits were bringing out a big cup or something at the end."

Aaron choked on his laughter then waved Savannah's curious glance away. "I'll explain later. But we need to get you to a game."

"That would be fun." She smothered a yawn then curled closer to him. He liked the way she felt next to him, with her head resting on his shoulder and her fingers tracing small circles on his chest. What would it be like to fall asleep with her next to him? To wake up with her body curled against his own?

No sooner had the thoughts come to mind then he shoved them away. He didn't need to be going there. Not now. Not for a long time. Maybe not ever.

And he had a feeling she'd agree with him. She deserved a hell of a lot more than he could give her. Why the hell would a woman like her even want to be with him? The end of his career was fast approaching. Not this year, maybe not even next. But it was coming, creeping along the horizon.

And he had two daughters to think of, too. A woman didn't want to be saddled with someone else's kids, especially when those kids wanted nothing to do with their own father. Maybe Isabelle didn't feel that way, but Brooke certainly did. And she—

Panic sliced through him and he pushed up on his elbow, his gaze darting to the clock on Savannah's nightstand. "Shit!"

"What is it?"

"The kids. They got home twenty minutes ago. Fuck." He rolled away from Savannah and jumped out of bed, searching for his clothes. "How did I completely forget about them? *Fuck*."

"I'm sure they're fine—"

"Brooke's probably set the house on fire by now. Or stole the car. Or both." He jammed one leg into his shorts, nearly tripped as he tried to shove the other one in.

"Well, I don't hear any sirens so…" Savannah's voice trailed off with a small chuckle.

"That's not even funny."

"That's not what I'm laughing at." She climbed out of bed, much more gracefully than he had, and reached for the shirt he'd been about to pull over his head. She turned it right-side out, gave it a sharp shake, then held it out to him. "I'm laughing because I don't think I've ever heard you cuss before."

"What?" Aaron poked his head through the shirt, embarrassment lancing through him as he recalled several of his more colorful word choices in the last five minutes. He stammered an apology, only to have Savannah interrupt him with a soft kiss.

"You have nothing to apologize for."

"Yeah, I do. I try to keep the locker room talk *in* the locker room. I didn't mean to—"

"I know. Don't worry about it. I'm not."

He grunted, thought about pulling her closer for another kiss, then changed his mind. He wanted more than a kiss, and he sure as hell didn't have time for it.

"Do you know where my shoes are?"

Savannah moved toward the stained cherry dresser, her back to him as she pulled out a pair of sweat shorts and a tank top. "If you had them, they're probably downstairs. But I don't think you were wearing any."

Aaron grunted again, this time in disappointment

as Savannah pulled her clothes on, covering all her soft curves. He jerked his gaze away from her ass and looked around the room once more, searching for shoes. "Are you sure I didn't have shoes on?"

"Pretty sure. If I find them, I'll bring them over. Now go." She placed her hand against the small of his back and guided him out of the room and down the stairs. She opened the patio door then leaned against it, a small smile on her face. Aaron stepped through, stopped, then turned and pulled her close for a deep kiss that ended entirely too soon.

"I had fun."

"Me, too."

"I mean it about lunch."

"You know where to find me."

"You're right, I do." He grinned and kissed her again, then forced himself to release her before he did something stupid—like toss her over his shoulder and carry her back upstairs.

He hurried across her yard and into his, slowing his steps as he approached the patio door. He hesitated, looking around for signs of destruction, listening for sounds that would indicate World War Three had recently erupted inside his house.

All was quiet. Maybe a little too quiet.

Cold air washed over him as he pushed the slider open. The large country kitchen was vacant but he could hear the sound of the television coming from the living room beyond. He moved across the room, his steps quiet, and peeked around the corner. A heavy sigh of relief left him when he saw Isabelle curled in the corner of the sofa, a closed book in one hand as she watched some kind of science show on the big screen television mounted on the wall.

"Hey, Sweet Pea. How was school?"

"Good." Her face scrunched up in a frown. "They gave us homework. On a weekend!"

Aaron bit back a smile. He totally agreed with her indignation but he couldn't let her know that. "Then don't you think you should be doing that instead of watching television?"

"This is part of it. We have to watch this show then answer these stupid questions." She waved a paper in front of her face then sat back with a deep sigh, making him bite back another smile.

"Then I guess I'll let you get back to your show."

"It's okay. It's on again tomorrow."

"Getting it out of the way early, huh?"

"Yeah, I guess." Isabelle tilted her head to the side, studying him with a quizzical look. "Why's your hair all messed up?"

"My hair?" Aaron ran a hand through his hair, smoothing it down and wondering if his ten-year-old daughter could see him blushing. Christ, he hoped not. "Um, where's your sister?"

"Upstairs. I think she's on her tablet."

"She better not be. I took that away from her two nights ago." He moved to the bottom of the stairs and raised his voice. "Brooke? Get down here."

He waited a minute then called again, louder this time. "Brooke. Now."

He heard something slam against the wall, then the loud sound of feet stomping across the floor. A few seconds later, Brooke appeared at the top of the stairs.

"What?"

"Are you on that tablet?"

"I need it for homework."

Aaron frowned, not missing the way she had

phrased it. "You went into my room to get it? Without permission?"

"I said I needed it for homework."

"Without permission?"

"But I—"

"We went over this already. If you need it for homework, you ask me to get it. And then you do your homework down here in the kitchen, where I can watch you."

She stomped her foot and jammed one fist on her hip. "That is so stupid! You're treating me like a little baby."

"When you start acting like an adult, I'll treat you like one. Now get the tablet and bring it down here."

"I don't—"

"Now!"

Brooke muttered something under breath, just low enough that he couldn't hear—which was probably a deliberate calculation on her part. He listened as she stomped down the hall into her room, heard something else hit the floor. Then, right when he was ready to go upstairs after her, she stomped back up the hall and down the stairs, brushing by him as she moved to the kitchen.

He followed her in, his back teeth grinding when she slid the chair across the tile floor. She dropped into the chair and slid back in, scraping the floor with each little bounce as she moved closer to the table.

"Hand it over."

Brooke's eyes narrowed, anger rolling from her thin shoulders as she stared at him. He half-expected her to shove the chair back and storm from the room, screaming that she hated him again. But she didn't, just shoved the tablet across the table to him.

He tapped his finger against the screen, waking it, and immediately scrolled through to see which apps had been opened. Everything looked innocent enough—which meant absolutely nothing. He'd removed most of them, but that didn't mean Brooke couldn't add them back on or delete them before he had a chance to check. God knew, she was a hundred times better with the damn thing than he was.

He handed the tablet back to her. "Don't ever go into my room again. Is that understood?"

"But I needed—"

"Is that understood?"

"Maybe if you had been here instead of next door with your stupid girlfriend, I wouldn't have had to go into your room!"

The words acted like a slap to his face. How in the hell could Brooke know anything? Or was she just guessing? Had she looked out her bedroom window? Had she seen him kissing Savannah? Her room was at the back of the house, her window overlooking the yard. It was possible she might have seen, he wasn't sure.

No, she couldn't have. The angle was all wrong.

Did it matter?

Not right now, no. His personal life—what little he had—was his own business. But there was something about the way Brooke was watching him, something about the hooded expression in her eyes, that made him uncomfortable.

He ignored the sensation, denied the subtle accusation. "Savannah is a friend. I was helping her with something."

"Yeah, right."

"Just what is that supposed to mean?"

"Nothing."

"Brooke, what's going on?"

"Nothing. Can I go now?"

"I thought you had homework."

"I'm finished already."

Aaron didn't buy that for a minute but he decided to let it slide—for now. "Then you may go. But you're punished this weekend."

"What? Why? I didn't do anything!"

"For going into my room when you know you're not supposed to."

"But I needed—"

"Then you should have waited."

"That's not fair!" She pushed away from the table so fast, the chair tilted back and would have hit the floor if he hadn't caught it.

"Brooke—"

"It's not fair!" She yelled the words and stormed across the room, stopping long enough to throw him a dirty look over her shoulder. "I ha—"

"Yeah, I know: you hate me."

Her eyes widened, then narrowed in anger. "I hate you!" She yelled the words, screeching them before tearing up the stairs.

Aaron sighed and sat down, his gaze on the blank screen of the tablet. He ran his hands through his hair then tilted his head back, following the sounds of Brooke's angry steps as she stomped to her room and slammed the door, her words still ringing in his ears and ripping a hole in his heart.

CHAPTER EIGHT

Tessa poked her head around the door of the refrigerator, a frown creasing her face. "So he seriously hasn't been back for seconds?"

"Tessa! Do you have to phrase it like that? You make it sound like I'm some kind of all-you-can-buffet."

"Sorry." She closed the refrigerator door, a fresh bottle of wine in her hand. Savannah frowned, wondering how smart it was to open a second bottle. The first one had disappeared too quickly, and she couldn't exactly blame it all on Tessa.

She peered into her wine glass, studying the mouthful of liquid at the bottom, then shrugged and tossed it back before sliding her glass across for a refill. She was in her own house. She wasn't driving anywhere. She didn't have any place she had to be.

And she was brooding.

Not brooding. *Pouting*.

If this didn't call for wine, she didn't know what did.

Tessa refilled both glasses then slid into the chair across from Savannah. "Have you at least talked to him?"

"Yes, of course. He lives next door. Of course, we've talked."

"I don't mean that casual neighbor stuff, like a wave or a nod across the yard. I mean like talked. Spent some time together. All that fun stuff."

"I know what you meant." Savannah took a small sip and swished the wine around her mouth. This one tasted different, not quite as sweet. She leaned forward and peered at the bottle, reading the label. No, it was the same kind, a crisp Riesling. So why did it taste different?

She shrugged and took another sip, longer this time.

"Well?"

"Well, what?"

Tessa blew the hair from her face with a heavy sigh then reached for Savannah's glass.

"Hey! Give that back."

"Not until you answer me. And maybe not even then."

"Just give me the wine back."

"You're going to have a headache in the morning."

"I don't care. I'm pouting." Savannah snagged her glass and curled both hands around it, just in case Tessa tried to take it from her again.

"No kidding. Are you going to answer the question?"

"What question?"

Tessa stared into her own glass, frowning. "I don't remember. Oh, wait. Yes, I do. Have you talked?"

"To who?"

"To Aaron. You know, the neighbor you've had the hots for? The one you had wild monkey sex with?"

"It wasn't monkey sex."

"Okay, whatever. It was sex. Have you talked to him since then?"

"I told you I did."

"No, you told me there hadn't been an encore performance. What I'm asking is, has he completely ignored you since then?"

"No, we've talked. Kind of. And he took me to lunch two weeks ago."

"But no fun stuff, huh?"

"Nope." Savannah's lips smacked together, turning the p-sound into two long syllables. There hadn't been any fun stuff at all. Yes, he'd taken her to lunch, but it had been a short one because he had to go meet with Brooke's teachers. And then she'd been out of town again for a few days and he'd been busy getting ready for some kind of camp and before she realized it, a few weeks had gone by and—

Savannah took a long swallow of wine, trying to force the depressing thoughts away. Yes, she was definitely pouting—which was silly. She hadn't been looking for a relationship, knew that probably wasn't even a possibility. He had a lot more responsibility than she did, especially with his daughters. And she wasn't looking for a family, ready-made *or* from scratch.

But she had really been looking forward to more sex. And she had thought that maybe he had been looking forward to the same thing.

She pushed out of the chair and grabbed the wine bottle.

"Where are you going?"

"Outside. It's too nice a night to be cooped up inside."

"But it's chilly!"

"It's not chilly, it's gorgeous. And I can get the

firepit going. Come on, let's sit outside."

"Are you sure you don't want to just sit out there so you can watch for him?"

"Positive." Savannah adjusted her grip on the bottle and her glass, using her elbow to open the door. "You coming?"

"Yeah, in a minute. I'm going to raid your refrigerator for some food."

Savannah rolled her eyes but didn't say anything. Food would probably be a good thing. Yes, definitely a good thing. Some cheese and crackers. Maybe some of that hard salami, sliced nice and thick.

She ignored the slight rumbling in her stomach and moved out to the patio, leaving the door cracked open because her hands were full. The night air was cool, the heat of summer finally giving way to the crisp weather of autumn. In a few more weeks—maybe just a few more days—she'd need a jacket to sit outside, but right now, it was nearly perfect.

She sat her glass and the wine bottle on the edge of the propane fire pit then leaned down, turning it on and hitting the ignition switch. It finally caught on the third try, small flames leaping to life around the lava rocks. She adjusted the flame then took a seat in the oversized chair, sinking into the overstuffed cushions with a soft sigh. The swivel rocker would have been her first choice, but if she sat there, she'd have a view of Aaron's house and yard. The last thing she needed to do was stare at his house, searching for signs of life, hoping to catch a glimpse of him.

Sex. She snorted, the sound filled with derision. She could tell herself that sex was all she wanted but she'd had too much wine to lie to herself. No, she wasn't looking for a relationship—she was honest about that much. But she really liked Aaron and had thought…

Well, it didn't matter. They were neighbors. Maybe even friends…who just happened to have had sex. Once. It happened. She'd just have to snap out of this depressing funk she'd been in and deal with it. If it happened again, great. If not…

She reached for her wine, pushing thoughts of *if not* from her mind as she leaned her head back and stared up at the night sky. Stars winked overhead, glittering points of sharp light against a background of velvet blackness. The small community she lived in was on the outskirts of town and had, at one time, been a sprawling farm. Only the farmhouse remained, the property divided into twenty large lots.

Her house—and Aaron's—were at the very end of the small development, isolated from the others because of the small stream that ran nearby. That was why she had decided on this house when she bought it, although she had at first thought it odd that the builders had placed the two houses so close together. It hadn't been enough of a deterrent to stop her from buying it, though.

Would she sell it in a few years, move somewhere else? Maybe. The house was large enough to grow into, with three bedrooms and two-and-a-half baths and a den and a full finished basement. Yes, it was entirely too big for one person, she knew that. But the price had been ridiculously low and she had been thinking about the future, planning ahead in case she decided to entertain clients. That was still a possibility, but the longer she lived here, the less inclined she was to invite clients into her personal space.

"Wake up."

"I am awake."

"Then why are you sitting there with your eyes closed?"

"Just thinking." Savannah sighed and lifted her head, her vision swimming just the tiniest bit. She grabbed the chair arm and shifted, blinking until the spinning stop.

"Uh-oh. Here, eat this." Tessa pushed a plate into her hand. Cheese, crackers, salami, fresh cauliflower, and carrot sticks. Savannah stacked some salami and cheese on a cracker and popped it into her mouth, slowly chewing.

"Do you think this house is too big?"

"Yes. I told you that before you bought it. Why? Are you thinking of moving?"

"No. I was just curious." She took a sip of wine then popped more food into her mouth.

"Maybe you should switch to water."

"I'm fine."

"Just remember that when I call you bright and early tomorrow morning."

"Ha. Like you'd even be awake."

"Unfortunately, I will. I have to—" Tessa was interrupted by a loud squeal, followed by clear laughter. Savannah jumped and wine sloshed over the rim of the glass, coating her hand. She muttered and put the glass down, wiping her hand on her pants leg as she twisted in the seat.

She could make out several shadowy forms in the yard next door, their silhouettes slightly darker than the surrounding night. Aaron's house was completely dark and for a brief second, she wondered if the power had gone out. But that couldn't be, not when the light from her living room spilled out onto the patio.

"Miss Savannah! Turn your lights out. Hurry!"

"What in the world?" That had been Isabelle's voice, filled with excitement. She squinted and leaned forward, watching as the young girl jumped up and down before darting across the yard. A second silhouette, taller and broader, slowly followed.

Savannah swallowed back a small groan and looked at Tessa, silently asking for help. She didn't want to see Aaron, not now, not after she'd been drowning her sorrows in wine. No, she wasn't drunk, but she was definitely feeling the beginning effects of it.

But Tessa just sat there, trying to hide the stupid grin on her face behind her own glass of wine.

"Miss Savannah, turn out your lights and come see."

Aaron stopped behind his daughter, his hand on her shoulder. He stood just outside the fall of light from her living room, his broad shoulders and chest somehow looking bigger in the semi-darkness. "Isabelle, Miss Savannah's busy, you shouldn't bother her. And she doesn't need to turn out her lights, we can see just fine."

Savannah pulled her gaze from Aaron's face and looked at the little girl. "See what?"

"The space station is going to be flying over and we'll actually be able to see it. We don't need a telescope or anything." Isabelle turned and grabbed Aaron's hand, trying to pull him back into his yard. "Daddy, come on."

"This is so stupid."

Savannah leaned to the side, saw Brooke walking toward them, her steps slow and reluctant. Even in the shadows, she could see the teenager's frown. And she could definitely hear the attitude in her voice.

"Brooke, please." Aaron's voice sounded tired, almost defeated. "Ten minutes. Can you just lose the attitude for ten minutes?"

"But I don't care about any stupid space station. I don't even know why I have to be out here."

"Because I said so, okay?"

"Then what are we doing over *here*?"

"I just wanted to see if Miss Savannah wanted to watch it with us."

"Sweet Pea, Miss Savannah is busy. I don't think—"

"Savannah would love to watch it with you. Wouldn't she?" Tessa narrowed her eyes at Savannah, her unspoken message not quite as clear as she probably thought it was. That didn't matter because Savannah was able to decipher it anyway. She started to shake her head, to tell her friend that her lame attempt to do whatever she was trying to do was a bad idea—a really bad idea.

"I don't think—" But Tessa was already moving. She grabbed Savannah's hand and pulled her from the overstuffed seat, causing her to stumble before catching her balance.

"Tessa—"

"I'll just go turn out the light and hang out inside while you guys watch. I was getting chilly anyway."

"Tessa—"

"In fact, it's about time for me to head home anyway. I've got an early day tomorrow."

"Tessa—"

"Come on, Miss Savannah. I already picked out the perfect spot." Isabelle grabbed her hand and tugged, leaving Savannah no choice but to follow. Her toe caught on the edge of a paver and she stumbled again, would have fallen if Aaron hadn't caught her with one steadying hand on her arm.

"Great. She's drunk."

Savannah opened her mouth to deny the accusation but Aaron spoke first, his voice harsh. "Brooke. Enough. She just tripped."

"Yeah, right." The girl didn't say anything else, which made Savannah wonder if Aaron had given her some kind of silent warning. She glanced over her shoulder but couldn't make out his expression in the dark—because it truly was dark now, the only light coming from the small flames of the firepit on her patio.

Isabelle lead her across the yard then stopped and released her hand. "Right here. Now all we have to do is wait. How much longer, Daddy?"

"Just a few more minutes." Aaron's voice was right behind her, so close she imagined she could feel his breath on her neck. She closed her eyes, refusing to let her thoughts stray down that particular path, and focused on the feel of the grass under her bare feet. Cool, damp, just rough enough to tickle the soles of her feet. She wiggled her toes in the short blades then caught herself as she swayed to the side.

No, it was Aaron who caught her, his large hand resting on her waist and steadying her. She glanced over her shoulder, saw the brief flash of his smile in the darkness. He leaned toward her, his mouth close to her ear, his voice pitched to a low whisper.

"Are you feeling okay?"

"Mhmm."

"A little buzzed?"

Savannah raised her hand, thumb and forefinger

spread a half an inch apart. "Maybe a little."

He chuckled, the sound dangerously low and warm. Her skin pebbled and heat unfurled in her belly, traveling through her body and settling between her legs. She pulled in a deep breath and tried to put more distance between them. Aaron's hand tightened around her waist and pulled her against him, her back flush against his body. Warm. Solid. And tempting. God, so tempting. She closed her eyes and breathed in the scent of him, reveled in the touch of his hand as he traced small circles against her hip. It would be so easy to lean her head back, drape her arm around his neck as he kissed her, touched her. Dampness spread between her legs as she imagined the feel of those large hands dipping down the front of her pants, the feel of those long fingers teasing her hardened nipples.

"Okay, look west. It should be any second now."

Savannah's eyes snapped open, her body stiffening at the sound of Aaron's voice. Dear God, what was she doing? They were standing in his yard, with his daughters not three feet away, looking for a flash in the night sky, and all she could think about was his hands on her naked body? Savannah uttered a silent prayer of thanks for the blackness of night, knowing it hid the embarrassment burning her face.

"There it is! I see it! I see it!" Isabelle jumped up and down, her finger pointed skyward, following the trail of the steady dot of light as it moved overhead.

And quickly disappeared.

"That was lame."

"Was not!" Isabelle turned toward her father, excitement still clear in her voice. "Daddy, can we go to the Air and Space Museum this weekend? I want to see all the spaceships and stuff."

"Maybe Sunday, we'll see."

"Miss Savannah, do you want to go with us?"

"No, stupid. Why would she do that? She doesn't care about stupid space stuff. Nobody does."

"I'm not stupid!"

Cool air washed over Savannah's back as Aaron stepped away from her. "Both of you, enough. Get inside and get ready for bed, I'll be back in a few minutes. I'm going to walk Savannah home."

"That's okay, I don't need—"

"I said, I'll walk you home."

"You heard her. She said she didn't need you to." Brooke's voice was laced with bitterness. Savannah couldn't make out the expression on the girl's face, but she had no trouble imagining it: the unseen scowl was as clear as the displeasure in her voice.

"Doesn't matter, because that's what a gentleman does. Now inside, both of you. It's already past your bedtime."

Both girls groaned but the argument Savannah expected didn't come. That didn't stop either one of them from muttering under their breath as they headed toward the house and disappeared inside.

Aaron breathed a sigh of relief, his muttered words too low to make out. Savannah bit back a grin and started walking back to her house. "I take it that means progress is being made?"

"Maybe. I'm afraid to get my hopes up, though."

"Like I said, it just takes time." The pavers of her patio were cold under her feet as she moved to the firepit and turned it off. Pitch black darkness surrounded them and she blinked, trying to restore her night vision. She turned and collided with one of the chairs, stubbing her toe in the process. Aaron's hand wrapped around her elbow, his warm chuckle echoing in the chill air around them.

"I guess it's a good thing I did walk you home."

"You didn't have to. I'm fine." And she was—she even found the back door with no problem. She curled her hand around the handle and started to push the door open. Strong arms wrapped around her, spinning her around. And then Aaron's mouth was on hers, the kiss hot and wet, demanding. Needy. She sighed and leaned into him, her hands clinging to his arms for support.

He pulled away too soon, leaving her breathless and needing more. She felt his hand caress her face, felt his fingers trail through the strands of her hair before tucking them behind her ear.

"That's why I walked you home."

"I—" She swallowed, nodded, swallowed again as she tried to catch her breath. "Okay."

She saw the quick flash of his grin then his mouth was on hers again, just as demanding, feeding the frantic desire spiraling out of control. She leaned into him, ran her foot up his leg and back down, wanting to leap into his arms. Wanting to wrap her legs around his waist, wanting to feel him deep inside her.

Needing to feel him.

But once again he pulled away, his breathing harsh and ragged. She heard him swear, the soft words disappearing into the surrounding night. "I need to get back."

"Oh." She swallowed her disappointment. Of course, he needed to get back. She knew that. Of course she did.

But God, how she wished he didn't.

"Our home opener is Saturday. Did you want to

go? I can get tickets."

Savannah blinked, her hazy mind not making the connection right away. His game. He was talking about his game. "Oh. Um, sure. Okay."

"Did you want me to get a ticket for Tessa?"

"For who? Oh. Yes. I mean, if it's not too much trouble."

"It's not." He leaned forward, kissed her again, slow and deep. "About Sunday."

"Hm?" And God, why was she having such a hard time following his conversation? It had to be the wine, even if she wasn't drunk.

"Would you mind hanging out with an old man when he takes his two daughters to the Air and Space Museum?"

Was it her imagination, or was that hesitant hope she heard in his quiet voice? It must be her imagination. Or maybe the wine again.

And she should say no. She really should. This was different than going to lunch, or sneaking a kiss in the darkness on her patio. This was almost like…she wasn't sure, didn't know if she really wanted to analyze it that closely.

It didn't matter because she should still say no.

"Okay, yeah. That'll be fun."

Aaron chuckled, the sound just a little surprised. "I don't know about all that, but we can always hope." He caught her mouth again, the kiss entirely too short before he stepped away.

"I'll bring those tickets over tomorrow."

And then he was gone, leaving Savannah standing there in the darkness, wondering what she had just agreed to. And cursing herself for having that fourth glass of wine, even if she hadn't finished it.

CHAPTER NINE

Legs stretched, muscles burned, lungs struggled to pull in air. Aaron clenched his jaw and pushed through it, ignoring the pain, forcing his body forward.

Move. Move, dammit.

He bent at the waist and slid right, pain shooting through his knee with the move. He forced the pain to the back of his mind and reached around with his stick, shoving at the puck. His blade tipped it, sending it sliding to the left and earning him a hard elbow in the ribs for his efforts. He ignored the hit, ignored the way his breath left in a sharp hiss, and spun around. He jabbed his elbow behind him, catching the player from Syracuse in the side, then took off up the ice.

Just a little bit of payback.

Jason moved forward with the puck, dodging to the left, crossing into the zone. Aaron was right behind him, Harland to his right, racing to get into position.

"Emory!" Aaron called Jason's name and tapped his stick against the ice, the clacking sound muted and hollow. Jason pivoted, shot the puck toward Aaron, a perfect pass against his tape. He moved forward, his mind registering the activity exploding around him. Syracuse's d-man, coming in hard and low. Harland, spinning around and getting into position. Syracuse's goalie, already anticipating Harland's shot as he slid to the right, dropping to one knee.

And Jason, wide open on the left. Aaron tightened his grip on the stick, flicked his wrist, and sent the puck straight to Jason's tape. The other man turned and shot, sending the puck straight to the top shelf.

Something heavy crashed into Aaron from behind, sending him sprawling face-first as the blare of the horn ripped through the cheers filling the arena. He got to his knees, moving slower than he wanted, then jumped to his feet, his stick and gloves already flying. The ref was there before he could throw the first punch, pulling him back as Harland and Jason and Ben and Dustin Rios rushed to his defense, ready to join in the fight.

But there was no fight, because the ref had acted too quickly, stopping it before they got the chance to start.

"Stupid fuck." Aaron muttered the words under his breath as he shot a stream of spit to the ice. And okay, maybe the words were louder than they should have been because the idiot from Syracuse spun around, ready to charge him again. Aaron just laughed, collecting his gear from Harland before making his way to the bench.

The kid was new, playing his first year, and had been trying to prove himself the entire game. Prove what, Aaron had no idea. He was hitting too late, anticipating the wrong moves, waiting too long to pass or take a shot. Yeah, it was the first game of the season, there was plenty of time to smooth the rough edges. But if the kid had dreams of getting called up—and Aaron knew he did, hell they all did, that's what they were here for—then he needed to work a little harder on finessing those rough edges.

He slid to a stop in front of Syracuse's bench, jabbing Scotty Wells on the side of the arm. He was another old-timer, just like Aaron. Fuck, probably older. They had played together for two seasons in Buffalo, a lifetime ago.

"Your boy needs to work on his timing."

"Yeah, no shit." Scotty leaned to the side and spit, then grinned at Aaron, revealing a hole where his front tooth had once been. "Noticed he still put you on your ass, though. Old man."

"Not as old as you. Or as fucking ugly."

"Yeah. Says who?"

"Your wife."

Scotty threw his head back and laughed, then reached out and bumped Aaron's fist with his own. "We'll catch up later."

"Sounds good." Aaron skated forward and pushed through the door of the Bombers' bench, resting his stick against the boards behind him and reaching for a water bottle. A sharp pain shot through his side and he winced, straightening with a hiss.

Travis Bankard slid closer, his brow lowered in concern. "You okay, Pops?"

"Yeah, fine." Aaron yanked at his jersey and pulled it up, craning his neck to study his side. A bruise was already forming, mottling the flesh along his lower rib cage. He gently poked at it with the tips of two fingers, pushing and prodding around his ribs, lower along his side, back up again. Didn't feel like anything was broken. That was always a positive sign.

He let the hem of the jersey fall back into place then accepted the water bottle Travis held out to him.

He took a long swallow, his gaze meeting Coach Torresi's. The other man moved toward him, his green eyes carefully blank.

"Everything good?"

"Yeah."

"Need tape?"

Aaron glanced at the scoreboard and noted the time. "It can wait."

"You going to be pissing blood?"

"Don't think so."

Torresi nodded, the motion short and efficient. "Let me know if anything changes."

Aaron nodded then turned his attention back to the game. They were just over a minute away from the end of the second period, and the Bombers were still two ahead on the board. Not a bad start for their first game.

And not a bad way to impress Savannah. Maybe. The woman knew absolutely nothing about hockey so she might not be impressed at all.

He resisted the urge to look around for her, figuring he'd catch even more shit from the guys if he did. He had let it slip earlier that he had a guest here tonight, that she might be joining him at Mystic's after the game. From the stunned looks he received, you'd think he had just announced that Mr. Hockey himself had been resurrected and was coming to York to be their new coach. And Christ, if he had known it was going to be that bad, he would have never said a word.

The horn sounded again, long and loud, signaling the end of the period. Aaron rose to his feet with everyone else and grabbed his stick, waiting to follow the rest of the team back through the tunnel. He shifted his gaze to the left, trying to study the crowd without being obvious about it. It didn't matter because he couldn't see a damn thing, not with the way everyone was standing and moving around, heading out to the concourse for refreshments or to use the bathroom, or whatever the hell else people did during intermission.

The interrogation started near the end of the intermission, after Torresi had given them his usual spiel, after cuts had been bandaged, ice packs handed out, and Aaron's ribs had been taped. He felt like he was holding court, right there from the bench as he pressed his arm against his side and willed the pain to go away.

Six of the guys hovered around him, curiosity mingled with concern as they watched him holding his side. Well fuck, did he look that bad?

He dropped his arm and eyed his teammates, wondering if he should just draw fucking numbers to see who went first. It didn't reach that point because Jason broke the ice by jumping right to the point.

"Okay, Pops. Who's this date and why haven't we heard about her?"

Aaron blinked, ready to shake his head at the stupid question. Zach beat him to it by elbowing Jason in the side hard enough to cause the other man to stumble. "You are fucking stupid. You know that, right?"

"What?"

"Are you really that unobservant? It's his neighbor, you stupid fuck."

"His neighbor?"

"Yeah. Remember her? You should, you fucking walked in on them at Aaron's house this summer."

Recognition finally flared in Jason's pale eyes, a

quick grin spreading across her face. "So you guys are together now? Cool."

Aaron swallowed back his choked laughter and resisted the urge to roll his eyes. One of these days, things would finally click for Jason. Until then, Megan had her hands full.

"We're not *together*. I just got her tickets for the game tonight, that's all."

"If that's all, why are you bringing her to Mystic's?"

Aaron glanced to his right, his gaze meeting Travis' solemn one before sliding away. "I just invited her along. You guys are reading too much into it."

"Bullshit, I know better." Zach dropped to the bench beside him then leaned forward, stretching his back with a few sharp *pops*. "What about the girls? You're not actually going to bring them to Mystic's, are you? I mean, I don't think you can. It's a bar."

"Isabelle and Brooke are home. My mom's watching them." He still felt a little guilty about that, and probably would have changed his plans if his mother hadn't insisted. Brooke had been throwing a fit about coming tonight anyway, telling him every chance she got that hockey was stupid and she didn't want to waste a Saturday night watching him play some stupid game.

Yeah, because spending it in her room was so much more exciting.

Isabelle had been the one who was disappointed—until he gave her a choice between staying up late and going to the game tonight, or going down to DC tomorrow. The Air and Space Museum had won, hands down.

But yeah, he still felt a little guilty. Would it always

be this way? His gaze slid to Harland, the only other guy on the team with a kid.

Harland looked up, one brow raised. "What?"

Aaron shook head. No, he wasn't going to ask Harland now, not in front of everyone else.

Ben nudged his skate against Aaron's own, pulling his attention from Harland. "So this is your first date in how long?"

"Are you kidding? They didn't have dates when Pops was growing up." Banky started laughing at his own joke, the laughter dying in his throat when everyone just stared at him. His ears turned red and he looked away, mumbling to himself.

"It's not a date."

"Yeah? Then what do you call it?"

"We're just getting together for drinks. That's it."

"Really?" Zach's voice was filled with doubt. "Bullshit. If you wanted to get together for drinks, you'd take her somewhere else. But you're taking her to Mystic's. With *us*. That's a date. Hell, it's more than a date, that's like declaring your intentions. And you know it, so don't go bullshitting us. Or yourself."

"Guys, it's not—" Aaron snapped his mouth closed, frowning as he worried about saying too much. Oh, fuck it. These guys were his family, as much as his daughters were. "It's not that simple. I'm divorced. I'm still adjusting to taking care of two daughters I barely know. Savannah doesn't want to get in the middle of shit like that. No woman would."

"Then why are you bringing her tonight?"

"Like I said, it's just drinks. Nothing else."

Aaron didn't have to worry about trying to convince anyone he was telling the truth, because Coach Torresi poked his head around the corner, a frown creasing his chiseled face. "You lazy fuckers going to get out there and play? Or are we just going to call it a night and let Syracuse go home with the win?"

Activity exploded inside the locker room as everyone grabbed their gear and headed out, Aaron and Zach the last two in line. Aaron was just ready to step onto the ice when Zach grabbed him, his dark gaze too intense.

"You know I call bullshit, right?"

"Doesn't matter, Mummy. It's just drinks. Nothing more." Aaron pulled his arm from Zach's grip and headed toward center ice, knowing the other man didn't believe the words any more than he did.

CHAPTER TEN

Savannah stopped just inside the door, her eyes adjusting to the dim lights of the bar. The interior was more spacious and modern than she had expected, with polished high-tops strategically placed around the floor and bench seating framing the back wall. Smaller groupings of tables that could be pushed together if needed were placed between the bar to her right and the stage to her left. The stage was empty except for two microphone stands and a karaoke machine set up between them. A guy dressed in all black sat on a stool in the back corner, headphones over his ears as he studied the large tablet in his hand.

She hoped someone had gotten here before them, because even without a band playing, almost every table was filled. The buzz of conversation was loud enough that it nearly drowned the music coming from…somewhere. A jukebox, probably.

Aaron placed his hand on the small of her back and guided her through the crowd. She noticed the tables pushed together in the corner, most of the seats still empty. Aaron led her to the two seats on the far end, across from another couple. He held the chair out for her and she shrugged out of her jacket, draping it over the back of the chair before sitting down. She studied the other couple from beneath her lashes, finally recognizing them from Aaron's party almost two months ago. At least, she recognized the woman. She had been the one with the cute little boy, who happened to be the spitting image of the man sitting with her.

Savannah searched her memory, finally latching onto the two names as Aaron leaned across to talk to the other man.

"I'm not used to seeing you here anymore."

Harland laughed, the sound low and mellow. "It's been a while, yeah. But it's the first game. I can't break tradition."

"Besides, we both need a break from Noah." Courtney turned to her husband, amusement flashing in her eyes as she leaned forward and pressed her mouth to his. Savannah looked away, feeling like a voyeur. And how silly was that? It was just a simple kiss, one that couldn't even be described as a public display of affection.

No, it wasn't the kiss. It was the intensity of the expression on Harland's face, like his entire life was devoted to the woman next to him, like he'd do anything in the world for her. Seeing that made Savannah feel like she was intruding on something private.

And made her wonder what it would be like to love like that. To be loved like that in return.

"Did you want anything to drink?"

She turned, nearly bumping noses with Aaron because he was so close. Of course, he was close—that was the only way she'd be able to hear him. That didn't stop her from jumping back in surprise, though.

"That depends. Who's driving?" She didn't have her car—Tessa had picked her up before the game, and she'd be driving home with Aaron, since they lived right next door to each other. But if he was going to be drinking, she figured she should stick to soda or water.

"I have a one beer limit so you're good to go."

"Then I'll have a glass of white wine."

"One wine coming up." He pushed away from the table, already reaching for his wallet as he threaded his way to the bar. Savannah let her eyes follow him, her gaze taking in the way his suit jacket fit his broad back, the way the dress trousers hugged his firm ass. What was it about a man in a tailored suit?

Especially *this* man.

She sat back in the chair with a small sigh of appreciation then looked to her left, her gaze meeting Courtney's. The woman offered her a small smile, letting her know she had been caught. Savannah shrugged and smiled back, not denying it. Why should she? Aaron was attractive, well-built, and sexy as hell. What woman wouldn't look?

He returned a few minutes later, a glass of wine in one hand and a bottle of beer in the other. She accepted the glass and took a small sip, studying him over the rim as he sat down beside her. Did she imagine the wince? Or the way he almost grabbed his side before letting his hand drop? No, she didn't think so. In fact, she'd be surprised if he *wasn't* hurt. She'd seen how he'd been hit tonight, more than once. The game had been too fast for her to follow but she didn't have any trouble missing the physical aspects of it. She had cringed more than once and wondered how the players did it, how their bodies survived it. Aaron had been playing for seventeen years, more than that, really.

It was a miracle he didn't have more scars and bumps than he did.

The table quickly filled as more players showed up, the conversation getting louder with each addition. A few of the faces she recognized and was better able to put names to each time Aaron made introductions. What surprised her was when a waitress came to their table, her long legs encased in slim-fitting jeans tucked inside a pair of worn cowboy boots. She hadn't been introduced at the party in August, but there was no missing that long, curly red hair.

Aaron draped his arm behind her chair and leaned forward, his mouth pressed against her ear as he spoke. "That's Haley. Zach's girlfriend."

"She works here?"

"Yeah. That's how they met."

She shouldn't be surprised but she was. For some reason, she hadn't expected a hockey player's girlfriend to be a waitress in a bar.

Which only proved she had some seriously snobbish, preconceived notions she needed to work on.

She turned to say something and almost bumped noses with Aaron again. She smiled, ready to apologize, except the smile wavered on her face. He was watching her so closely, the brown of his eyes so warm, her insides started to melt. She dropped her gaze to his mouth, to the thin scar that ran from the corner of his mouth down to his chin, barely noticeable in the ever-present stubble that covered his jaw, adding to his rugged appeal. His lips curled in a quick grin and she leaned forward, just a little, wanting to press her mouth against those sinfully soft lips, wanting him to kiss her.

"Hey, Pops. Come sing with me."

Aaron jerked back, sliding away and dropping his arm. Savannah swallowed a groan and reached for her wine, surprised to see her hand trembling.

"I'm not singing, Banky."

"Come on. I need someone to go up with me."

"You're a big boy, you can do it on your own."

"Nah. I'd be too embarrassed."

One of Aaron's teammates—Ben, she thought his name was—leaned forward, humor glittering in his eyes. He was attractive, with his jet-black hair and square jaw and hazel eyes, but there was something about him. Almost like he *knew* he was attractive and wasn't afraid to let everyone know it. "Oh, for fuck's sake, Banky. You just played in front of eight thousand people. Why would you be embarrassed to get up on stage and sing in front of a hundred?"

"It's not the same, is all."

Savannah bit down on her lip, hiding her smile at the blush that stained the other man's ears. There was something so endearing about him, something that made her want to cuddle and protect him. She had been surprised when he walked in, certain he wasn't old enough to drink, but Aaron had assured her he was twenty-one.

Legal, but barely.

A lot of teasing and pushing and shoving ensued, none of which Savannah understood. Then two of the guys grabbed the younger player and dragged him to the stage, where they studied a binder filled with song choices.

"Oh man, get your phones ready. This is going to be good."

Savannah smothered her laugh and took another sip of wine. She wasn't sure if it would be *good* or not, but it certainly couldn't be any worse than some of the other people who had been up there so far. Not that she would ever criticize because it took a lot more guts than she'd ever have to do something like that. Not to mention a lot more alcohol.

Everyone shifted in their chairs, facing the stage. More than one of the players had their phones out, ready to start recording. Savannah turned her chair around and curled one leg under her, settling in for the show. She heard Aaron move his chair behind her, smiled when he shifted closer and draped his arm around her shoulder. It was silly, for something so small and inconsequential to make her smile like she was, but she couldn't help it. They were with his teammates, so in a way, it was like he was claiming her.

And God help her if she ever said that to Tessa. Her friend would read her the riot act on how being an independent, successful woman—or just a *woman*, period—meant no man was able to claim her.

Tessa was probably right. But that didn't stop the little thrill of excitement shooting through her and pebbling her skin.

The music finally started and the three guys up on stage started singing—out of tune and out of sync. Good-natured laughter erupted around the table, as well as the light from several flashes. Travis groaned and shook his head, motioning for everyone to stop.

He moved back to the guy in black, their conversation lasting long enough that the other two guys started complaining. Travis moved back to the microphone, uncertainty flashing across his face. He looked over at Aaron, some kind of silent communication passing between them.

"Go for it, Travis. You got this."

Savannah tossed a questioning glance over her shoulder, but Aaron just smiled and shook his head. She turned back to the stage, wondering what was going on as music drifted from the expensive sound system.

And then Travis started singing and the entire bar grew quiet.

She heard the whispers of amazement from Aaron's teammates, quickly glanced around and saw the expressions of surprise on each face. She was certain the expressions matched her own. He had a beautiful voice, rich and mellow, the vocal range astounding as he belted out the words to "When A Man Loves A Woman".

Her throat tightened at the emotion in his voice, at the way he made the audience *feel* the music, *feel* the lyrics as he sang about holding on to what he needs. And just like everyone else around her, she jumped to her feet to clap and cheer when he was finished, forgetting for a moment that she wasn't at a concert, but in a bar she had never heard of, surrounded by a bunch of hockey players.

She sat back down then eased her chair around, pulling in a shaky breath. "That was—" The words died in her throat when she met Aaron's gaze. The way he was watching her, the expression in his eyes. Dark. Sinfully intense.

Filled with need.

He leaned forward, his lips brushing against her ear, his breath warm against her skin. "Do you want to leave?"

Savannah couldn't speak. She could barely breathe.

All she could manage to do was nod her head.

CHAPTER ELEVEN

Savannah pushed the door closed, the soft click echoing in the silence of the house like a shot. Aaron didn't wait—he *couldn't* wait, not when his entire body burned for her. He reached for her, spun her around and claimed her mouth in a searing kiss.

He heard a small thud, a crashing jingle as her purse and keys hit the floor, then felt her palms press against his chest. Was he being too rough? Assuming too much, too soon? Was she going to push him away?

No.

Her fingers trembled as she undid the buttons of his shirt, missing one then undoing two at a time. He shrugged out of the suit jacket, his mouth never leaving hers, and let it drop to the floor, right there in the entranceway.

Savannah moaned, the sound a sigh of disappointment as her fingers bunched in the plain white cotton of his undershirt. He tried to free his arms from the dress shirt, damn near strangled himself because the stupid fucking tie was still around his neck. He started to pull away but Savannah grabbed him, holding him still, and deepened the kiss. She pushed against him, her body soft and pliant and warm. Her kiss, her touch, everything about her…she drove him wild, forcing all thoughts from his mind.

All thoughts except this woman in his arms. Here. Now. With *him*. Rubbing against him, like she was consumed with need to get closer.

He knew the feeling.

He tightened his hands around her waist and spun, bracing her supple body against the wall. Another sigh escaped her, sharp and needy, unleashing something inside him. Something primal, hungry, desperate. Something he never knew existed until now.

Until Savannah.

He shoved her coat off her shoulders, grabbed the hem of her sweater and pulled it up. Knuckles grazed soft skin, smooth and warm. Were his hands too rough? Too callused? Should he stop—

Savannah closed one of her smaller hands around his and dragged it up, placing it on the soft swell of her breast. Aaron swallowed back a groan of need, his tongue plunging into her mouth over and over as his thumb grazed the tight peak of her nipple poking against the lace of her bra. And fuck, it wasn't enough. He needed to feel bare skin, needed to touch and taste.

He dipped his fingers into the cup of her bra and pulled the lacy material down, baring the rounded flesh to his touch. Her back arched as he ran his thumb across the hard nipple. He flicked the tight peak with the edge of his nail then gently pinched. She sighed again, the sound sharp and desperate. Her hips thrust against his, rubbing against the hard length of his aching cock.

His hands dropped to the waistband of her pants, searching for a button or snap or zipper. Anything. He needed them off her. Now. Needed to see her, touch her, taste her, with a searing intensity he'd never experienced before.

Savannah reached down, nudged his hands out of the way, then pushed the slacks down past her hips to her thighs. Trembling fingers closed around his hand, guiding it between her legs.

God, she was so fucking wet. Slick and hot. He ran the tip of his finger along her clit, swallowed a groan when her hips jerked against his touch. She pulled her mouth from his, her lips damp and swollen from his kisses. Her lids fluttered open, revealing eyes glazed with burning need. Her gaze met his as one breathy word fell from her lips.

"Please."

He caught her mouth again, the kiss hard, possessing. Then he dropped to his knees, grabbed the waistband of her pants, and yanked them down. Her fingers dug into his shoulders, searching for balance as she kicked off her shoes and stepped out of the tangled material of her slacks.

Aaron grabbed her leg and draped it over his shoulder, mesmerized at the sight in front of him. The small patch of tightly-trimmed curls, their color slightly darker than the thick strands of hair that framed Savannah's face. Soft flesh, swollen and pale, the delicate folds parted to reveal the darker pink flesh beneath. Aaron reached out, trailed his finger against the hard nub of her clit. Her body quivered, her nails digging deeper into his shoulders, her breath rushing from her in a soft cry as he lowered his head and ran his tongue over her clit.

Sweet, so fucking sweet. He pulled the hard flesh into his mouth, sucking, heard her moan again, louder. Fingers tangled in his hair, pulling him closer. Her hips rocked against his mouth, faster as he licked. Sucked. Tasted.

He reached out, using two fingers to spread the damp flesh, and flicked his tongue against her clit. Over and over, faster, her hips matching the rhythm of his mouth, his tongue. He reached behind her with his free hand, squeezed the round globe of her ass, then slid a finger along the cleft, down, down further, tracing the cleft to the hot entrance bared before him. He slid his finger into her tight heat, slow and deep. In, then out. Again, a second finger joining the first. Filling her, stretching her, over and over as he sucked and teased with tongue and teeth.

Her hips rocked, thrusting, seeking. Faster, tiny little moans and pleas falling from her mouth. Her muscles tightened, squeezing, pulling his fingers deeper. Her hands twisted in his hair. Her body stilled, stiffened for a fraction of a second, then a harsh cry filled his ears as her hips bucked against his. Her inner muscles convulsed around his fingers, hard and fast as her climax exploded.

"Aaron." His name was a harsh plea, ragged and desperate. "Please. Now. Fuck me. Now."

Hunger, blinding and desperate, tore through him. He eased away from her, steadying her with one hand as he tore at his trousers with the other. Belt, button, zipper. His mouth closed over hers, swallowing her cries as her hips continued their desperate thrusting, and shoved his pants down. His cock thrust free, hard and aching. He closed his hands around her waist, lifted, and plunged into her, burying himself deep in her wet heat.

She ripped her mouth from his, his name falling from her lips in a breathless scream. Her head tilted back as her hips rocked and thrust, riding his cock. Harder, faster. Over and over, driving him to the edge, driving him insane.

He clenched his jaw, braced a hand against the wall on one side of her head, and searched for control. Struggled, begged, pleaded, as sweat beaded on his forehead from the strain. He lowered his head, resting it against his arm as Savannah's body slowed. Stilled.

She dropped her head to his shoulder, her harsh breathing echoing around them. Trembling fingers traced his arm, his jaw, sending him even closer to the edge.

He couldn't—

Fuck.

He absolutely. Could not. Lose control.

"Don't move." Desperation filled his harsh growl. Savannah stilled, but only for a second. She shifted, pressed a kiss against his jaw, then lifted her head. He knew she was watching him, felt her confusion.

He sucked in a deep breath, held it, praying the last thread of his control wouldn't shatter as he forced the words from his throat. "I'm not wearing a condom."

Would she get pissed? Push him away and demand he leave? Because he knew, just like she did, that it was already too late. It wasn't just about birth control—it was about safe sex. Wasn't that the rule now? And he'd been the one to break it, to lose control and forget. But fuck, he wasn't used to this, had been out of the fucking game for too fucking long now.

Didn't matter. He knew better.

He held his breath, his jaw still painfully clenched as her body shifted against him. And fuck, if she didn't stop moving like that, if she didn't stop wiggling against him, it really would be too late.

Except she wasn't moving *against* him—she was easing away from him, unwrapping her legs from around his waist. Would she push him away? Demand he leave?

He held his breath, waiting, his heart pounding so fucking hard, he expected it to jump out of his chest. And still he struggled to maintain control as she slid down his body.

"Savannah, I'm sorry—"

"Sh."

He struggled to lift his head, to open his eyes. He needed to see her, to see the expression on her face because he didn't understand the sound she had made, had thought it sounded like some kind of reassurance. And he didn't understand why her hands were trailing down his body, couldn't make sense of anything because he was still struggling to hold onto that last fucking thread of control.

And then she was on her knees in front of him, her nails grazing the flesh of his ass. And then, fuck, her mouth was on him. Hot and wet around his cock, her tongue swirling around the engorged tip. He shuddered, forced his eyes open, looked down—

And met her blazing gaze as she looked up at him, her head tilted back as the last inch of his hard cock disappeared into the hot recesses of her mouth.

He groaned, the last bit of control shredding as he wrapped a fist in the silky strands of her hair and thrust his cock deeper into her mouth.

CHAPTER TWELVE

Aaron's eyes drifted closed, sleep beckoning him. It would be so easy to drift off, to fall asleep with Savannah sprawled on top of him, her body still wrapped protectively around him, cradling him with her slick heat.

How long had it been since he felt this way? Too long. Not since—

No, not even then.

Never.

He ran his hand along her back, tracing the ridges of her spine with the tip of one finger. She sighed against his shoulder, a sleepy sound of contentment as she snuggled even closer. A small smile curved his mouth at the sound, almost like she was purring. She was the most caring, giving, uninhibited woman he'd ever been with. Not afraid to tell him what she wanted. Not afraid to seek her own pleasure in his body and demanding he do the same.

He wanted to stay here all night, just holding her. Wanted to wake her in the morning by raining soft kisses along her body, to feel her come alive as he slowly entered her. Filling her. Stretching her.

Christ, he needed to stop thinking like that, not

when he was already inside her, seconds away from growing hard again.

He forced his eyes open and turned his head, blinking at the glowing numbers on Savannah's clock. It was later than he thought, although he shouldn't be surprised. They had made love two more times, long and slow, their bodies moving together as if they'd been meant for each other.

Intense. Driven.

He ran his hand along her arm and pressed a gentle kiss against the slope of her shoulder, then gently eased her away from him. Her eyes opened, filled with sleepy need. She wiggled her hips against him, a playful smile on her face.

"Going somewhere?"

"Yeah. I need to get home."

The smile faded, the sleepiness leaving her eyes. He thought he saw disappointment in her gaze but he couldn't be sure because she blinked and looked away. She moved her leg, slid off him, propped her head on her hand. Her gaze was focused on his chest when she spoke.

"You can stay here if you want. I don't mind."

Christ, he wished he could. He wanted nothing more. "I can't."

"Oh." There it was again, that flash of disappointment. But she quickly hid it behind a brief smile. She started to roll away but Aaron put a hand on her shoulder, stopping her. He leaned forward, holding her in place with his body, and captured her mouth in a slow, deep kiss.

"I want to, Savannah. I do. But I can't. The girls are home."

"I thought your mother was watching them."

"She is. But I can't stay gone all night. I won't do that to them."

"It's okay. I understand." The words were nothing more than empty reassurance. She *didn't* understand. She might think she did, but she didn't. She couldn't, because she didn't know.

He settled beside her and pulled her closer, held her gaze with his when she would have looked away.

"Savannah, it's—" He hesitated, not knowing how much to tell her, not knowing if he could even explain. "Their mother did that. All the time. I won't—"

She placed her fingers against his mouth, silencing him. "You don't have to explain, Aaron. You don't owe me anything."

He frowned, not liking the way the words sounded, not liking the flash of sorrow he saw in her eyes. He wrapped his fingers around hers and pulled them away. "The hell I don't."

"Aaron—"

"Let me finish. Please." He waited for her to argue, to tell him again that he didn't owe her anything. But maybe she saw the need in his eyes, the desperation to explain, because she slowly nodded and settled against him.

He took a deep breath, his gaze focused on the pillow beneath Savannah's head, on the spill of her hair against the creamy fabric. "Amy hated that I played hockey. Hated the sport, the travel, the time I spent on the road. Hated the moving. Hated everything about it."

"Then why did she marry you? She had to know what it would be like."

He smiled at the defensiveness in Savannah's voice. "The money. And the glamour—at least, what she thought would be glamour. I wasn't a superstar, not even close, but I was young enough that she thought I would be. Hell, so was I, if I'm going to be honest about it."

"Then that's her own damn fault."

"Not all of it. Not back then. I was too young to know better, convinced I'd be a superstar in no time. But it didn't work out that way, and she wasn't happy with the reality. And she really wasn't happy being stuck at home with a baby when I was on the road all the time."

"*Stuck?* I'm sorry, but isn't that part of being a parent?"

"She didn't see it that way. It's not—" Aaron frowned, searching for the right words. It would be so easy to lay all the blame at Amy's feet, but that wasn't the case, not entirely. "It wasn't just her. We were both too young to get married, too young to start a family. We were ready to call it quits before Brooke was even born."

"Why didn't you?"

"The money. She didn't want to give it up that easily."

"Prenup?"

"Yeah, but only because my agent insisted. You see, at that time, we still thought I was going to make it big. That didn't happen, though. By the time reality reared its ugly head and Amy decided it was better to cut her losses, she was pregnant with Isabelle."

He'd never shared these many details with anyone else before, not even Harland. So why now? Why was he telling Savannah?

Because of the way she was looking at him, understanding in her eyes. Because of the way she reached up and cupped his cheek with one hand, because of the way she slowly traced the curve of his lower lip with her thumb. Because of the way she made him feel, grounded and peaceful. Sane.

Because he wasn't afraid to be himself with her.

And Christ, he didn't want to think about what that meant. Not now. He couldn't.

He pushed those last thoughts from his mind then leaned forward and pressed a quick kiss against her lips.

It was time to finish his story.

"Looking back, I think I probably would have stayed married, even now. Just dealt with it and hoped for the best."

"But?"

Aaron closed his eyes, swallowed back the pain and anger that were still so clear in his mind, in his gut. "She was screwing around. I think I always knew, but I didn't care enough to do anything about it. Until I came home one morning and she wasn't there. She got my schedule screwed up and left the kids with a babysitter while she spent the night with her latest boyfriend. The babysitter was our fifteen-year-old neighbor."

"How old were the girls?"

"Brooke was six, Isabelle was three. I hired an attorney the next day and filed for a legal separation and that was that."

"But the girls lived with her."

"Yeah. That's, uh—" He cleared his throat and looked away, unable to meet Savannah's eyes. "I convinced myself that it would be better for them. I was never home, always on the road. By that time, I'd been traded a half-dozen times already and was spending most of my time with the minors. I saw the writing on the wall, knew what was coming. They needed stability, and I thought Amy would be able to give that to them in a way I never could."

"Did she?"

"For a little while. Maybe. We didn't divorce right away, so I was still able to see them. Then Baltimore picked up my contract five years ago and assigned me here, to the Bombers. Amy decided she didn't want to stay in St. Louis so she moved back with her parents. We, uh, we finally divorced three years ago."

"Were things better then? When she moved back to her parents?"

Aaron was silent a long time as he searched for the answer, needing to find the truth as he knew it. He sighed and shook his head. "I don't know. I like to think so. She loved the girls, tried her best, in her own way. At least, that's what I kept telling myself. And I know the girls were never alone, not when Amy was living with her parents. But…she never changed, still liked to go out and have too much fun."

Savannah pressed her hand against his cheek again and leaned up to kiss him. Her mouth was soft and gentle, the kiss meant to reassure. And when she pulled away, he saw understanding in her eyes, knew that he didn't have to finish.

But he did anyway, needing to explain.

"That's why I won't hire a nanny or a babysitter. That's why I won't leave them alone, Savannah. Not even with my mom watching them. It's going to be bad enough with my schedule. I have practice during the week. Games every weekend, even some weeknights, here and on the road. I just—I can't. Not after everything they've been through. I can't leave them like their mother did."

"It's okay, Aaron. I understand." She leaned forward and kissed him again, then looked at him with a sad smile that tugged at his heart and twisted his gut. She *did* understand, maybe even more than he did. His girls were his priority now. They had to be.

And she understood, even if he didn't say the words.

She climbed out of bed, her steps slow and graceful as she moved to his side and tugged his hand. "I'm officially kicking you out, Mr. Malone. Now go. I need my beauty rest."

A chuckle escaped him, surprising him. How could he laugh now, after everything he had told her? How could he even *feel* like laughing? It was because of Savannah. Her smile. Her clear gaze. Her understanding and acceptance of the words left unspoken.

Only Savannah could make him feel this way.

He stood up and reached for her, pulling her in close for a kiss. Deep and slow and over way too soon. He grabbed his pants, stepped into them then reached for his shirt. "You should come over for breakfast."

"When?"

"Tomorrow. Or rather, today." He glanced over his shoulder, frowning at the clock. "In four hours, to be exact."

"I don't think—"

"It's French toast day. And I make a killer French toast. Besides, you can't go to the museum on an empty stomach."

"Are you sure that's a good idea?"

"What? Eating?"

"No. Me, going to the museum with you."

His fingers fumbled with the buttons of the shirt

and he looked up, frowning. "Why wouldn't it be?"

"Don't you think it might be better if it was just you and the girls? I mean, after…" Her voice trailed off, her hand waving absently at the bed.

"After…?"

"After everything you told me. I don't want to intrude."

Aaron closed the distance between them in two long strides. "You won't be intruding. I want you there. And so does Isabelle."

"I'm not—"

He cut her off with a quick kiss. "Eight o'clock. Breakfast. Then we head down to DC to play tourist."

Savannah opened her mouth, then quickly shut it at his look. He held his breath, waiting to see if she'd make another argument against going. She finally sighed then darted a pointed look at the clock. "In that case, I really am kicking you out. And I'm telling you right now, don't expect much from me on less than four hours' worth of sleep."

"Fair enough. We can take turns napping in the exhibits." He kissed her again then grabbed his shoes and jacket, telling her he'd lock up on his way out.

Then he made his way from her yard to his, trying not to dwell on the expression he'd seen in Savannah's eyes when she said she didn't want to intrude.

CHAPTER THIRTEEN

Savannah smothered a yawn, then looked around to see if anyone had noticed. She didn't know why she bothered—nobody was paying attention to her. In fact, nobody was paying attention to *anything*. How could they, when it took all of their focus on simply breathing through the thick tension that permeated the SUV?

She glanced out the window, barely seeing the trees rush past as they raced down 295 toward Washington. Not for the first time, she wondered what she was doing here, why she had agreed to come along.

Especially since the tension had been brewing from the second she walked into Aaron's house to join them for breakfast. Brooke had taken one look at her, shot an accusing scowl at Aaron, then loudly proclaimed that she wasn't going if *she* was. Savannah had stopped where she was, in the process of closing the sliding glass door, and almost turned around to leave right then and there. What had she ever done to the teenager to make her talk to her that way?

Nothing that she could think of. She barely even spoke to Brooke, knowing her attempts would have been thrown back in her face with every ounce of attitude the girl could muster. She didn't need to subject herself to that, not today, not when she'd only had two hours' worth of sleep—

Because her mind had been going over and over every word Aaron had said. Dissecting. Analyzing. And it didn't matter how many times she studied them, she came to the same conclusion. Yes, his daughters came first, as they should. She didn't fault him for that, not in the least. But it was the underlying message that had been loud and clear: they were a package deal, and there wasn't room for anyone else.

At least, she thought that's what he was telling her. She wasn't sure. How could she be? Especially when, in the next breath, he was insisting she join them on this outing today.

Had she given him some sign, some unintentional indication that she was interested in something more permanent? No, not that she knew of. Because she *wasn't* interested in anything more permanent. Wasn't interested in settling down with a family.

So why did his words, spoken and unspoken, bother her so much? Why did simply thinking about them leave a small ache in the hollow of her chest?

Because she needed sleep, that was why. If she had been smart, she would have made an excuse and turned around to leave. But Aaron's mother must have sensed what she was ready to do because she came over and grabbed Savannah's arm and guided her to the table with a bright smile. Then she sat across from her, her ringed hands curled around a steaming mug of coffee, and started talking.

About everything.

Before Savannah knew it, she'd finished three slices of French toast, two cups of coffee, and was being herded out to Aaron's SUV with everyone else.

The woman was sneaky, definitely sneaky.

Savannah loved her already. Too bad she wasn't joining them on this outing. There was no doubt in Savannah's mind that Carol Malone would have banished the suffocating tension with one simple command.

"I still don't understand why I have to go. This is stupid."

Savannah sighed and glanced at her watch. Five minutes had passed since the last time Brooke had said those same exact words—almost a record.

"We've been over this before, Brooke."

"You could have left me home."

"Not by yourself."

"I'm old enough."

"Not when you keep acting the way you are."

"It's not fair!"

"Life's not fair. Get over it."

Savannah glanced toward the front seat, saw Aaron's hand clench the steering wheel. Sympathy welled inside her, along with an odd burst of humor. Not at the situation, but at his comeback. It struck her as such a *parent* thing to say.

Maybe because she'd heard her own parents tell her the same thing when she was growing up.

Life's not fair. Get over it.

Couldn't get much simpler than that. Maybe that's what *she* needed to do: get over it. She liked Aaron, had been fantasizing about him for a year. They were neighbors. Casual friends, maybe even more than that—but still only friends. And they were having sex.

Steamy, hot, intense sex. The man had stamina— a *lot* of stamina. And he knew exactly what he was doing, even if he had been almost shy at first. No, not shy. Reserved, maybe. Or maybe even a little old-fashioned, like when he had stammered and blushed during their condom conversation last night, when she told him she was on birth control and was clean and asked him the same.

A small smile curled her lips at the memory, at the way he'd blurted out his admission. Definitely a little old-fashioned when it came to discussing those kinds of details.

But not with anything else. Even now, she could feel the tenderness in her muscles, a gentle ache between her legs that reminded her of the night before.

Her face heated and she turned back to the window, hoping nobody noticed her blush or the way she shifted in the leather seat.

Ninety minutes later, after driving around looking for a parking garage and walking an untold number of blocks, they finally reached the National Mall—at the wrong end. Brooke grumbled and muttered when Isabelle insisted on having their picture taken in front of the Washington Monument, then complained when Aaron told her they had to walk to the other end to reach the Air and Space Museum. For once, Savannah found herself agreeing with the girl.

At least it was a nice day out, the sky a bright blue, the air warm for early October but without the humidity. Isabelle and Brooke ran ahead, weaving around the joggers on the path before doubling back and telling them to hurry then running ahead again. Savannah shrugged out of her windbreaker and tied it around her waist, trying to match her shorter stride to Aaron's longer one.

He paused, turning to wait for her, his hand pressed against his side. She frowned and he immediately dropped his hand then resumed walking, slower this time.

"Does it hurt?"

"What?"

"Nice try. I might be tired but I'm not blind. Does your side hurt?"

"Not much. Just a twinge here and there."

"Liar."

A smile curved his lips. "I may have overexerted myself last night."

Heat filled her face at the memory and she forced herself to keep her gaze focused forward. "Is that a complaint?"

"Hell no. Not even close."

There was something in his voice, something low and needy, that made her stop and turn toward him. Her pulse soared, heat unfurling low in her belly as need coursed through her. How? How could he do that to her with just a look? And God, she wanted to lean up on her toes and kiss him, to thread her fingers through his and walk along the mall, hand-in-hand, like the dozens of other couples strolling past them enjoying the beautiful day.

Dangerous. So dangerous. She couldn't do that, shouldn't *want* it. They weren't a couple, not in that sense. Not in any sense.

Were they?

No, they weren't. They couldn't be. Aaron had given her that message in the dark hours of the morning. And that wasn't what she wanted, anyway.

Was it?

"Daddy! Miss Savannah! Come on, hurry up."

Isabelle's clear voice called out, shattering whatever spell had been weaving around them. Aaron jerked away from her, shoving his hands into his pockets as he started walking again.

Savannah took a deep breath and followed behind, her steps a little slower now as she tried to calm the thoughts racing through her mind. She wasn't paying attention and lost track of time, but only minutes. It was enough. She looked up, only to see that Aaron and Isabelle were further ahead, the younger girl tugging on her father's hand, pulling him along.

But Brooke was right in front of her, walking backward, her blue-green eyes focused on Savannah.

"He doesn't love you, you know."

Savannah paused, trying to hide the shock she felt at the words. "Excuse me?"

"You heard me. He doesn't love you."

"Brooke, really, this isn't a conversation I'm having with you."

"I know he was at your house last night. I know you were having sex."

Savannah couldn't stop the heat filling her face, any more than she could stop her mouth from dropping open in surprise. Did Brooke know, or was she just guessing? And how in the hell was she even supposed to comment on that?

Simple: by not commenting at all.

"We need to catch up to your father." Savannah lengthened her stride, hoping the girl would turn around and leave, run ahead of her and leave her in peace to sort out her shock over the unexpected words. But she simply matched Savannah's pace, still walking backward.

"Why don't you like me?"

Savannah stumbled, almost stopped. Changed her mind and kept walking. "What makes you think I don't like you?"

"Because you don't talk to me like you talk to Isabelle. You don't talk to me at all."

Savannah heard the confusion in the teenager's voice, the pain hidden behind the tough words. Her heart squeezed, sympathy welling inside her. Brooke was right: she *didn't* talk to her the way she talked to Isabelle. She stopped, her gaze softening as she looked at Brooke.

"You're right, I don't. I'm sorry. But sometimes you don't make it very easy to talk to, not when you're always running away."

"I don't run away."

"Sometimes you do."

Brooke's gaze darted away, but not before she saw the doubt flash in the girl's blue-green eyes. Savannah reached out to put a comforting hand on the girl's shoulder. "Maybe we can change that. Maybe we can become friends."

Brooke jerked back, her jaw clenching in anger as she shook her head. "I don't want to talk to you. And we'll never be friends. That's stupid. And my father will never love you so you might as well just stay away."

The girl turned and hurried away, racing to catch up to Aaron and Isabelle. Savannah slowed her pace, finally stopped, needing to put more distance between them for a few minutes.

Needing those few minutes to sort through the sharp pain slicing through her as she tried to decide which of Brooke's hateful words hurt the most.

CHAPTER FOURTEEN

"Malone! Phone call!"

Aaron slid to a stop, his head swiveling in surprise. Phone call? What the fuck? He didn't get phone calls. And he especially didn't get phone calls when they were on the road, during game-day skate. *Nobody* got phone calls.

Immediately following that thought came another, this one curdling his stomach as fear squeezed his lungs.

Nobody got phone calls...unless it was an emergency.

He sprinted toward the bench, damn near tripping as he jumped the boards and shook off his gloves. Coach Torresi was standing there, holding the cell phone out to Aaron, an inscrutable look on his face.

"Make it quick."

Aaron nodded, trying to swallow past the lump in his throat as he pushed the helmet off his head. He moved into the tunnel, steadying himself with one hand braced against the concrete block wall, and brought the phone to his ear.

"Yeah?"

"Aaron, it's Mom. Nothing's wrong. Nothing you

need to worry about."

Fear released its stranglehold on his lungs. He drew in a deep breath as relief flooded him. Two seconds later, the fear was back. His mother wouldn't be calling if there wasn't anything wrong.

"What happened?"

"There's just been a little situation at the middle school. Brooke is fine. Nobody's hurt. But I need to go down there and I won't be able to get to your place in time to meet Isabelle's bus."

Aaron closed his eyes, his mind trying to make sense of the words. The only thing he could focus on right now was the fact that nobody was hurt. He reached up, pinched the bridge of his nose, and inhaled.

Situation. There was a situation at the school.

With Brooke.

Anger threatened to overtake him. Damn her. What the hell had she done now? And why? Things had seemed to be improving these last two weeks, ever since their trip to the Air and Space Museum. What the hell had happened to change that?

Then his mother's words about Isabelle's bus sunk in. The elementary school had early dismissal today, letting out three hours before the middle and high schools. He glanced around, searching the bare walls for a clock before lowering the phone and looking at the time at the top of the screen.

Isabelle would be home in thirty minutes.

And nobody would be there to meet her.

"Fuck!"

He heard what sounded like a low laugh, realized he had sworn out loud—right into the phone. And straight into his mother's ear. "I'm sorry—"

"Like I haven't said worse myself."

"I have no idea what to do. I can't get down there—"

"Well of course not. You're in Rochester. I just called to get Savannah's number, to see if she could meet with Isabelle and stay with her until I got there."

"I can't ask her to do that."

"You won't be asking her if you give me her number. And I'm sure she won't mind. Now, what's her number?"

"I, uh, I don't know what it is."

Silence greeted his admission, followed a long sigh. "Aaron, I'm disappointed. You're sleeping with the woman and you don't even have her number?"

Holy fucking shit, he did not just hear that. His *mother* did *not* just say that. No fucking way. He glanced around, hoping like hell that nobody was nearby to witness the heat of humiliation spreading across his face.

Or worse, close enough to hear his mother's voice through the phone.

No such luck, because Torresi was standing at the end of the tunnel, his arms folded in front of him. He didn't give Aaron any indication that he'd heard— which meant absolutely nothing.

Aaron turned, shifting so his back was toward the coach, and lowered his voice.

"I didn't say I didn't have it. I said I didn't know it. It's in my phone."

"Then can you call her? I need to get down to the school and this will save me time."

"I—" He stopped, glanced over his shoulder at Coach Torresi, then turned back around. "Yeah. I'll call her."

"Perfect. I know you're at practice so I'll let you go now."

"Call me later to let me know what's going on?" He waited for an answer but didn't hear anything. He pulled the phone away from his ear and looked at the screen. She had ended the call already.

Of course, she had.

"Everything okay?"

"Uh, yeah." He handed the phone back to Coach Torresi then looked in the direction of the locker room. Fuck. This was going to go over well. "I have a, uh, a childcare issue. I need to make a phone call. Just a quick one."

Was it his imagination, or did the coach's mouth twitch, like he was trying not to smile? No, it had to be his imagination.

"Go. You've got two minutes, then I want your ass back on the ice."

"Yes, Coach." Aaron hurried down the hallway, the blades of his skates making an odd squeaking-squishing noise against the rubber mat. Fuck. What would he do if Savannah wasn't home? What would he do if she couldn't get Isabelle from the bus and watch her? He didn't want to put her in an awkward position, even though he was almost positive she'd say yes.

Maybe.

But fuck, it wasn't like he had much choice. And he didn't even want to think about what he'd do if she weren't home.

Call Courtney? Maybe.

He just hoped like hell that Savannah was home, and that she wouldn't mind.

He hadn't had a chance to see her much the last couple of weeks, not with practices and games and taking care of the girls. And when he had seen her, she'd been a little preoccupied. Maybe even a little distant. He'd been too busy to give it much thought, hadn't taken the time to ask.

Because he was a fucking idiot.

He pushed through the locker room door and headed straight to his assigned cubby, pulling his bag from the shelf and digging through it. He grabbed his phone, powered it up, surprised to see there weren't any waiting voicemails. Had the school called his mother first?

Probably.

What the hell had Brooke done?

Part of him was afraid to find out.

He pushed all the worst-case scenarios from his mind as he scrolled through his contacts, tapping Savannah's number then holding the phone to his ear. It rang once. Twice. Three times. Fuck. She was busy. Or she wasn't home. Or she was in a meeting and couldn't answer the phone or—

"This is Savannah. May I help you?"

He closed his eyes, breathing a sigh of relief. "Hey. It's me. Aaron. Um, are you busy?"

"No, just working on another presentation. What's up? I thought you were on the road today?"

"Yeah, I am. Listen, there's been a problem at Brooke's school. My mom's on the way there now, which means she won't be at my place to get Isabelle off the bus. The elementary school gets out early today."

"Is everything okay with Brooke? Did something happen to her?"

"I don't know, Mom didn't say. Sounds like she got into trouble. I hate to ask but—is there any way you can get Isabelle off the bus and wait with her until my mom gets there?"

"Um…"

He held his breath, waiting, wondering at the hesitation he heard in her voice.

"Yeah. I can do that."

"You sure? If there's something else you need to do, let me know. I can try to call Courtney and—"

"No, it's good. I don't have plans until later tonight."

Aaron frowned, ready to ask her what plans. He stopped himself at the last minute, telling himself it wasn't his business.

Yeah. That's why his back teeth were grinding together.

He sucked in a deep breath, forced his jaw to unclench. "Great. Thanks. I owe you."

"Not a problem. That's what friends are for."

His jaw clenched again and he had to concentrate even harder to relax it this time. "Yeah. Sure. There's a key to the patio door in one of those small magnet boxes tucked under the grill. On the right-hand side."

"Okay. What time does her bus get here?"

"Um—" He pulled the phone away from his ear and checked the time, then softly swore. "In about fifteen minutes."

"Okay, I'll start heading over. Do you need me to do anything else? Does she need lunch or anything?"

"If my mom's not there in the next hour, maybe. But other than that, no."

"Sounds good. I'll head over now—"

"Actually, there is one thing you can do for me."

"Yeah?" Had her voice changed? Become a little more excited maybe? No, she was probably just walking, already heading to his place.

"Make sure my mom calls me and tells me what's going on? She didn't know. Or wouldn't say, I'm not sure which. I'm going to be thinking the worst until I hear."

There was a short pause, then he heard what sounded like a door opening and closing. Her voice sounded a little distant, maybe a little preoccupied. "Sure. No problem. I'll have her call you."

"Thanks, Savannah. I owe you one." He heard her mumble something then the call disconnected. He frowned at the screen, wondering what the fuck he had just missed.

And wondering what kind of plans Savannah had later.

CHAPTER FIFTEEN

"Number 15. Two minutes, tripping."

Aaron shook his head, ready to argue. One look from Zach convinced him otherwise. But dammit, this was a bullshit call. He hadn't tripped anyone. The dumb fuck had come from behind and tripped himself—over his own two damn feet, not Aaron's stick. The SOB should be getting two minutes for embellishment. But the refs weren't calling shit against Rochester, hadn't been since the middle of the second period. In the meantime, the Bombers were getting slammed, with everything from bullshit offsides and icing calls to goalie interference.

Now Aaron was heading to the sin bin for his fourth penalty of the game for another bullshit call. So far, their penalty kill had been able to keep Rochester from capitalizing on the man-advantage each time. Too damn bad they hadn't been able to get anything on the board themselves, because they were still down by one point.

Aaron dropped to the bench, his hand wrapped around his stick as he propped it between his legs. His gaze followed the play as it moved from center ice down to the Bomber's net. Fuck. Tyler was struggling, he could see it from here. Why the hell hadn't Torresi put Ryan Gardel in the net tonight? Tyler was holding his own, yeah, but he was also coming down with something, probably the fucking flu. The guy should be on the bench, hydrating and tossing back vitamin C tablets. He'd already blocked twenty-six shots tonight. From the way the play was unfolding, it didn't look like he'd make it twenty-seven.

And *fuck*.

Aaron jumped to his feet, leaning against the glass as he watched the Bombers' play break down in front of their own net. Jason reached with his stick, lost his balance, stumbled to one knee then quickly regained his feet. It was too late. One of the guys from Rochester darted around him, fast and low, and took the shot while Jason blocked Tyler's view. The light flashed red behind the net as the horn blasted through the arena's chilly air.

Shit. Dammit.

Aaron left the box, pausing before heading back to the bench. Jason and Tyler were standing too fucking close to each other, damn near chest-to-chest. Aaron could tell heated words were being exchanged. He couldn't hear them, not from center ice, but he didn't need to.

And wouldn't that just be the perfect fucking ending to an already shitty night? To have two guys from the same team going after each other on the ice. Yeah, that would be just fucking perfect.

Aaron took off down the ice, Travis right behind him.

Stupid fucking idiots. He was half-tempted to knock both their heads together. The mood he was in, it would be easy.

And too damn tempting.

He slid to a stop between the two men, placed one hand in the middle of Jason's chest to stop him from moving toward Tyler. No, Jason wasn't going anywhere—Travis was behind him, a hand wrapped around his arm, pulling him back toward the bench, giving him hell in that soft-spoken voice of his.

Aaron turned to Tyler, not bothering to hide his scowl. "What the fuck do you think you're doing? Are you out of your fucking mind?"

"I'm tired of his shit, Aaron. And I don't need him running his fucking mouth about the way I tend net."

"Then fucking ignore it."

"Easier said than done. The shit he says?" Tyler shook his head. "Not happening."

"You better make it happen. Now calm the fuck down and get your head back in the fucking game." Aaron turned his back on Tyler and skated away, not giving the goalie a chance to respond. Stupid fucking idiots. Both of them needed their heads knocked together for this stupid bullshit. It needed to end. Now.

Aaron understood what the issue was. Hell, all of them did. But it wasn't like Tyler had been using Jenny or stringing her along. Tyler wasn't like that. If it had been someone like Ben then yeah, he would have stood by in case Jason needed help kicking the man's ass. But fuck, Tyler and Jenny were married now. It was time for Jason to let it go and get the fuck over it.

He took his spot on the bench, leaning forward to glance at Jason. The man was sitting at the other end, a muscle ticking in his jaw, his pale eyes cold as a glacier as Nelson Richards, one of their assistant coaches, leaned down and spoke in his ear. Probably giving him an ass-chewing.

Which was probably just a warm-up for the ass-chewing they'd get once they reached the locker room when the game ended in five minutes. They'd been playing like shit all night—and he included himself in that analysis, maybe more than anyone else. But he'd been fucking distracted all night, wondering what the hell was going on with Brooke.

Wondering what Savannah was doing.

Wondering why the hell nobody had called him earlier to let him know what the fuck happened this afternoon.

Aaron was still pissed ten minutes later, after the game had ended with the Bombers down by three. And *ass-chewing* didn't even come close to what they got. Torresi must have been hoarding all the insults since the start of the season because he had plenty to hurl at them. Aaron was convinced the man would have kept going, too, if Richards hadn't leaned over and said something to him. Whatever it was couldn't have been good because Torresi's mouth flattened and those brittle green eyes scanned each face in the locker room before settling on Jason's.

And then moving to Tyler's.

"Emory. Bowie. With me. Now. The rest of you fuckers—" He shook his head in disgust. "I don't even want to fucking see you. Hit the showers and get on the fucking bus."

A collective sigh filled the room as soon as the coaching staff left, followed by Tyler and Jason. Aaron jumped from the bench and reached for his bag, digging for his phone, powering it up as soon as his hand closed around it.

"You think they're in trouble?"

Aaron looked over his shoulder, his gaze resting

on Travis for a brief second before moving back to his phone. "What do you think?"

"Yeah, probably."

"No 'probably' about it. Coach is pissed—and he should be. That was a stupid fucking stunt they pulled." He stared at the phone, waiting for the screen to come to life, waiting for the beeps and chimes that would signal a text message or a voicemail.

Nothing.

"Hey, Banky. You got reception in here?"

"I don't know. My phone's off."

"Can you turn it on and check?"

"Yeah." Travis leaned down and dug his own phone out. "You waiting for a call or something?"

"Yeah. Or something."

"From your girlfriend?"

"I don't have a girlfriend."

"Sure, you do. That woman you brought to Mystic's that night."

"She's just my neighbor."

"She looked like more than your neighbor from what I saw."

"What the hell are you talking about?"

"It was just the way she was looking at you and you were looking at her, is all. Like you were more than neighbors."

"We're not. I've got my hands full as it is. I don't have time for a girlfriend." Aaron clenched his jaw, trying to ignore the way his gut twisted when he said those words, wondering why it bothered him so much.

"You just have to make the time, is all."

"Banky, not now. Just let me know if you have reception." No sooner had the words left his mouth then Travis' phone started chiming and beeping, over and over and over.

Aaron looked down at his, the screen still disgustingly blank. "Dammit."

He tossed it back in his bag then grabbed his shower kit. There still weren't any messages by the time he got out of the shower. Or when they boarded the bus.

He finally called his mother, his voice pitched low because he didn't want everyone to overhear him. Her only response was that everything was fine and she would explain in the morning.

Which told him absolutely nothing.

In desperation, he sent a text message to Savannah. The message went unanswered. He tried telling himself it was because she was probably sleeping, or that she hadn't heard her phone, or that the message didn't go through right away.

Aaron finally stretched out in the seat, trying to get comfortable, telling himself he needed to stop worrying and get some sleep on the long bus ride back. Telling himself he should just put the phone back in his bag and not worry about it.

Instead of clutching it in his hand, waiting for a call or message that he knew would never come.

CHAPTER SIXTEEN

Aaron drew the hood of the sweatshirt around his neck and knocked on the French door again. The weather had turned cold overnight, more like winter than late October. The wind certainly wasn't helping. Sharp and cold. Biting. The kind that went straight through you and settled into your bones, making you feel like you'd never be warm again.

Still no answer.

He jammed his hands into the front pocket of the sweatshirt then walked to the far end of Savannah's patio and peered around the corner. Her car, a sporty blue coupe, sat in the driveway, untouched.

That didn't mean she was home. She could be out somewhere with her friend, Tessa. Or she could be working in the den at the far end of the house, or even downstairs. There could be a hundred different reasons she wasn't answering the door.

So why the hell was he so anxious?

Because he wanted to see her. *Needed* to see her, like a junkie needed a fix. And hell, that was such a bad analogy…but it fit. He felt like he was going through withdrawal and the only thing that would make it better was seeing Savannah.

The admission hadn't been easy to make. Hell, he'd fought it, tried to convince himself that there were a hundred other different reasons why he was so antsy and frustrated and short-tempered.

He was tired.

He was having trouble adjusting to the hectic season schedule.

His body was beat up.

He was worried about the girls. About Brooke. Worried he was screwing things up with them.

Yeah, that last item was a big one, the doubt eating him alive every damn day. Each time he thought things were getting better, something else popped up to change his mind, like Brooke getting in trouble for mouthing off to a teacher the other day.

Because she'd been bored.

Because the work was too easy.

Why the hell hadn't he known that? He should have. But the meeting he had yesterday afternoon with her guidance counselor took care of that oversight. Brooke was being moved into the advanced classes now, where she wouldn't be bored.

He hoped.

At least she hadn't copped her usual attitude about it. In fact, she almost looked happy. Which, in an odd way, worried him more—because he should have known Brooke was bored, should have known she wasn't being challenged in school. Just one more thing he worried about it, one more doubt.

The same doubts he'd been struggling with since April, when he brought the girls back here to live with him. That hadn't changed. That didn't explain his recent mood.

What *had* changed was not seeing Savannah like

he was used to, especially since that day they'd all gone to DC. He had chalked it up to the lazy days of summer being over, told himself it was nothing more than everyone being busy. But it was more than that, his gut instinct was sure of it.

And Wednesday night, during the bus drive back from their road game, he'd been forced to come to a realization: he missed Savannah.

Missed seeing her. Missed talking to her. Missed her easy smile and her reassurances. Her laughter and the way she teased him.

He just missed *her*.

He knocked on the door one more time, peering inside for signs of life. A single lamp was on in the living room, but that meant nothing. She always left that lamp on. Another minute, that's all he'd wait. If she didn't come to the door by then, he'd head back to his place instead of hanging out on her patio like some crazy person.

He had just given up and was stepping off the patio when he heard the door open behind him. He turned, got one good look at Savannah, and felt the smile of greeting die on his face.

"You look like shit."

She grunted, the sound weak and pathetic, and pulled a thick blanket tighter around her shoulders. Her hair was sleep-tousled, her eyes bright with fever, her face flushed. She turned to the side and pulled a corner of the blanket over her face as a deep cough shook her.

He nudged his way past her, closing the door behind him as he pressed the back of his hand against her forehead. Her skin was hot and dry—too hot. "Christ. You're burning up."

She made another sound, this one weak and tired, then shuffled toward the sofa and dropped onto it. "Sick."

"No shit. You've got the bug that's going around."

"Uh-huh." She tilted sideways against the arm of the sofa, her eyes drifting closed.

"Have you taken anything for it?"

"Uh-uh."

"Why not?"

She mumbled something, the words too soft to hear. He moved over to the sofa and sat next to her, reaching out to rub small circles on her back as she coughed again. "Tell me what you need."

"To get better."

Aaron almost laughed at that one. "As Brooke would say: Duh. Besides that, what do you need?"

She shrugged, the movement dislodging a corner of the blanket. She was wearing a thick hoodie and flannel pajama pants and wool socks—and she was still shivering. He pulled her toward him, ran his hands up and down her arms then held her close as she snuggled against him.

"You'll get sick."

"Nah. I've got the constitution of a horse. Besides, one of the guys already has it so if I get sick, I'll blame it on him." He heard her mutter something against his chest before another cough wracked her body. He pressed a kiss against the top of her head then eased her away from him, tucking the blanket around her. "You need to get some medicine in you. Is it upstairs?"

Another small murmur, softer this time. He took that as a yes and headed upstairs, hesitating for only a second before going through the medicine cabinet in the master bathroom, trying to shake the odd feeling that he was invading her privacy.

And maybe he was, but not on purpose.

It was still an unsettling feeling.

Moisturizer. Toothpaste. Mouthwash.

A box of condoms.

Deodorant. Q-tips.

Tampons.

Mature, Malone. Real fucking mature. Christ, he felt like a fucking teenager, the way he was blushing.

His hand closed over a small spray bottle and he pulled it out, frowning as he read the label.

Toy Cleaner.

He read it again then damn near dropped the bottle in the sink as an image filled his mind. Clear and potent. Powerful. Savannah, propped against her pillows, her knees drawn up and legs spread wide as she pleasured herself with a vibrator.

He put the cleaner back and slammed the cabinet shut.

She had everything but cold medicine. Not even ibuprofen or acetaminophen. A quick search of the guest bathroom revealed even less. Well damn. Where else would she keep cold medicine?

He headed back downstairs and into the kitchen, his gaze scanning the countertop before he searched a few of the cabinets. Nothing.

Well shit.

He moved into the living room, the urge to take care of her growing stronger when he saw her curled into a ball on the sofa. Savannah was a grown woman, living on her own. Independent. Professional. She didn't *need* anyone to take care of her. And if she were feeling like her normal self, she'd probably tell him as much. But she wasn't, she was burning with fever. Not exactly helpless but not really capable, either. Besides, who the hell didn't wish they had someone to take care of them when they were sick?

He leaned down, brushed his hand against her feverish cheek. "Savannah, I'm going to run next door, grab some medicine. I'll be right back."

She nodded her head then snuggled deeper into the cushions, coughing again. He made sure the blanket was still tucked around her shoulders, pressed a kiss to her cheek, then let himself out.

It didn't take long to grab everything he needed, and he was letting himself back into Savannah's ten minutes later. She was still curled into a ball on the sofa, wrapped in the blanket, her chest rising and falling with the shaky breathing of illness. Aaron walked into the kitchen, pulling things out of the reusable shopping bag and lining them up on the counter.

Nighttime cold and flu medicine in a liquid.

Daytime cold and flu medicine in caplets.

A small blue jar of vapor rub.

A bottle of blackberry brandy, mostly full. A bottle of Irish whiskey, mostly empty.

A jar of honey. A half of a lemon. A handful of teabags.

He stared at the collection of his mother's cold and flu remedies, wondering if maybe he'd gone just a bit overboard. Probably. But hell, it wasn't like they'd make her feel worse.

Aaron found a coffee mug in one of the cabinets and filled it halfway with water then popped it into the microwave. Once it was heated, he tossed in a teabag and let it steep for a few minutes. Then he added a healthy shot of whiskey and stirred in some lemon and honey. He grabbed the vapor rub, one of the kitchen towels, the cold caplets and the mug, then carried everything into the living room.

"Savannah, sit up, hon. I need you to drink this."

No response.

He placed the mug on the low glass-topped table and sat on the sofa by her feet. Let her rest a few more minutes, before he applied the vapor rub. Then he'd get her to drink some of the tea before bundling her up again.

He shifted, placing her feet in his lap, then removed the thick socks. Yeah, even her feet were hot to the touch. He grabbed the jar of vapor rub and uncapped it, the sharp tang of camphor and menthol and eucalyptus searing his nostrils. He winced and jerked his head back, breathing through his mouth for a second. He'd forgotten how strong that first whiff always was.

He scooped a small bit from the jar then rubbed some into the arch of each of Savannah's feet before putting her socks back on. She barely moved the entire time, not even a twitch of her foot when he applied the vapor rub.

Aaron wiped his hands off on the towel then placed his arms around Savannah and eased her to a sitting position. Her head lolled against his shoulder for a second, then her lids fluttered open. Her brows lowered over her glassy eyes and her face scrunched up when she sniffed.

"Stinks."

Aaron laughed and brushed the hair from her face. "It's the vapor rub. I put some on your feet."

She tilted her head back and stared up at him, like she wasn't sure what he was doing there. "Why?"

"For your cough. And because that's what my

mom always did when I was sick. She swears by it."

"Hm." She closed her eyes and let her head drop back to his shoulder.

"Not yet. I need you to drink some of this first. After that, I'll put you to bed."

Savannah raised her head again then slowly sat up, pulling the blanket around her shoulders. She looked around, frowning when Aaron held the mug out to her. "What is it?"

"Hot toddy. Drink up."

"But what is it?"

"Tea. Whiskey. Lemon. Honey."

She stared at the mug for a few more seconds then slowly reached for it, curling both hands around it. Aaron kept his hand close by, just until he was sure she wouldn't drop it, then tore open the blister pack containing the medicine.

"Here, take these."

Savannah held her hand out, not even looking at the caplets when he dropped them into her palm. She popped them into her mouth then took a long sip of the toddy.

"Don't you even want to know what that was?"

She drank more of the toddy then shook her head. "I trust you."

The words slammed into him, stealing his breath, making his vision swim. He rubbed a fist against his chest, the tightness confusing him. Worrying him at first. Then the tightness eased. Not just the tightness in his chest, but the tightness in his shoulders, his lungs. He felt…lighter. Like the stress and weight he'd been carrying around for months, for years, was gone. He sucked in a deep breath then started coughing as he got a deep whiff of camphor and menthol.

Savannah trusted him.

Yes, of course she did. She wouldn't have slept with him if she hadn't. He needed his fucking head examined for reading too much into it. What the hell was wrong with him? Of course, Savannah trusted him.

He watched as she finished the toddy, then took the mug from her and placed it on the table before she dropped it. She was already sliding to the side, her eyes closed as her body fought against the fever. He scooped her into his arms then stood, carrying her toward the stairs.

"You're going to hurt yourself."

He paused with his foot on the first step and looked down, his gaze meeting Savannah's feverish one. "I'm just going to tell myself that's the fever talking, that you didn't actually just insult me."

The corner of her mouth twitched in the barest of smiles before she closed her eyes and rested her head against his shoulder. He carried her upstairs, into her room, getting her settled in the bed. Then he sat next to her, his back against the headboard, and stroked her hair. She mumbled something and shifted, placing her head in his lap and draping her arm across his legs.

A few minutes went by before she shifted again, lifting her head to look up at him with a sleepy frown. "Don't you have to get the girls?"

"No." A small grin curled his lips, the motion filled with irony. "Mom's got them tonight since we hit the road early tomorrow."

"You don't have to spend your free night here, taking care of me."

"Actually, that's why I came over. I, uh, I was going to ask if you wanted to go out tonight."

Savannah blinked and damn if her eyes didn't start

tearing up. Panic sliced through him and he wondered what the hell he'd done wrong, what he had said to upset her. Then she sniffled and let her head drop back into his lap.

"That's so sweet. I'm sorry."

"Sorry? Why are you sorry?"

"Because I'm sick."

"Savannah, God." He swallowed back a small laugh. "Don't be sorry. Just rest your head and get some sleep."

"But I am." She yawned, then grimaced when another shiver shook her. The shivering stopped and she settled more deeply against him. "And thank you. For taking care of me."

He brushed the hair from her face and pulled the comforter over her shoulders, a rueful smile on his face. "Just remember you said that in an hour when your fever breaks."

CHAPTER SEVENTEEN

"Looks like you have company."

Savannah peered at Tessa through half-closed lids. Her friend was looking at the patio doors, her brows slightly raised, her mouth curled in amusement. Savannah looked over then blinked in surprise. Isabelle was standing by the door, her face pressed against the glass as she peeked inside. Aaron stood behind her, one large hand on his daughter's shoulder.

"Should I let them in?"

Savannah tightened the blanket around her shoulders and shot Tessa a disbelieving look. "Is there a reason you wouldn't?"

"God, you're grumpy when you're sick. Anyone ever tell you that?" Tessa made her way over to the door, opening it for the unexpected visitors. Isabelle bounded inside, a large container in her hands. She zoomed right past Tessa, ignoring the other woman as she moved straight to Savannah. She stopped in front of her, a bright smile on her face, and held the container out like some kind of offering.

"Miss Savannah, we brought soup! Grammy said it'll make you feel better."

Savannah looked at the container, then up at

Isabelle. "Oh. That's, um, that's very nice. Thank you." Her gaze darted to Aaron, her brow raised in silent question.

He shifted, ran a hand through his dark hair, then shrugged. One corner of his mouth tilted in a tentative smile. "The girls told her you were sick so she made some soup. Chicken noodle. Isabelle wanted to bring it over."

Savannah doubted the girls said any such thing—especially not Brooke. And how had they found out anyway? They hadn't been home Friday night. As far as she knew they weren't home all day yesterday, either, since Aaron had a game...somewhere.

Which meant Aaron must have said something to his mother. The thought that he had been talking about her with his mother left her feeling...odd. Vaguely unsettled but surprisingly giddy.

Which made no sense at all, and only proved her brain was still fried from the fever and chills. Yes, she was feeling better now, just drained and tired, but her brain obviously hadn't recovered yet.

"That's—" She stopped, cleared her throat, started over again. "That's very sweet. Thank you." She reached out to take the container from Isabelle then looked around, wondering what she was supposed to do with it now.

The kitchen. She should probably take it into the kitchen. She uncurled her legs from beneath her, kicking the blanket away so she wouldn't trip and fall. Tessa muttered something then came over, rescuing the container from her hands.

"I'll take it. Sit back down before you fall down."
"Still feeling bad?"
Savannah glanced over at Aaron, saw the concern

flash in his eyes as he moved toward her. His gaze darted to Isabelle. He stopped, jammed his hands into the front pocket of the sweatshirt, and rocked back on his heels.

Like he was afraid to come any closer to her. It couldn't be because she was sick—he'd been with her Friday afternoon, until the early hours of Saturday when he had to leave. Holding her. Taking care of her. Helping her shower and change when the fever finally broke and sweat had soaked her clothes.

No, he hadn't been afraid to come near her then. So why the hesitation now?

She didn't have to ask, she knew why: because of Isabelle.

Savannah swallowed against the hot pain scalding her throat and forced a smile to her face when Isabelle climbed onto the sofa next to her. The girl kneeled beside her, an expression of seriousness on her face as she reached out and placed her hand against Savannah's forehead. She started to jerk back in surprise, stopped herself at the last minute, afraid of hurting the girl's feelings.

"Isabelle, don't bother Miss Savannah."

"But Daddy, I think she feels warm. Come check."

Savannah would have laughed at the expression on Aaron's face—if it hadn't hurt so much.

Surprise. Indecision.

Guilt.

It was the guilt that hurt, more than she expected. Pain sliced through her, sharp enough that she gasped, the sound nothing more than a breathy hiss. Was he so ashamed of being with her, so embarrassed at what they'd done, that he couldn't even come near her in front of his daughter? That he wouldn't even touch her in the most casual way?

Savannah ripped her gaze from Aaron's, afraid he would see how much his actions hurt, see how badly his guilt had sliced through her. She forced a smile to her face, one that felt brittle and cold, and leaned away from Isabelle.

"It's okay. I'm fine. Just warm from the blanket." Except she wasn't warm—she was chilled, straight to the bone. Straight to her heart. She grabbed the blanket and tugged it over her shoulders, holding it tight in front of her.

Like some kind of inadequate shield that could protect her from the unspoken words in Aaron's sad eyes.

Isabelle was oblivious to the stifling tension suddenly blanketing the room. She bounced on her knees then finally sat back, that innocent smile still on her face. "Did you want to go trick-or-treating with us Tuesday night? Daddy said he'd dress up, too. And Grammy's coming over to hand out candy while we're gone and then we're going to come home and watch a scary movie."

"I don't think Miss Savannah wants to go trick-or-treating with us, Sweet Pea."

"But it'll be fun!"

Aaron's gaze darted to hers, his dark eyes filled with a confusing mix of yearning and indecision that left her mind spinning. Did he want her to go, or not? Was there a silent message there that she wasn't seeing?

What did he want from her? She couldn't read whatever was in his eyes, couldn't shake the feeling that the man in front of her had no idea what he wanted himself—

And no idea how to go about getting it.

In the end, it was Tessa who saved her from answering, saved her from making a fool of herself by accepting an invitation that hadn't even been issued. She moved into the living room, her shoulder braced against the doorframe, her arms crossed in front of her.

"Actually, we have a party Tuesday night." Her voice was clipped, her eyes cool and distant as she stared at Aaron. Did he notice? Did he sense Tessa's sudden hostility and understand the reason for it?

Maybe. Maybe not.

He darted another glance at Savannah, his weight moving from one foot to the other. "Come on Isabelle, time to leave."

"But—"

"No *buts*. I have to get ready to head to the arena. And Miss Savannah needs her rest."

Isabelle's shoulders slumped with her deep sigh. Then she jumped off the sofa and hurried over to the door, Aaron following more slowly. "Feel better, Miss Savannah."

"I will."

Isabelle skipped across the patio, disappearing from view. Aaron still stood there, one large hand wrapped around the edge of the open door, uncertainty in his gaze.

"If you, um, change your mind about Tuesday night, let me know. You're more than welcome to join us."

"She won't." Tessa's voice was clear, maybe a little too loud, the words sharp and precise. If Aaron noticed, he gave no indication.

"I hope you're feeling better. If you, um, if you need anything—"

"I'm fine." Savannah forced the words from her

throat, worried at what might come out of Tessa's mouth next. "Tell your mom I said thanks for the soup."

Aaron hesitated for another second then finally nodded and stepped onto the patio, pulling the door closed behind him with a sharp click.

A full five seconds went by before Tessa stormed across the room and dropped into the chair with a growl. "I take back everything nice I said about him. That man is an ass."

"Tessa, he's not—"

"Yes. He is. *What* is his problem? The way he just stood there, looking like he'd been caught red-handed? I mean, *God!* How could he just stand there like that? Like he'd rather cut open his femoral artery and go shark diving instead of touching you!"

"He doesn't want his kids to know anything's going on."

"Yeah? Then what about the mixed messages? What the hell is up with that? One second, he's afraid to touch your forehead. The next, he's staring at you like he wants you to pounce on his daughter's invitation to go trick-or-treating. Or like he wants to pounce on *you*. I don't get it."

"He's just—he's worried about his kids. I understand it." That was the worst part: she really *did* understand.

"Why are you defending him?"

"Because I understand."

"Well, *I* don't."

"That's because you didn't get bounced from one parent to the other when you were growing up. You don't know what it's like, being that young and thinking your parents cared more about their personal life than they did you. *I* do. So yeah, I understand. He's putting his kids first. There's nothing wrong with that." But God, she wished things could be different.

"That doesn't excuse his mixed messages. He can't have it both ways."

Savannah forced a smile to her face, trying to act like it didn't bother her. But she couldn't quite meet Tessa's knowing gaze when she spoke. "It's not a big deal. I knew what I was getting into. It's just sex. That's all."

"No, it's not. I saw the expression on your face, Van. I saw how much you hurt."

"Then you were seeing things."

"Liar."

Savannah didn't say anything. She couldn't, not when she knew Tessa would see right through any denial she uttered.

CHAPTER EIGHTEEN

Aaron sat outside on the front porch, Harland on his left. They each had a beer in their hand, enjoying the relative peace and quiet of the cool night. Trick-or-treating was done, the kids inside comparing their loot under the watchful eyes of Courtney and Aaron's mom. He figured they'd be running around, bouncing off the walls for another hour at least.

He knew he should go inside and get them settled down, knew he shouldn't let them stay up past their bedtime. But what the hell. They were behaving—even Brooke, who had been on her best behavior since getting into trouble last week.

And he didn't want to spoil their fun, not when there was finally peace in the household and everyone was getting along. He could wait a little bit longer to play the bad guy. Besides, they'd be tired soon enough from all the walking they'd done.

They had started the evening with pizza. Then they headed out, just as the sun was sinking below the horizon. Courtney and Aaron's mom had stayed behind, holding down the fort and manning the overloaded candy bowl, so it had been just the five of them: Aaron and Brooke and Isabelle, Harland and

Noah. They had walked up the street then turned the corner, heading into the main section of the neighborhood. It might be a small community, with less than two dozen houses, but they were spaced far enough apart that it had taken almost two hours to make the rounds. They had hit every house, some of them twice because the adults were trying to get rid of the candy.

No, not every house. Not exactly.

Aaron raised the bottle to his mouth, his gaze shifting to Savannah's house next door. The porch light was on now, casting a soft glow across her front steps and part of the yard. A bucket of candy sat on the bottom step of the small porch, alone and unattended. Aaron knew she was home, getting ready for whatever party she was going to.

He lowered the bottle, thought about maybe going over and…and what? Say hi? Tell her to have fun? Yeah, right. After that stupid fucking move he'd made the other day? Freezing the way he had, afraid to get too close to her.

Because he had wanted to do nothing more than scoop her into his arms and carry her upstairs. To put her to bed and hold her while she slept. And that's exactly what he would have done if he had gotten close, if he had touched her.

And he couldn't, not with Isabelle standing right there. Not with Savannah's girlfriend in the next room.

Yeah, he had fucked up. Again. Royally.

He should go over and apologize. Tell her he was sorry for acting like an ass. He started to stand, ready to do just that, when her front door opened and Savannah stepped outside, pulling it closed behind her and hurrying down her steps. She must have sensed him watching because she paused then glanced over her shoulder. She hesitated, turning slightly toward him, her hand raised in a small wave.

Aaron sat back down. Hard.

Holy fuck. What was she wearing? He wasn't sure if he wanted to run over and cover her with his coat—

Or tear the outfit from her.

With his teeth.

She was wearing a curve-hugging black gown, the shiny material clinging to each curve and dip of her body like a second skin. A long slit split the side of the gown from the hem all the way to her upper thigh, revealing a shapely leg encased in black fishnet. He blinked, trying to pull air into his lungs as his gaze traveled from the creamy skin peeking out just above the thigh-high stocking to the sinfully high heels of her shiny black shoes.

How the fuck was she even walking in them?

And the front of the gown...holy shit, how was she not falling out of it? The two scraps of material clinging to her firm breasts were held together by nothing more than a thin black string crisscrossed between the panels, baring a wide expanse of creamy skin. And it was cut low. Way low. *Too* low, revealing a hell of a lot more cleavage than he remembered her having.

A ridiculously long black wig completed the outfit, the straight ends hanging down to her waist. She brushed a few strands of the fake hair from her face, gave him another wave, then climbed into her sporty little car and drove off.

Harland chuckled then nudged him in the side. "You need me to a grab a towel?"

Aaron sucked in a strangled breath, his lungs

finally filling with much-needed air. He turned to Harland, frowning. "What?"

"A towel. For the drool running down your chin."

Aaron actually reached up to wipe his chin before he realized Harland was just joking around. He frowned again then raised the bottle to his mouth and drained the beer in two long swallows.

And fuck, he didn't think he'd ever get the image of Savannah's costume out of his mind. He wasn't sure he wanted to. In fact, he was pretty damn sure he'd be pulling that image from his mind in the lonely hours of the night, when the household was sleeping.

"So how are things going between you two?"

Aaron forced his mind away from images of Savannah in his bed, on her back, wearing nothing but those stockings and heels and tried to focus on Harland's words.

Easier said than done.

"There's, uh, there's nothing going on."

"Man, you are so full of shit, it's not even funny. Who do you think you're kidding?"

"Seriously. There's nothing going on. We're just neighbors."

"Uh-huh. Right."

"Why does everyone think there's something going on?"

"Hm, let me think." Harland held up one finger. "Jason caught you making out in your kitchen." He held up a second finger. "You brought her to Mystic's. You, who—from what all the guys are saying—haven't been seen with anyone in years."

"That's not—"

Harland silenced him with a shake of his head and held up a third finger. "You damn near had a heart attack when she walked out the door. Now don't tell me there's nothing going on."

"Think what you want. I told you, she's just my neighbor."

"You're not sleeping with her?"

Aaron opened his mouth, snapped it closed. He raised the bottle to his mouth then frowned when he realized it was empty. Then he clenched his jaw when Harland started laughing again.

"Yeah, thought so."

"It's not what you think."

"Yeah? Then what is it?"

"We're just friends."

"Friends with benefits?"

"It's not—" Aaron stopped mid-sentence and looked away. He sighed and shook his head, nodded, and finally shrugged. "Yeah. Sure. I guess."

"You guess?"

"You heard me."

"Yeah, I heard you. But I heard what you're *not* saying more. So what's the problem? I mean, not that there has to be a problem, not if that's what you both want. I just get the feeling that isn't exactly the case."

"Has nothing to do with what I want, and everything to do with what's best right now."

"Meaning?"

"Meaning—I have Brooke and Isabelle to think of."

"Yeah? And?"

"And nothing. That's it."

"I'm not following."

"There's nothing to follow." Aaron stared down at the empty bottle, wondering why his voice had been so sharp. He inhaled, forcing himself to calm down, then exhaled. "Brooke and Isabelle come first. Simple as that."

"Yeah, I get that. But again, what the hell does that have to do with you seeing someone?"

"It has everything to do with it."

"It's not an either-or situation, you know. You can do both."

"No, I can't. Their mother pulled that shit, running around every night, leaving them with a babysitter, and then with her parents after we split. I'm not going to do that to them, too."

Harland was quiet for a long time, so long that Aaron figured the subject was dropped. He leaned against the railing and closed his eyes, trying to banish the lonely desperation that always seemed to hover nearby.

No, not always. Not when he was with Savannah.

"I'm going to say something, and I don't want you to take this the wrong way."

Aaron groaned and opened his eyes, frowning at Harland. "Then do us both a favor and keep it to yourself."

"Yeah, not happening."

"Day-glo, I swear to fuck—"

"Why are you punishing yourself?"

"What?"

"You heard me. Why are you punishing yourself?"

"What are you talking about?"

"You can be a parent and have a life, too, you know. They're not mutually exclusive."

"I told you—"

"You told me what your ex did. Somehow, I don't see you foisting the girls off every night to go out partying. There's a difference. A big difference."

"You don't understand."

"You're right, I don't. I saw you with Savannah, saw the way you watched her, so don't tell me you're just friends with benefits. I know better." Harland grabbed Aaron's empty beer bottle then rose to his feet. "Punishing yourself, denying yourself happiness, isn't going to make up for whatever your ex did. It's just going to make you a miserable old bastard. Is that how you want your kids to see you?"

"I'm not—"

"That was a rhetorical question. Just think about it. I'm grabbing another beer. Want one?"

"Yeah, sure."

He watched Harland disappear inside, thought about everything he'd just said.

Was he punishing himself? No. Putting his girls first wasn't a punishment. But what about everything else Harland had said? Was he turning into a miserable old bastard? Is that how the girls saw him?

And fuck. If that was the case, what the hell was he supposed to do about it?

He didn't have the answer to that. And he was still searching for it an hour later, when Harland and Courtney took Noah home. And later still, after the girls were sound asleep and his mother had decided to spend the night in the guest bedroom instead of driving home.

Telling him she'd keep an ear out for the girls in case they needed anything. In case he needed to step out for a little bit.

Christ. Even his own mother was convinced there was something more going on than there was.

But that didn't help with finding an answer. Any answer.

And he was still searching hours later, at one in the morning when the headlights of Savannah's car drifted across his living room wall, lighting up the dark room as she turned into her driveway.

CHAPTER NINETEEN

"Savannah."

She spun around, a scream lodged in her throat, and lashed out with her keys. The quick movement caused her to wobble in the ridiculous heels and she stumbled back, falling against the door as a dark figure emerged from the shadows.

Aaron, his face wreathed with concern.

Her throat finally cleared, the stuck scream leaving in a breathless rush of air. But her heart didn't stop its frantic race. If anything, it sped up even more—and not from fear.

"Damn you! Are you trying to scare me half to death?"

"I thought you heard me."

"No, I didn't hear you. How could I hear you when you're sneaking around like that?" Savannah sucked in a shaky breath, the strength finally returning to her legs. She studied his face, the angles somehow sharper in the light and shadow falling over him. His eyes were hooded, his gaze too...too focused. Too intense.

Her heart slammed against her chest once more and she forced herself to look away, to jam the key into the lock of her door. Her hands were shaking so much, it took her three times to get it unlocked. "What are you doing out here anyway? It's past midnight. Don't you have a game tomorrow?"

She pushed the door open and stepped inside, expecting him to be right behind her. But he wasn't. He hadn't moved, not a single step.

"Aaron, if you want something, out with it. I'm tired, my feet are killing me, and all I want to do is take this stupid outfit off, throw it in the trash, and go to bed." Her voice was sharper than she had intended, both from the fright he had given her and from the horrendous evening she'd just suffered. She should have never gone to that stupid party wearing this stupid costume. It was supposed to be a sexy costume party, attended by adults.

Technically, she guessed it had been. Most everyone in attendance had been wearing variations of sexy costumes. And yes, everyone had been over twenty-one. That didn't mean they were adults.

They sure as hell hadn't acted like it.

She'd spent most of the night with a napkin held in front of her, glaring at the men who kept making lewd suggestions and talking into her chest.

"Bad night?"

"You could say that, yeah."

He finally moved forward, stopped with one foot on the bottom step. "I'm sorry."

"Why? It wasn't your party. And it wasn't your fault I stayed so late."

"Not about the party." He climbed the first step, then the second and the third, finally stopping at the threshold. But he didn't move closer, didn't try to follow her into the house.

She stepped back, her hand curling around the edge of the door. A tingle danced along her spine, pebbling her skin. Not from fear, never from Aaron. No, this was much deeper than fear.

"Then—" She stopped, her tongue darting out to wet her suddenly dry lips. Aaron's gaze dropped, something flaring in his eyes as he stared at her mouth. "Then apologize for what?"

His gaze slid from her mouth to her eyes. "For being an ass. For being a miserable old bastard."

"I—I don't understand."

He finally looked away and ran a hand through his thick hair, those broad shoulders slumping in defeat. No, not defeat—it was like the weight of the world rested on his shoulders, and he was struggling to hold it up by himself.

He looked back at her, those full lips curling in a humorless smile that did nothing to banish the shadows from his eyes. "Never mind. Goodnight, Savannah."

"Aaron, wait." She moved toward him, grabbing his arm before he could leave. "Why don't you come in and tell me what's going on?"

"I can't."

The rejection stung, even if she did understand the reason for it. "The girls. I forgot—"

"No." He shook his head, that humorless smile stretching his lips once more before quickly fading. "No, this has nothing to do with Brooke and Isabelle."

"Then why?"

"Because if I come in, it won't be to talk."

Savannah gasped, unable to hide her surprise, helpless against the sudden desire that washed over. Hot. Sharp with need. She glanced down at her hand, still wrapped around his arm. Muscle, hard as steel, bunched under her palm, humming with tension.

If she were smart, she'd let go. If she didn't, things would change between them. She wasn't sure how she knew that, wasn't even sure *how* they'd change...but they would. She had never been more certain of anything in her life.

Yes—if she were smart, she'd let him go.

She tightened her hand on his arm instead and pulled him inside.

"Savannah—"

"No. Don't talk. Not now." She didn't want words, not right now. She didn't need them, not with the way Aaron was looking at her, not with the desperate need burning in his eyes.

She trailed her hand up his arm. Across his shoulder. Traced his lower lip with the tip of one finger, felt the heat of his breath against her skin, heard the pounding of her heart echo in her ears. She moved closer—

And Aaron pulled her into his arms. The embrace wasn't gentle, and neither was his kiss. This wasn't a shy meeting of lips and tongue, or a hesitant seeking of permission. This was Aaron, claiming her. Demanding. Possessing.

His hands closed around her head, his fingers tangling in the strands of her hair as he tilted her head back and drank from her. Hot, deep, his tongue thrusting against hers, demanding she respond in kind.

And she did. Oh, she did.

Her hands twisted in his shirt as she rubbed against him, reveling in the feel of his hard cock straining to meet her thrust. She needed to get closer, her skin dancing, burning, yearning for his touch.

Desperate, so desperate she felt like she could crawl out of her skin and into his. She moaned, the sound a whimper of need in the back of her throat, and ran one foot up his leg.

"Please."

Did she say the word out loud, or only think it? It didn't matter, not when Aaron lifted her in his arms and carried her upstairs. The muscles of his chest and arms bunched and moved against her. Strong. Smooth. Powerful. Igniting a frantic yearning that intensified with each step he climbed, with each second that passed.

She expected him to ease her down onto the bed but he didn't. Instead, he let her body slide down against his, steadying her as she balanced on the too-high heels. He pulled away, his gaze burning into hers, and reached for the black string—nothing more than a long shoelace—holding the front of her costume together.

The tip of his finger grazed her skin as he freed the lace from each hole. Slow. Agonizingly slow. Her lungs burned with each deep breath. Her breasts pulled tight, her nipples so hard, so achingly tender, the brush of fabric against them was almost painful.

But Aaron never looked away, his gaze searing her. It was too much, too...too powerful. Too demanding. Too intense. She started to close her eyes, needing to look away, needing to break whatever spell he had on her.

"No."

Just a single word. Not a command. If it had been a command, she would have been able to ignore it. But this was a plea. Harsh. Desperate.

And she couldn't ignore it.

She stood there, held captive without being touched. Aaron stepped back, pulled the shirt over his head and tossed it to the side, baring his chest to her. Broad, sculpted, hard. Marred by scars and bruises, both old and new, but no less perfect. Her fingers itched to touch each inch of skin. Her palms tingled with the need to stroke, to caress, to memorize.

And then he shed the sweatpants, kicking them off to the side, and she forgot about everything else, nearly forgot to breathe.

She had seen him without clothes before, had reveled in the hard contours of his body. But this...this was different. There was something about the way he stood before her, baring himself to her. Proud. Strong.

Vulnerable.

How could a man be so rugged and so beautiful at the same time? Flat stomach, lean hips. Strong thighs, thick with muscle. Not muscle-bound, the way weightlifters were muscle-bound. But solid, powerful.

Her gaze wandered from his legs, up to his cock. Hard, thick, the smooth tip glistening in the dim light. She wanted—needed—to touch him. To taste. To feel. To ride.

And then he closed one large hand around the thick length and stroked. Slow, from the base to the tip, back and forth.

Savannah's knees buckled and she fell against the edge of the bed, catching herself at the last minute. It was the shoes, it had to be the shoes. It couldn't have anything to do with the unexpected sight of Aaron stroking his own cock.

The beautiful, magnificent, sight.

And oh, God, she was such a liar.

Her mouth watered with need. She swallowed,

reached down to pull off one shoe, her eyes never straying from that wondrous sight. But she must have blinked, must have looked away, because Aaron was suddenly right in front of her, his hands on her waist, his eyes boring into hers.

"No. Leave them on."

She blinked, her mouth parting in a silent gasp of surprise. He claimed her mouth, his tongue sweeping against hers until she fell against him, her fingers digging into his bare shoulders as she struggled to stay upright.

He dragged his mouth along her throat, nipped at the corded muscle between her neck and shoulder, teased the lobe of her ear with his teeth.

"Were you serious about throwing this in the trash?"

Savannah frowned, her mind struggling to make sense of the question. The costume. He was talking about the costume. She nodded, her eyes fluttering open to meet his. "Y-yes."

"Good." He grabbed the plunging neckline and pulled. The sound of material ripping apart echoed around her like a shot, not stopping until the gown hung around her, gaping open like a ragged robe. She gasped, her muscles quaking with sharp need as liquid heat pooled between her legs. Wet, so wet.

Aaron pushed the remnants from her shoulders, his callused hands following the fall of the material until she stood there in nothing but the stockings and heels. The tip of one finger traced the cleft of her ass, the flare of her hip. Then he reached between her legs and cupped her with his palm, gently pressing.

The climax crashed over her, stealing her breath, so sudden and surprising. Unexpected. She called his name, the sound of her voice odd to her own ears. Strangled. Breathless.

Pleading.

He swallowed her cries and dropped to the bed, pulling her down on top of him. She expected him to plunge inside her, needed to feel his thick cock filling her.

His hands closed over her hips and he lifted her, dragging her further up his body until his head rested between her legs. She reached for the edge of the headboard, the wood digging into her palms as she struggled to balance herself. And then his mouth closed over her and there was no balance. No thought. Just sensation, sharp and biting in its clarity. She flew apart, her body exploding into a million shards as Aaron demanded response with each taste, each touch, each softly whispered command.

And then she was on her back, struggling to breathe, clinging to him as he drove into her. Hard, deep. Over and over, until she could no longer tell where she ended and he started.

Until she truly and completely lost herself.

Aaron called her name, his voice a hoarse cry of need as he pumped into her. Once. Twice. His body stilled, his head thrown back, the muscles of his neck corded with strain. Savannah reached for him, wrapped her arms around his neck and pulled him down, forced his gaze to hers.

His body convulsed, his hips thrusting with his own climax. He fell on top of her, his harsh breathing mingling with her own. She could feel the heart pounding in his chest, could feel her own heart beating in the same heavy rhythm.

Minutes passed by, maybe longer. She might have

dozed, she wasn't sure. But Aaron finally shifted off her, moving to the side. He leaned down, removed her shoes and stockings, then stretched out beside her and pulled her against him. She turned her head, sighed when his mouth closed over hers in a soft, sweet kiss.

He had to leave. She knew that, understood it. But a part of her wanted him to stay, needed to feel his body next to hers as she drifted off to sleep.

She opened her eyes, expecting to find him watching her. But his eyes were closed, his face relaxed as he breathed in the deep rhythm of sleep. He looked so relaxed, so peaceful. She didn't want to disturb him, didn't want to wake him.

But she had to.

"Aaron." She placed one hand on his shoulder and gave him a gentle shake. "Aaron, you need to wake up."

One eye peeled open and he stared at her. "Why?"

She blinked in surprise. "Because—Brooke and Isabelle, aren't they home?"

"Yeah. Sleeping."

"Don't you need to get back over there?"

"My mom's with them."

"But—"

Aaron opened his other eye then propped himself up on one elbow. He leaned forward and pressed a quick kiss against her mouth. "I just need to be back home before they leave for school."

She was afraid to read into whatever he was saying. She couldn't—under any circumstances—read into it. If she did, she'd starting hoping...and that was the last thing she could afford to do. "But aren't you worried they're going to wonder where you were?"

His gaze was steady on hers, pulling her in, deeper and deeper, fanning the hope to life. "No."

It was the answer she had wanted to hear...and the answer she was afraid of hearing. She looked away, her gaze resting in the middle of his chest.

"Did you want me to leave?" His voice was quiet, filled with uncertainty. She met his eyes, saw the same hope she felt blossoming in her chest flare in their depths.

"No."

"Good." He kissed her again then pulled her against him, guiding her head to his shoulder. She curled closer, feeling safe and protected in his arms.

She had just started to drift off when he spoke again.

"Are you doing anything Friday night?"

"No." She yawned and grabbed the edge of the comforter, pulled it up to her waist. "Why?"

"Would you like to go out with me? On a date?"

The words, so unexpected, so shy and hesitant after everything they'd done, pushed her over the ledge she had been teetering on for weeks, for months. Maybe longer. She felt herself falling, fast and hard. But there was no fear, not when Aaron held her so securely in his arms. And instead of panicking, she simply smiled a sleepy smile and pressed a kiss against his chest. "I think I'd like that very much."

CHAPTER TWENTY

Aaron tilted his chin up, watching his reflection in the mirror, focusing on the deft movement of his fingers as they went through the motions of tying the silk tie. He saw Isabelle's reflection behind him as she kneeled on the edge of his bed, bouncing up and down as she watched him. Brooke stood just inside the room, leaning against the doorframe.

Both girls were frowning.

He finished the knot, straightening the tie before pulling the shirt collar down. Then he turned and faced both girls, a knot forming in his stomach. "Why are you both staring at me like that?"

They exchanged a quiet look, neither one of them saying anything. He sighed and moved over to the bed, sat on the edge and wrapped one arm around Isabelle's shoulder. He patted the mattress next to him, motioning for Brooke to join him.

She looked like she wanted to refuse, like she wanted to shake her head and run from the room. He held his breath, waiting...

She finally heaved a sigh, a heavy one filled with all the teenage drama she could muster, then shuffled over to the bed.

Aaron took a deep breath, let it out in a rush, then asked the question that worried him the most. "Are you sure you guys are okay with this?"

"Would it matter if we weren't?" The question came from Brooke, her voice injected with a combination of sulkiness, disbelief, and just a hint of attitude. Aaron shifted, his gaze meeting his oldest daughter's. She looked so much like her mother, with those deep blue-green eyes and thick golden hair. She was already showing signs of the stunningly beautiful woman she'd become, with those slightly exotic eyes and her mother's slender curves.

But God, she was only thirteen, just barely. The thought of her growing up, the thought of any boy showing interest in her, scared the living hell out of him. And he prayed, every damn night, that her looks were the only thing she inherited from his ex, that she was better able to handle the attention she would receive—might already be receiving—than her mother ever had.

For Amy, the attention had become an addiction, something she craved, something she needed as much as she needed air to breathe. His ex had constantly been seeking attention, searching for that superficial validation even after they had married. It didn't matter where it came from, as long as she had it.

He pushed away all thoughts of his ex-wife, banished the sorrow and regret of mistakes made—by both of them. That was in the past, and it was time to let it go.

That didn't stop the urge he had to lock Brooke in the basement until she got older. Like, say, maybe until she turned forty.

He gave himself a mental shake, forcing his mind

back to the here-and-now, to answering Brooke's question.

"Yeah, it would matter."

She made a small snorting sound and rolled her eyes. "Yeah. Right."

He turned toward her, placed one hand on each of her shoulders, and peered into her eyes. "Yes, it would. If you—either one of you—aren't comfortable with this, let me know."

"And what? You'll cancel your big date?"

"Yes, I would." It would kill him. His gut was already twisting into a knot at the idea—but he'd do it. "You girls come first. Always."

Brooke watched him for a long minute, her gaze so intense, seeing too much for a girl her age, that he almost looked away. Then she rolled her eyes and snorted again, nothing more than a normal teenager once more.

"That's stupid. I mean, it's not like you haven't already—" Her mouth clamped shut and she darted a quick glance at Isabelle before looking back at him, her eyes not quite meeting his. "Kissed."

Brooke's observation slammed into him, knocking the breath from his lungs. Not so much what she had said—no, it was what she *didn't* say. And Christ, how could she know? How did she even know about that shit anyway? She was a *girl*, too young to have any knowledge of kissing, let alone knowledge of…of *sex*. A sickening thought twisted his gut and he quickly shoved it from his mind.

No. Oh, no. No fucking way. He wasn't even going there. The idea that his little girl may have already…that she wasn't—oh no. No, no, no. Absolutely not.

"Daddy, are you going to marry Miss Savannah?"

Isabelle's innocent question, asked on the heels of Brooke's observation, sent him over the edge. He damn near jumped from the bed, his fingers working the knot of the tie that was suddenly strangling him.

"No, Sweet Pea. We're not getting married. We're not even going out. I'll call and…and—" Fuck. He needed to cancel the date. He didn't want to, but he had to. And then he was going to barricade himself in the house with the girls until they turned fifty.

Or until he died, whichever came first.

The way he felt now, he just might keel over from a heart attack in the next thirty seconds.

Isabelle and Brooke both started talking at once, their high-pitched voices coming at him from both sides. But it was Brooke's louder voice that cut through the din, demanding attention.

"Dad! What are you doing? You can't cancel!"

He paused, the ends of the tie dangling from his hands. "I think I need to."

"Why?"

Why? Good question. Too damn bad he couldn't come up with an answer. At least, not one he could give to the two young girls sitting on the edge of his bed, watching him with identical expressions of bewilderment. So he settled on his mother's favorite standby, the explanation she had given for everything when he was growing up.

"Because."

Aaron yanked the tie off and moved to the closet, hanging it on the rack with all his other ties. He reached up, undid the top button of his dress shirt, and pulled in a deep breath.

"That's just stupid."

"Yeah, Daddy. That's stupid."

He spun around, frowning at both his daughters. "Okay, no more 'stupid'. I am so tired of hearing that word around this house. Come up with something different."

Brooke jumped to her feet then promptly stomped one against the floor. "But it *is* stupid! Why would you even do that?"

"I don't think it's a good idea."

"That's just stu—" Brooke's lips pursed and her eyes narrowed, her mind obviously searching for another word. "Dumb."

"You need to go, Daddy. Miss Savannah'll be sad if you don't."

"I'm not going. Not if you girls aren't okay with it."

"But we are!"

If the comment had come from Isabelle, he might have believed it. But coming from Brooke? No. He couldn't. "Brooke, how am I supposed to believe that when I know you don't even like her?"

"I never said I didn't like her."

"Brooke. Really?"

She lowered her head, a faint blush coloring her cheeks. "She's okay. I guess."

Aaron wanted to believe her, he really did. But he knew better. He shrugged out of the suit jacket and placed it on a hanger, then undid the buttons of the shirt sleeves. "Why don't you two run downstairs and help Grammy out? I'll be down in a few minutes. After I change."

And call Savannah to cancel their date. And Christ, he hadn't expected the wave of disappointment that crashed over him. Hadn't expected to feel so hollow and empty.

He felt a hand tug on his arm, looked down to see Brooke standing next to him, her eyes big and round and filled with tears. "Daddy, I'm sorry. Don't cancel. Please? I'll be nicer to Miss Savannah. I promise."

"Brooke—" He had to stop and clear his throat because, fuck, the sight of his daughter staring up at him, looking like *she* was the one to blame for his decision, slayed him. "Brooke, this isn't your fault. Okay? It's just—this whole dating thing. I'm not ready. I'm too old. I'm not—"

He stopped before he said too much, remembering that this was his daughter he was talking to. His *thirteen-year-old* daughter. "It'll be fine, okay?"

"No, it's not okay. I want you to go. We both do." She turned to Isabelle. "Tell him, Isabelle."

"Brookie's right, Daddy. We want you to go."

His head started to spin, trying to make sense of the sudden change of heart. Not from Isabelle—although he wondered if he needed to worry about that comment she had made about getting married. But Brooke…this wasn't like her, especially when he knew she wasn't overly fond of Savannah. He hadn't pushed the issue, hadn't asked why, had just chalked it up to one of those things.

Maybe he should have pursued it before now.

"Why, Brooke? Why is it suddenly so important to you?"

"Because—" She looked away, chewed on her lower lip for a few seconds, then heaved another long sigh as the words left her in a rush. "Because you like her and I guess she's really not that stupid and you smile a lot more when she's around so that makes it okay."

And damn if Aaron's throat didn't fucking close up. He closed his eyes, pinched the bridge of his nose and sucked in a ragged breath. Then he pulled Brooke in for a hug, felt her stiffen for a brief second before she relaxed and wrapped her arms around his waist. He looked over, crooked his finger at Isabelle, then grunted when she crashed into them, joining in the hug with a laugh.

Brooke was the first one to pull away. "So you're going to go?"

"Yeah, I'll go." He redid the buttons on his sleeves then reached into the closet for the suit jacket.

"Dad, no. You can't wear that."

"Why can't I wear it? It's a suit. There's nothing wrong with it."

"Because that's what you wear to work!"

He blinked against the surprise he felt at Brooke's comment. Yeah, sure. He wore a suit to and from the games, that was their dress code. But it's not what he wore *for* work.

He really needed to start bringing the girls to more games.

"There's nothing wrong with a suit—"

"But Dad, that's all she's ever seen you in. That and sweatpants or gym shorts or those stupid cargo shorts you always wore during the summer."

"What's wrong with cargo shorts?" The question popped out before Brooke's comment completely sunk in. Before the *truth* of the words sunk in. And shit, she was right. Sweatpants. Gym shorts. Cargo shorts. That's all he wore around Savannah because he was always *home* when he saw Savannah, and he dressed for comfort when he was home. Didn't everyone?

He stared at the suit jacket dangling from his hand,

then looked at his two daughters. "Then what am I supposed to wear if you don't want me wearing this?"

Brooke and Isabelle exchanged a look. Identical grins spread across their faces, filling him with a dread he didn't quite understand. Then the girls shoved him out of the way and started digging through his closet, tossing clothes over their shoulders in search of a daughter-approved outfit for his first date in forever.

CHAPTER TWENTY-ONE

Savannah laughed when Aaron finished the story. He had felt like an ass at first, wondering if maybe he shouldn't have even started telling it. It was embarrassing, admitting that his daughters had dressed him for the evening. But they had just been seated at their table when she looked over and complimented him, telling him she'd never seen him in anything but sweatpants or his suits.

Yeah, definitely embarrassing. He'd have to pay closer attention when he got dressed each day, instead of just reaching for the closest pair of sweatpants when he rolled out of bed.

He pulled the wine bottle from the small bucket perched on the edge of the table and refilled her glass before topping his off his own. "Just don't tell them I told you. I'll never live it down."

"Don't worry, your secret is safe with me." Savannah sipped the wine then reached up to tuck a strand of hair behind her ear. Candlelight reflected off the diamonds in her lobes, shooting rainbow fire back at him. She looked poised. Relaxed. Beautiful. The knit sweater draped her body, the scooped neckline showing him just a hint of creamy cleavage. Black jeans hugged her body, down to where they disappeared into the top of the knee-high leather boots she wore. The denim clung to her, molding to her curves, something he had noticed—and appreciated—as they made their way to their table.

And he really needed to stop thinking about getting her out of her clothes. Their date had just started, with a casual dinner at this small Italian restaurant. They still had hours ahead of them—he hoped. Dinner. A movie. Drinks afterward. And then, maybe, when he took her home—

He had to stop thinking about *later*. That's not why he asked her out tonight. Not even close.

Savannah grabbed a breadstick from the small wicker basket and broke it in half. "It sounds like things are getting better with Brooke."

"Yeah. I think. I mean, it's been over a month since she told me she hates me so..." He shrugged, letting the words trail off.

"A whole month, huh? Progress." A small smile teased her mouth as she nibbled on the breadstick.

"I worry about her, you know? About both of them, but especially about Brooke."

"You're their father. You're supposed to worry about them."

"It's more than just that. I worry about her growing up too fast, you know? She's been through so much. And I think she had a harder time adjusting to everything than Isabelle. Brooke—" Aaron paused. What the hell was he doing? He was on a date. With Savannah. There were a hundred other things he could be talking about. "Sorry. You don't want to hear me talking about the girls."

"Why not?"

"Because. I mean, we're on a date. We should be talking about something else. It's just..." His voice trailed off. He ran his finger up and down the handle of the knife resting in front of him, then started flipping it over. Front-to-back, front-to-back. He realized what he was doing and quickly dropped his hand to his lap.

"Sorry."

Savannah leaned forward and grabbed his other hand, her fingers threading with his. "You keep saying that. Why?"

"Why am I saying it? Or why am I sorry?"

"I don't know. Both."

"Well, I'm saying it because I *am*. And I'm sorry because I have no idea what to say. This...it's been so long since I've been on a...an actual *date*. I'm not sure how to act. I'm pretty sure I'm not supposed to be sitting here, talking about my girls, though."

Savannah squeezed his hand then sat back. Did his admission surprise her? If it did, she didn't let on. And she either didn't see the heat filling his face, or she chose to ignore it. "Aaron, this isn't exactly a first date. I mean, we're not strangers. We've known each other for a year now. And we've already—"

She stopped, her gaze darting away from his. His face wasn't the only one sporting a small blush.

"I guess, uh, guess we started things out of order, huh?"

"Yeah, I guess we did." She laughed, the sound light and musical, and sipped some of her wine. "What I'm trying to say is that you shouldn't worry about talking about the girls. They're your daughters. I expect you to talk about them. I'm just glad things seem to be getting better between you and Brooke."

"Yeah. Me, too."

"Is she, um, is she okay with this? With us going out tonight, I mean."

"She says she is. I think she knows that we—" He cleared his throat and looked away. "You know."

"Oh, God. No." Savannah groaned then lowered her head, covering her face with both hands. And shit, why the hell had he said anything? He leaned forward, nearly knocking her wine glass over as he reached for her hand.

"I didn't mean—I'm sorry, I shouldn't have said anything."

Savannah finally looked up, a blush glowing on her face. "She actually said that?"

"Not exactly, no. But the message was pretty clear."

Savannah shifted in the chair, sighed, then reached for the wine glass and took a small sip. "Brooke said something similar to me. I, uh, I thought she was just making a wild guess. I guess not."

"She *what*? When?"

"That day we went to DC."

Aaron opened his mouth, snapped it closed again. A few seconds went by before he could finally speak. "How? How would she...that scares the hell out of me. She's thirteen. How the hell does she know about any of that stuff?"

Savannah's brows arched above eyes sparkling with amusement. "Because she's thirteen. She's in school. Sex ed. Plus I'm sure all the kids talk."

Reality sucker-punched him, kicking the bottom from his stomach. He opened his mouth—to shout a denial, to bellow his disbelief—but the only sound that came out was a wheeze. He grabbed his wine glass and downed the contents, nearly choking when he swallowed.

"Christ. She's only thirteen. She's not supposed to—" He looked over at Savannah, not hiding the real fear on his face. "You don't think she—I mean, would she…" Christ, he couldn't even think the words, let alone get them out.

"Are you asking if I think she's sexually active?"

"Shit. Shit!" He hissed the words, glancing around in a panic to see if anyone had heard Savannah. Nobody seemed to be paying any attention to them. "Don't even say that!"

Why did he get the impression she was biting back a smile? The impression grew when she raised the wine glass, using it to hide her mouth. "If it makes you feel better, no. I don't think she's sexually—"

"Yeah. Okay, got it. No need to say it out loud again. Christ."

"Poor Aaron." She laughed again. "What are you going to do when they start dating?"

"*They?*"

"Yes, *they*. You have *two* daughters, remember?"

"Oh hell no. Isabelle is just a baby. Not happening. They're not dating. Neither one of them. I'll kill any boy that even thinks about asking them out."

Savannah smiled again and he wondered if he was overreacting. No wondering about it—he was. But shit, how could he not? These were his *daughters* they were talking about. And he wasn't so old that he couldn't remember how he had been, a lifetime ago, back when he was a teenager. Hockey had been a top priority when he was growing up, but that had certainly never stopped him. In fact, playing hockey had only helped with the girls.

He reached for the glass, frowned when he discovered it empty, then sighed and leaned back in the chair. "I guess I'm going overboard, huh?"

"You're a dad. It's expected."

"Was your dad the same way?"

Savannah shrugged but she wouldn't meet his gaze, and he kicked himself in the ass for even bringing it up. "In his own way, I guess. When he thought about actually paying attention."

"I'm sorry. I shouldn't have said anything—"

"Don't worry about it. Things are better with them—both of them—now that I'm older. I understand a little more now. I mean, they both loved me in their own way—they still do." She offered him a smile that didn't quite meet her eyes then looked away. She pulled the wine glass closer to her, running her fingers up and down the stem. "But when I was growing up, they were both so busy, I kind of felt like an afterthought."

He reached for her hand, curled his fingers around hers and squeezed. "You could never be an afterthought, Savannah. Not even close. And especially not to me."

Her gaze shot to his, her eyes widening in surprise. At his words? At the huskiness in his voice? Or was she surprised at the expression he knew was glowing in his own eyes as his gaze held hers? He didn't know, and he didn't care. He meant the words, every single one them—spoken and unspoken.

Her tongue darted out, swept across her lower lip. She opened her mouth, ready to say something, only to be interrupted when the waiter approached with their salads.

Talk about absolute shitty timing.

And when he finally left, the spell had been broken, whatever words Savannah had been ready to say gone forever. Instead, she offered him a small smile filled with humor he didn't quite understand and shook her head.

"And to think you were nervous about not knowing what to say."

CHAPTER TWENTY-TWO

The noise surrounding them was growing louder as more and more people made their way into the arena, filling seats that had been empty ten minutes ago. Savannah's gaze swept the area around her, taking everything in as she sipped fountain soda from a straw. This was her second hockey game, ever, and so completely different from her first that she wasn't sure what to make of it.

For starters, she was sitting in a different section, just a few rows behind the bench where the players would be when they came out. She knew that because Courtney had told her as much.

And Tessa wasn't here tonight, either, so she felt even more out of place, like she was by herself. How silly was that? To feel that way when she was surrounded by all these people.

Because she most definitely wasn't by herself. Courtney was in the row in front of her, little Noah climbing from her lap to his seat and back again. Three other women sat with Courtney: Haley, Megan, and Jenny. She'd been officially introduced as each woman settled down. Four women, all of them so completely different from each other but still friends because of the men they dated. Or, in Courtney and Jenny's cases, married.

It felt a little weird, sitting behind them the way she was. Like she didn't quite belong. Not that they ignored her—they each turned in their seats, trying to draw her into the conversation, trying to make her feel welcome.

And if she was honest with herself, she didn't feel out of place because of the women in front of her.

It was because of the two girls sitting on either side of her.

She turned her head, studying each one for a brief second as she tried to figure out how she had ended up here. Aaron had invited her to the game tonight, a week after their first official date. It was supposed to be Savannah, his two daughters, and his mother.

Except his mother had succumbed to the same flu bug that had knocked Savannah on *her* ass a few weeks ago and wasn't able to make it. If she had thought, for even a fraction of a second, that she'd be here with the girls by herself, she would have taken Aaron up on his offer of that extra ticket for Tessa.

But she hadn't, and Tessa had already made plans for tonight, refusing to cancel no matter how many times Savannah begged and pleaded. So here she sat, between Isabelle and Brooke, feeling out of place and oddly alone.

Both girls were wearing Bombers jerseys, with Aaron's last name—*their* name—in big block letters on the back, above the number 15. Brooke had rolled her eyes when Savannah asked what the number was, then explained it was Aaron's number.

Duh.

Duh, indeed.

The girls weren't the only ones wearing jerseys. The women in front of her had them on, too, only with different names and numbers on the back. So did little Noah. A lot of people in the arena were wearing them.

Savannah had felt out of place enough that she had asked Courtney to keep an eye on the girls then dashed out to the concourse and purchased an oversized hooded sweatshirt with the Bombers logo on the front. She wasn't sure what made her do it, but she bought a jersey, too, with the name MALONE on the back in block letters above the number 15. The jersey was rolled into a tight ball and double-bagged, sitting under her seat.

No way was she going to put it on, not with the girls right there. She didn't want to subject herself to their questioning looks, didn't want to risk Brooke saying something sarcastic or scathing. She hadn't forgotten that one encounter with the girl, when Brooke had told her quite plainly that Aaron would never love her and she should just leave.

Did Brooke remember that conversation from a little more than a month ago? If she did, she didn't act like it. And she had actually been nice so far, for the most part—except for that whole *duh* thing, which Savannah figured she had deserved.

Savannah wasn't going to risk changing that by putting on Aaron's jersey.

Which made her wonder why she had bought it in the first place.

Jenny turned in her seat, glancing at Savannah then leaning closer so everyone could hear her. "Does anyone else have one of those feelings about tonight?"

"Yes."

"No."

Haley and Megan both spoke at the same time, contradicting each other. Courtney glanced at Noah then turned to Jenny, a frown creasing her face. "I refuse to think about it. And if it even looks like something is going to happen, I'm taking Noah out to the concourse. He doesn't need to see that again."

Savannah glanced at the two girls, but they looked as confused as she did. "See what? Is something supposed to happen?"

Haley brushed her long hair over one shoulder and turned to look at Savannah. "I hope not. But from the way Zach was acting before he left this afternoon, I'm not sure."

"Tyler was the same way. Acting like some macho prizefighter on the way to the ring. I told him not to even think about it."

"Do you think it worked?"

Jenny's mouth curled in a wide, mischievous smile. "Nope."

"OhmyGod, you're actually enjoying this, aren't you? You're hoping something happens!" That had come from Megan, who Savannah had learned was dating Jenny's brother. The two women seemed close, which was odd because Aaron had told her that the men they were each seeing had come close to blows a few times already.

Savannah didn't waste time trying to figure out whatever weird interpersonal dynamics were being played. "What am I missing?"

Courtney grabbed the back of Noah's pants, holding him in place as she answered. "They're playing Bridgeport tonight."

She looked as if that explained everything. In fact, all four women looked like that was answer enough. To them, it probably was, but Savannah was clueless. "I don't get it. What's that mean?"

Jenny twisted in her seat, bracing her arms along the back of the chair. "The last time we played Bridgeport, there was a huge brawl on the ice. Gear was thrown everywhere, fists were flying. It was a bloodbath."

"A bloodbath?"

Megan nudged Jenny in the side. "Don't look so happy. The whole thing happened because Tyler was defending your honor."

"Why shouldn't I be happy about that? Viktor had it coming." Jenny turned back to Savannah. "I used to, um—" Her gaze darted to the girls then quickly looked away. "—*date* one of the guys that plays for Bridgeport. He started running his mouth and things just got a little out of hand from there."

Haley laughed. "A little? That's one way to put it."

"You weren't even here!" A second passed before Jenny's smile died. The color drained from her face, and she leaned around Megan to put her hand on Haley's shoulder. "Oh God, I am so sorry. I wasn't even thinking—"

"Oh please. Stop. You're as bad as Zach. I'm over it already."

"Then you're stronger than me because I don't think I'd ever get over it. What Jimmy did to you—"

Haley cleared her throat, the noise long and loud and exaggerated. Her green eyes darted a meaningful look at the girls sitting on either side of Savannah before she gave her head a quick shake. Jenny sat back, biting her lower lip as color rose in her cheeks.

Courtney must have seen Savannah's confusion—and her curiosity—because she reached back and gave her leg a quick pat. "Let's just say that night was filled with more excitement than any of us needed and leave it at that."

Savannah wanted to ask for details, knowing she had missed so much, but she couldn't. And not just because the girls were sitting there. The lights dimmed and music blared from the arena loudspeakers. Spotlights lit up the ice, swirling back and forth in a crazy pattern as an announcer's deep voice boomed around them.

Everyone jumped to their feet as the players came out to the ice, skating around for a few minutes before lining up for the anthem. And then the game started, an explosion of action and noise.

Not five minutes had passed, and Savannah could already tell that something was different from the last game she'd attended. The last game had been fast, filled with action and excitement.

This game was just as fast, but there was something else going on. Some kind of tension that even she could feel. She knew she wasn't imagining it because the women in front of her seemed nervous, too. Antsy. Even Isabelle and Brooke could sense it. Isabelle's hand had grabbed Savannah's arm once or twice already, both times when Aaron had been hit. And Brooke had jumped, moving a little closer to Savannah when some guy slammed Aaron from behind and sent him sprawling to the ice.

It was brutal, the hits and taunts that she could hear even from where they were sitting. There had been a break in the game and some guy in orange and blue was led to another bench across the ice. Savannah jumped when the sound of the slamming door echoed around the arena. Now both teams were lining up at the other end of the ice, away from Bombers' net.

Courtney leaned back, her attention divided between the ice, Noah, and Savannah. "We're on the power play, so we have one more player on the ice than Bridgeport."

"Is that good?"

"For us, yeah." Jenny answered the question instead of Courtney. "We just need to capitalize on the man-advantage. And crap. Shit, shit, shit."

"What? What is it?" Savannah looked at the ice but the only person moving was some big guy from the other team, who was skating toward the other players down by the net.

"They just put Viktor in for the penalty kill. He's not known for his speed or endurance, which means there's only one reason they'd use him right away."

"Why?"

"To get physical."

Savannah stared at the ice, wishing she understood the game better, wishing she knew what Jenny was talking about—especially when the guy stopped right in front of Aaron.

She leaned closer, ready to ask, but then the ice exploded with action. Savannah narrowed her eyes, trying to see every detail, wondering if she should look at the giant screen hanging above the ice instead. But she couldn't take her eyes off the action, afraid to even blink in case she missed something.

She saw someone pass the puck to Aaron, watched as he caught it and did some kind of graceful slide-twist-spin move on his skates. The crowd surged to their feet, clapping and cheering as he skated behind the net. A hand gripped hers, squeezing. Not Isabelle—Brooke. Savannah didn't take the time to wonder what it meant, she couldn't, not when she was so focused on the game. She simply squeezed the girl's hand in return, her breath held, certain that Aaron was going to shoot the puck into the net.

And then she saw a flash of orange and blue, hurtling like some kind of rocket straight toward Aaron. She opened her mouth, wanting to scream his name, needing to warn him, but it was too late.

There was a sickening thud as the orange blur collided with Aaron, knocking him flat on his back. The other player landed on top of him and they both slid across the ice, coming to a sudden stop as they slammed against the half-wall bordering the ice with a loud thud. The player who had knocked Aaron down jumped to his feet and made a mad scramble for the puck, dashing away from the net. But Aaron didn't move. He just lay there, deathly still, his back wedged against the wall, his arms outstretched.

Brooke's hand tightened around hers. Isabelle grabbed her around the waist, clinging to her.

"Daddy!"

Savannah didn't know who said it. Isabelle. Brooke. Maybe both. She wanted to reassure them, know she needed to tell them that Aaron was fine, that he'd back on his feet any second, but she couldn't get the words from her mouth.

Because he *wasn't* fine, and he *wasn't* getting back to his feet. The noise around them slowly died, fading to an eerie silence. A whistle blew somewhere, the sound too sharp, too loud. Several of Aaron's teammates knelt by his side. Two more helped some man shuffle across the ice. More people headed toward him, carrying large tackle boxes.

And all the while, people looked on in silence. The

only sounds Savannah could hear were Isabelle's sobs—and Brooke's plaintive whisper, repeated over and over in desperation.

A whisper Savannah knew Aaron couldn't hear. "Daddy!"

CHAPTER TWENTY-THREE

She was trapped in a nightmarish hell that showed no signs of ending. Stuck on a ride that kept spinning faster and faster, until her vision swam in front of her and nausea welled in her stomach.

Savannah jerked upright, pressed her hand against her middle, and closed her eyes. Tight, tighter, willing the spots behind her lids to disappear, waiting for her stomach to settle.

She took a deep breath, opened her eyes and looked around. Floors covered in an industrial gray carpet. Walls painted an indistinguishable color. Chairs, an ugly slate blue with straight backs and hard seats and wooden arms, their illusion of comfort nothing more than a mockery.

What was she doing here? She didn't belong here, didn't understand why she wasn't at home, snuggled under her downy comforter, her head cradled by a soft pillow.

Dreaming, instead of being stuck in this never-ending nightmare.

Savannah turned her head, her gaze landing on the two young girls beside her. Their heads, one dark and one light, so close together they nearly touched.

Brooke.

Isabelle.

Both of them sound asleep in those awful chairs, their legs curled under them in nearly identical poses, a thin blanket tossed over their shoulders. Pale faces, streaked with dry tears.

They were the reason she was still here. She wouldn't leave them, couldn't take them home. Not yet. Not until they heard news about Aaron.

Bile erupted in her stomach again, rising into the back of her throat. She swallowed, pushed it away, tried to close her mind against the image of Aaron being carried off the ice on a stretcher to the sound of applause from thousands of cheering fans.

And oh God, how could they cheer and clap that way, when his daughters were shaking with fear, tears sliding down their faces as he was carried out? Couldn't they see? Didn't they care?

Savannah stared at the curled fists in her lap, forced her fingers to relax. On some basic level she didn't really understand, she knew why the crowd was cheering. Not because Aaron had been hurt, but because they were wishing him well, hoping for the best.

And she knew Aaron had heard them, had seen the small wave he offered the crowd. Not really even a wave, more of a lifting of his arm, his hand outstretched. Seeing that wave had been the only thing keeping her from falling apart.

The wave—and the knowledge that she had to take care of the girls. Aaron's daughters.

Things were a blur after that, nothing more than quick snapshots of memory.

Being escorted through the stands.

An elevator taking them downstairs.

Halls painted black and white. The cold concrete of a parking garage. Being helped into a shiny SUV.

Arriving at the hospital. Being escorted into this hell disguised as a private waiting room.

Waiting.

Always waiting.

And through it all, holding the girls. One at a time. Together. It didn't matter. Whatever they needed. Until they had grown so sleepy—exhausted from crying, still in shock over seeing their father hurt—that they'd finally fallen asleep.

People had come to see the girls, to talk to Savannah. Men she didn't know, didn't recognize. Two, maybe three, all of them in suits, none of them wearing a lab coat or surgical scrubs or even something as basic as a stethoscope around their necks.

Not doctors. The men worked with Aaron. One of them—she couldn't remember his name, only the piercing green eyes that glowed with reassurance—had seen her twice. Offering comfort. Assuring her everything was fine. Talking to her about tests and precautions. Asking if she needed anything.

He'd been the one to finally get the blanket for the girls.

How much time had passed? She didn't know, didn't see a clock on the wall and she didn't wear a watch. She couldn't even check her phone because she wasn't sure where it was. In her purse, she thought.

But she had no idea where that was.

People started drifting in, big men in suits, sporting cuts and bruises on their faces and hands. Savannah blinked, a few of the faces coming into focus. She recognized some of them, or at least she thought she did.

One of the men walked over to her, his thick hair sliding over his forehead and falling to his eyes. He bent down on one knee and brushed the hair from his face. His hand was cut, his knuckles scraped and bruised. His eyes looked familiar...

This was Noah's father. Courtney's husband. Her sluggish mind searched for a name, finally found it as soon as he introduced himself in a low voice.

Harland. Harland Day.

He glanced at the girls then looked back at Savannah. "Any word yet?"

She shook her head, wondering why he was asking *her*.

"How are the girls doing?"

"Sleeping." Her voice was nothing more than a croak, the word barely audible. She didn't bother repeating herself, knowing the answer hadn't made sense, not just because it sounded off to her own ears, but because of the way Harland was looking at her.

A few seconds went by then he offered her a gentle smile, patted her on the leg, and left. Several minutes later, another man in a suit approached her. He looked younger, almost boyishly innocent despite the cut on his chin and the mottled flesh swelling under one smoky gray eye. He sat down in the chair next to her, holding out a paper cup filled with steaming liquid. Savannah stared at the cup then looked back at him, not understanding.

"It's hot tea. Lots of sugar."

He was soft-spoken, maybe even a little shy. She recognized the voice, remembered hearing him sing that one time she'd gone out with Aaron. But she still didn't understand why he was telling her about his tea.

A small blush fanned across his cheeks as he reached for one of her hands and curled it around the cup. Heat seeped into her chilled fingers, both from the warm liquid inside the cup and from the hand he kept around hers. Her hazy mind finally understood what he wanted her to do and she raised the cup to her mouth, took a cautious sip, then another. Hot liquid, strong and sweet, drizzled down her aching throat to her stomach. Heat filled her, slowly thawing the numbness that had been gripping her.

And with the thawing came emotion.

She blinked against the sudden tears burning her eyes, swiped at the single tear that fell over her lashes and trailed down her cheek. The man beside her made a low sound of panic in his throat and awkwardly patted her on the arm. Then he muttered something in his soft voice and wrapped one arm around her shoulders, murmuring awkward words of comfort she couldn't quite make out.

How much time went by? The minutes dragged on, the room filled with the low drone of hushed conversation. She finished her tea and stared into the empty cup, idly wondering what she should do with it. Something changed in the air around her, a subtle shifting of energy as conversation drifted to a stop. Savannah raised her head, her eyes falling on the newcomer entering the room. He walked over and talked to the man with the green eyes for a few long minutes then turned and walked out. The man with the green eyes said something to someone else, who said something to the man next to him. On and on, the hum of conversation growing a little louder with each passing second.

But Savannah couldn't hear what was being said,

couldn't make out the words. Her heart lodged in her throat as the man with the green eyes walked toward her. She tightened her hands around the empty cup, squeezing until the cardboard collapsed in her grip.

Brooke and Isabelle stirred beside her, waking as the man stopped in front of them. Savannah dropped the cup to the floor as two pairs of hands grabbed hers, seeking reassurance.

"He's fine. Nothing is broken and he only has a mild concussion. They're keeping him overnight for observation." A grin curled the man's mouth, there and gone in a flash. "You can go back to see him now."

The girls squealed in excitement and jumped from their chairs, halfway across the room before they stopped and ran back to her. Isabelle grabbed her hand, tugging her from the chair. "Miss Savannah, come on."

She hesitated, not knowing what to do. She wasn't family. Didn't they have rules about those sorts of things?

But nobody seemed to care as she followed the girls across the small waiting room and through a set of double doors. A nurse led them down the hall, then paused in front of a partially closed door and smiled at Savannah.

"He's all yours. And he'll be good as new in a day or two, if not sooner."

Savannah blinked. Did the nurse think they were—? She must, if the sparkle in the woman's eyes meant anything. She opened her mouth, ready to correct the nurse's assumption, but she was already walking away.

And the girls were already running into the room.

Savannah followed them, her steps much slower as she entered the dim room. Aaron was propped up in the bed, his dark hair tousled around his head, a hospital gown stretched across his broad chest and shoulders. An IV line ran from the back of his left hand to a clear bag hanging from a pole next to his bed. His mouth curled into a brief smile as the girls ran toward him.

"Daddy! You're okay!"

He winced then patted the bed next to him, motioning for Isabelle to climb up. He leaned forward and kissed the top of her head. "Of course, I'm okay. Just, um, just use your inside voice, okay?"

"Are you really okay, Dad?"

"Yeah, I really am." His glance darted to Savannah then moved back to Brooke. He shifted, wincing with the movement, then patted the bed on his other side.

"Dad!" Brooke drew the word out, giving it three syllables. "I'm not a little kid like Isabelle."

"I know you're not."

Brooke hesitated for only a second then made her way over to the bed. Savannah bit back a smile as the young teenager climbed up next to Aaron and hugged him.

She stood there for a long minute, watching the three of them. Isabelle, her eyes already closed, her small arms holding onto her father like she was afraid to let him go. Brooke, curled up on his other side, doing her best to act like she didn't care. She could have pulled it off, too, if not for the way her lips trembled.

And Aaron, his strong arms wrapped around both of them, his eyes closed as pain and weariness pinched the features of his face. Savannah hesitated, feeling like an intruder, not sure what to do. Should she take the girls home now? If she took them home, was she supposed to stay with them? Call Aaron's mom? But Carol was sick, in no condition to babysit.

Or maybe the team had someone to do that, someone to worry about and take care of the details. Which meant she should probably leave. Go home and finally get some sleep and try to forget the horror of this night and—

"Hey."

She looked up at Aaron's soft whisper, blinked to bring his face into focus. He watched her for a long minute, long enough that she could tell he was in more pain than he had let on with the girls. Then he raised his hand and held it out to her, palm up. She hesitated, took a slow step toward him. One, then another, then another, not stopping until she stood by his side.

His hand closed over hers. Warm, comforting. Big and solid. He pulled her even closer, raising her hand to his mouth and brushing a soft kiss across her knuckles, his eyes never leaving hers.

"You okay?"

"Me?" Savannah almost laughed. "You're the one in the hospital."

"Maybe. But you look like you're ready to collapse."

"I'm fine. Just tired."

"You should sit down before you fall down."

"I've been sitting all night and—"

"Please."

There was something about the way he said it— the soft plea in his voice, the quiet need in his eyes. Or maybe Savannah was simply so exhausted, she was seeing things. It didn't matter because she lowered herself to the cushioned chair next to Aaron's bed, his hand still wrapped around hers.

Savannah glanced over at the girls to see if they were watching, if they saw the way she was holding their father's hand. Both girls had their eyes closed, their breathing deep and steady. Asleep? Maybe. It had been a long night so it was possible.

She looked back at Aaron, studying him, looking for signs of pain or discomfort. Could he read her mind? Or was it simply because her worry was that evident on her face? Maybe both, because he squeezed her fingers and gave her a small smile that was meant to reassure.

"I'm okay."

"Are you sure? They said something about a concussion—"

"Just a mild one. Not the first time I've had one."

"But you weren't moving for so long."

Aaron laughed, the sound quickly morphing into a brief moan. His mouth pinched tight and he closed his eyes, taking a quick breath through his nose. He shifted then reopened his eyes, one corner of his mouth curling into a quick grin. "That's because I had the wind knocked out of me. It was a hell of a hard hit."

Savannah knew he was leaving a lot out. Because of the girls? Probably. "But you're sure you're okay?"

His gaze caught hers, the brown of his dark eyes swirling with warmth, with unspoken messages she was afraid to read. He tugged on her hand, pulling until she was leaning across the bed, her face close to his.

"I am now." He caught her mouth in a gentle kiss, just the barest brushing of lips. Then he closed his eyes and rested his head back with a soft sigh.

Savannah shifted, turned her head to the side and caught Brooke's gaze. The young girl watched her for a long minute, those deep blue-green eyes so intent on hers that Savannah felt herself blushing.

Brooke glanced at Savannah's hand, still clasped in Aaron's larger one. Savannah started to pull away, worried about what the girl would think, worried about creating more tension between father and daughter.

But Brooke simply smiled then rested her head on her father's chest and closed her eyes.

And Savannah stopped worrying.

CHAPTER TWENTY-FOUR

"Welcome back, Pops." Ben tapped Aaron on his thigh with the blade of his stick, earning him a glare and a grunt. If Aaron heard one more person call him *Pops*, saw one more smug smile sent his way, he was going to start slamming bodies into boards.

Not that he hadn't expected the comments or the teasing. This was his first practice back. Of course, he was going to get a fair amount of ribbing. But fuck, he'd been on the ice for a grand total of five minutes and already he was fucking tired.

Nine days. He'd been out for nine days because of the fucking headaches. It shouldn't have taken that long, would have never taken that long a few years ago. But protocols had changed—

And so had his body. He didn't recover as fast, not like he used to. It wasn't just the headaches—his entire body felt like he'd been hit by a freight train.

Probably because he had been.

The hit had been hard. Too fucking hard. He hadn't said anything in front of Savannah or the girls, but he'd had a hell of a lot more than just the wind knocked out of him. He hadn't moved after Krasnoff knocked him flat on his ass and slid him into the boards because he was afraid to, afraid he'd punctured a fucking lung because it hurt so much to breathe. Afraid he'd snapped his neck or cracked something in his back. No, he hadn't said anything to anyone, not even the guys on the team, but there had been a few terrifying minutes where he'd been afraid he might not play again.

Apparently, he hadn't been the only one who had been terrified. His chest still got all tight when he remembered the expressions on the girls' faces, the glimpse of fear when they had bounded into the hospital room, followed by the pure relief shining in their eyes.

And Savannah—yeah, she'd been scared. They hadn't talked about it, he hadn't asked her. He didn't need to, not when he could see what she'd gone through in the reflection in her hazel eyes. Even now, more than a week later, he would catch a glimpse of it, whenever she thought he wasn't looking.

But there had been a few good things come from it. Brooke seemed to have done a complete turn-around. No more arguing, no more shouting or stomping, no more attitude. Well, mostly—Aaron figured the occasional attitude was probably normal, since she was thirteen. And her attitude toward Savannah had changed, too. They actually talked now, the beginnings of a tentative friendship.

Christ, he hoped so. He wanted that more than he would have thought possible, even a month ago.

Because he wanted Savannah. Not as a neighbor, not as a friend. Not as someone he was simply dating. He wanted her in his life. In the girls' life.

Long-term.

He just needed to work up the courage to talk to

her about it and hope like hell she felt the same way. He thought she did. Maybe.

Christ, he hoped so.

Maybe this afternoon, when he got home from practice. He could run next door and figure out a way to bring the subject up. And maybe they could make time for things other than talking.

An image of Savannah, naked, straddling him, popped into his mind and he closed his eyes, savoring it. The sway of her hair against her shoulders as her head tilted back. The long column of her throat, the pulse beating fast against her delicate skin. Firm, round breasts, dark nipples pulled tight with excitement.

He swallowed back a groan and shifted his hips, trying to adjust the length of his hard cock against the binding of the protective cup. Fuck. What the hell was his problem? He knew better. God help him if any of the guys even so much as suspected what he was thinking right now.

But nine days had gone by. Nine long days. He'd seen Savannah nearly every single one of those days—

But they hadn't had so much as five minutes alone.

Which meant he was pathetic. He'd gone longer than nine days before. A hell of a lot longer.

But that was before Savannah.

He slid to a stop in the corner, bent over at the waist, and stretched his back. Two laps around the ice and he was covered in sweat, the muscles of his legs already burning.

It wasn't just nine days without alone time with Savannah that had taken its toll on his body. Nine days off the ice, nine days without working out at all, had left him feeling shaky and weak.

Maybe that was a slight exaggeration, but hell, he

was definitely feeling it.

Which meant he just needed to push himself a little harder because he wasn't ready to call it quits just yet.

Aaron made one more lap around the ice then headed over to Coach Kroncke, who put him through a conditioning routine that left him drenched in sweat and sucking in gulps of air. A quick break then he was back on the ice, running through drills, getting his second wind.

Ignoring the good-natured teasing of his teammates. Focusing on the feel of the stick in his hands. The precision of weight balanced on the blades of his skates. The sharp bite of metal cutting into ice as he raced from one end to the other. Back and forth, dodging and weaving. Passing. Receiving. Shooting.

Ready to pass out when the whistle finally blew, signaling the end of practice.

Aaron skated over to Coach Torresi, met the other man's steady gaze and held his breath, waiting. The man looked him over, studying him with those piercing green eyes.

"How're you feeling?"

"Good."

"You sure about that?"

"Yeah. A little tired but still good."

The other man finally nodded, just a small up-and-down motion of his head. "You going to be ready for Saturday's game?"

"Yeah, I'll be ready."

Torresi nodded again. "I'm going to take you at your word, Malone. You've been around long enough to know better than to bullshit about something like that."

"I'm good. No bullshit."

"Alright. Go. Get out of here."

Aaron nodded then headed off the ice, hurrying back to the locker room to change and clean up. He was tossing the small duffel over his shoulder, ready to leave, when Harland stopped him.

"Hey, I meant to give you this when I stopped by the other day and forgot."

Aaron looked down at the rolled-up plastic bag in Harland's hand. He could see the bottom of the Bombers' logo emblazoned on the wrinkled surface, recognized it as one of the bags from the arena's concession stands. "What is it?"

"No idea. Courtney found it under one of the seats after the Bridgeport game and told me to give it to you."

Aaron took the bag and started unrolling it, thinking maybe it belonged to one of the girls. Another bag was inside the first one, this one carefully rolled up as well. He shoved the empty bag at Harland then unrolled the second and reached inside. His hands closed around a wad of material and he pulled it out, surprised to realize it was a jersey.

He shook it out, saw his name and number on the back, and grinned.

"I thought the girls already had your jersey."

"Yeah, they do." He held it up so Harland could see the size. "This isn't for them."

"You think it's Savannah's?"

Aaron's grin turned into a full-blown smile. "Must be."

Harland glanced at the jersey then looked at Aaron and burst into laughter. "Yeah, you've got it bad. No doubt about it."

CHAPTER TWENTY-FIVE

Savannah had just stepped out of the shower when she heard the knock on the door. Steady. Insistent. She grabbed a towel and quickly dried off, wrapped it around her hair, then grabbed another one to wrap around her body. A glance at the clock on the nightstand told her it was too early for Tessa to be here. Her friend wasn't due for another forty minutes. Of course, Tessa was always early so maybe it *was* her.

God, she hoped not. Savannah still had to pack. She was running behind, had lost all track of time as she put the finishing touches on the new presentation she was giving to her client tomorrow morning in Philly. Packing wouldn't take long—just a change of clothes and toiletries—but Tessa would still tease her about being distracted.

Savannah didn't need the teasing, not when she knew Tessa was right—she *had* been distracted.

Worrying about Aaron as he recovered, trying not to go overboard and smother him when all she wanted to do was never let him out of her sight. Helping around the house, listening as his mother shared stories of his childhood and early career. Helping the girls with their homework. Listening as Brooke shyly confessed to her crush on some boy she had met, the brother of some girl in her class.

Analyzing her feelings, trying to convince herself she wasn't in over her head when she already knew she was.

Just like she knew it wasn't Tessa at the door.

She hurried down the steps, tugging the towel tighter around her. Tessa wouldn't be knocking because she had a key. She'd just rap her knuckles against the door then walk in, like she always did. And the knocking was coming from the back door, not the front.

Savannah almost slipped on the bottom step, had to brace her hand against the wall to catch herself at the last minute. She readjusted the towel, trying to push away the anxiety pummeling her. If the knocking was coming from the back door, that meant it had to be either Aaron or one of the girls. Today had been Aaron's first day back at practice. Had something happened? Was he okay?

She slid the curtain across the patio door and unlocked it, stepping back as Aaron walked in.

"Is everything okay? Did something happen?" The words fell from her in a breathless rush.

Aaron opened his mouth then snapped it shut, frowning as his gaze traveled from the top of her towel-wrapped head down to her bare feet then back up again. "Why are you answering the door wearing nothing but a towel?"

"I thought it was Tessa. Then I thought something might have happened and I—" Savannah stepped back, finally noticing the flare of heat in Aaron's eyes. She looked away, her skin burning, and saw the bag in his hand. "What's that?"

"You left it at the game the other night." He pulled the jersey from the bag and held it up, his eyes smoldering as he moved toward her. "I was going to ask you to model it for me. Wanted to see how you looked wearing nothing but my name and number but I think I like the towel better."

He tossed the jersey to the side then quickly closed the distance between them. One arm snaked out and closed around her waist, pulling her toward him as he reached up with the other and eased the towel from her head. Savannah swallowed back a groan, heat pooling between her legs when she felt the hard length of his cock pressing against her.

He tilted his head, his mouth claiming hers in a hot kiss that robbed her of breath. He dragged his mouth from hers, kissed her neck, her shoulder. She dug her hands into his arms, to keep herself from collapsing, and swallowed back another groan.

"Tessa will be here soon. She's—" She gasped as Aaron nibbled her ear, sending a tidal wave of sensation crashing over her. His breath was warm against her skin, his voice a soft whisper of need.

"She's what?"

"She's, uh—" And God, she couldn't think, not when his mouth and tongue and hands caused flames to dance across her skin. "Um…train station. Taking me…meeting tomorrow."

"When?"

"Hm?"

"When will she be here?"

"An hour. No, less than that. I—I can't think when you're doing that."

Aaron chuckled, the sound throaty and hoarse and strained. He pulled back, need simmering in his eyes.

Not just need, something more, something that made her heart leap and soar.

"I think I can remember how to manage a quickie." The brown of his eyes deepened, pulling her in. "Or do you want me to stop?"

Savannah reached between them, palmed the hard length of his cock under the nylon of his track pants, and shook her head. "No."

Aaron hesitated, but only for a second. Then his mouth crashed against hers. Hungry, demanding. He yanked the towel away and cool air washed over her, replaced by the heat of his hands as he touched every inch of her. He broke the kiss, his breathing harsh and raspy. Instead of picking her up and carrying her upstairs as she expected, he reached for his shirt and pulled it over his head, tossed it to the side. Leaned down, shed shoes and socks and pants, his hungry gaze never leaving hers. Then he grabbed her again, flesh-to-flesh, his mouth devouring hers.

She moved against him, their feet tangling as he turned and dropped onto the sofa. He shifted her body so she was straddling him, his fingers digging into her hips as he rocked her slick heat against the rigid length of his cock.

He bent his head, pulled one tight nipple into his mouth, and drove into her.

Her head fell back, his name falling from her lips in a breathless scream as the climax swept her away. He held her through it, whispering her name, kissing her, still driving into her. Hard, deep. So deep. Then slower, until her senses gradually returned, until her breathing evened out.

He hooked his hands under her knees, pushed up with his powerful legs and turned, reversing their positions so he was on top of her, pressing her into the sofa cushions. He braced one knee on the sofa and thrust into her, faster, harder, driving her to the edge once more.

She grabbed his shoulders, nails biting into flesh, searching for an anchor against the desperate need battering her. Close, so close, ready to fly apart, to lose herself.

Her eyes fluttered open as he rocked into her, driving her deeper and deeper into the maelstrom. She looked up, her gaze meeting his. Tried to look away but couldn't.

"I love you, Savannah."

The words sent her flying, her body shattering into so many pieces, she was afraid she'd never find herself again. But she wasn't lost. Could never be lost as long as Aaron held her. Safe. Secure. Protected.

Loved.

She opened her mouth to say the words, heard only her sharp gasps and shallow screams. Aaron's mouth closed over hers, swallowing each little sigh and moan. Then his body tensed, his arms tightening around her as his own release crashed over him, filling her.

Consciousness slowly returned as her breathing slowed, as she became aware of her surroundings.

The hum of the refrigerator in the kitchen ten feet away.

The play of the afternoon sun on the carpet and the arm of the sofa near her head.

The tangle of her legs, wrapped tight around Aaron's waist.

The rise and fall of Aaron's chest as his body pressed against hers. Hard, strong. Solid.

The look in his eyes as he stared down at her, so open and honest, hiding nothing.

She reached up and cupped his cheek with one hand, felt the scratch of stubble against her palm. A smile curved her mouth. She pulled in a deep breath, needing to say the words. To give him the same honesty he had given her.

But the sound of keys jangling in a lock distracted her. She heard the door open, heard a quick rap of knuckles against wood.

Savannah stiffened, looked at Aaron in desperation as she heard the first footsteps in the front hallway.

"Hey, Van. Are you almost ready? I know I'm early—"

"Tessa, no! Don't—" She pushed against Aaron, frowning when she noticed his shoulders shaking in silent laughter. She pushed again, harder, but it was like trying to budge a concrete wall. "Tessa, wait. Just give me a—"

"Whoa. OhmyGod. Van! Really? Really!" Tessa's shriek filled the room. Savannah couldn't see her, she couldn't see anything past Aaron's broad shoulders, but she didn't need to. She could picture her friend's reaction perfectly, imagined her standing in the middle of the room, her eyes rounded in shock, her mouth hanging open.

"Tessa, go! Now!"

"Holy shit. Okay. I'll be outside. Just—Jesus."

"Tessa!"

"I'm going." She heard the sound of footsteps heading back to the door and breathed a sigh of relief. The relief was short-lived when she heard the footsteps return, heard Tessa's voice, dripping with feminine appreciation.

"Okay, I just need to say, for the record. Aaron, that is one amazingly fine ass."

Savannah waved her hand, blindly pointing her finger in the direction of the door. "Out!"

The door closed and she dropped her head back on the cushion, her face flaming. Aaron's head fell forward, his shoulders shaking as warm, rich laughter filled the room.

Savannah did the only thing she could think of: she reached behind him and smacked his amazingly fine ass.

CHAPTER TWENTY-SIX

Tessa swore under her breath as she struggled to step through the door with the plastic tub in her hands. She tripped, swore again, then finally stepped onto the patio. She dropped the tub then brushed the hair from her face and fixed Savannah with a dirty look.

"Tell me again why I'm doing this?"

"Because you owe me."

"I said I was sorry!"

"Doesn't matter. You still owe me."

"If you didn't want me catching an eyeful, you shouldn't have been doing the wild thing in the middle of the living room. Especially when you knew I was coming over."

"That's not the point."

"Oh, please. It's not like a saw anything."

Savannah braced one hand on her hip, her brows shooting up in disbelief. "You complimented him on his ass!"

A wide smile stretched Tessa's mouth. "Can you blame me? Good God, I'll be dreaming about that ass for months."

"Tessa!"

"Sorry. But seriously, what did you expect? It was

right there in front of me. How could I not look?"

"Again, you're missing the point." Savannah leaned down and grabbed a string of lights, frowning as she tried to untangle them. She gave up ten seconds later and dropped them back into the tub. "I was getting ready to tell him I loved him."

"There was nothing stopping you from telling him after I walked out."

"Nothing except the fact that you completely killed the mood."

"Mhmm. You sure it has nothing to do with you chickening out?"

"Positive."

"If you say so." Tessa sat down on the wicker loveseat with a small sigh and stared at Savannah. "So. You love him, huh?"

"Yeah. I think."

"You *think*? Or you *know*?"

Savannah stared at the tub of lights, frowning. Then she blew out a deep breath and sat across from Tessa. "I know."

"You sure about that?"

"Yes."

"Like, really sure? Not just lust, but love?"

"Yes."

"We're talking full-time commitment here. The settling down, getting married, and having babies kind of love."

"Yes. I think." Savannah stared down at her hands, frowning. Then she sighed again and looked at Tessa. "I don't think. I know."

"What about swearing off having a family? Has that changed? Because there's a big difference between starting one of your own and jumping into a ready-made one."

"I know that."

"And that doesn't scare you?"

"It terrifies me."

"But not enough to run and hide." It was a statement, not a question.

"No."

"Well, as long as I get to be maid of honor, okay."

"Tessa! You're getting a little ahead of yourself, aren't you? I haven't even told him how I feel yet, and here you are, planning the wedding."

"Yeah, so?"

"So…he might not even want to get married."

"But you said he told you he loved you."

"That doesn't mean he's making long-term plans."

"Van, trust me. From what I've seen of that man, if he said he loves you, he's making long-term plans."

"The only thing you've seen of him is his ass."

"And can I just say again what a fine ass it is?"

"Tessa! God, I can't believe you. Is that all you can think about?"

"Generally speaking, no, but since we're talking about him—"

"Okay, okay. Enough." Savannah leaned to the side and grabbed the tangled string of lights from the tub then tossed them at Tessa. "Here. Make yourself useful."

"Tell me again why we're doing this."

"Because you owe me."

"Yeah, I get that. But I still don't know *why*. It's not even December yet. You never decorate this early."

"Because it's nice out and I don't want to wait until it gets cold again."

Savannah grabbed another strand of lights, her

fingers mindlessly working at the tangles as she thought about Aaron. Tessa was right: she should have told him. It didn't matter if the mood had shifted. She should have cupped his face between her hands and told him she loved him.

Instead, she chickened out. Now two days had gone by, and she was worried that maybe he regretted saying the words in the first place.

No, Aaron wouldn't have told her if he didn't mean it. That was just her own doubt, her own fears, coming to the surface. So, she'd tell him tonight, after he got home from practice and the girls got home from school. They were having dinner tonight, just simple chicken on the grill since the weather had turned warm. After dinner, once the girls had finished their homework and gone to bed—that's when she'd tell him.

Or maybe she should just tell him as soon as he got home. Go over and wait on his porch and tell him—

"Hey, Van."

"Hm?"

"Did schools let out early today?"

Savannah looked up, noticed Tessa staring at Aaron's yard with a frown on her face. "No, why?"

"Because isn't that Aaron's oldest daughter stumbling across the patio?"

"What? Where?" Savannah jumped from the chair and moved to the corner of the house so she could see. Sure enough, Brooke was making her way toward the back door, walking with the deliberate care of someone who'd been drinking. A teenage boy was right behind her, his hand resting at the top of Brooke's ass.

Savannah's hand tightened around the string of

lights as she watched the pair disappear into the house. "What the hell?"

Tessa stood beside her. "Maybe it's not what we're thinking."

"She's been drinking!"

"You don't know that for sure." Savannah turned on Tessa, not bothering to hide her anger and disbelief. Tessa stepped back, her hands held out in front of her. "Okay, Momma Bear, calm down. So she's been drinking. That doesn't mean anything."

"I can't believe this. She's *thirteen*. What does she think she's doing? And bringing a boy to the house? If Aaron catches her—" She didn't want to think what Aaron would do. He'd act first and think later, and probably say something he'd regret. And if he caught that boy in the house…

Savannah dropped the lights and hurried across the yard, Tessa right beside her. She noticed the car parked along the curb between the two houses and quickened her steps. That meant the kid was at least sixteen. What the hell was a sixteen-year-old doing with a kid Brooke's age?

Forget about what Aaron might do. Savannah was going to kill the kid herself.

She reached the sliding glass door and tugged on it, only to find it locked.

Tessa looked at her, the same concern Savannah felt reflected on her face. "Now what? You know they'll just ignore it if we knock."

"We don't need to knock. I know where the key is." She moved over to the grill, bent down and felt underneath for the small magnetic box. She pried open the lid, her fingers closing around the key as she tossed the box to the ground. Five seconds later, she was easing the sliding door open, Tessa right behind her as they stepped inside.

Savannah paused, her head tilted to the side as she listened. The house was quiet except for the whispered voices coming from the living room.

"I—I feel kind of funny." Brooke's voice, confused, the words a little slurred. A sharp hiss of breath, a small moan, the rustle of fabric.

"Shh. It's okay. You'll like it. Feel how much I want you?" Another moan, almost guttural. Another rustle of fabric, followed by a sharp hiss.

"K-Kevin, stop. T-that hurts. I don't—"

Savannah charged into the room, her vision clouded by a red haze. She saw Brooke standing in the middle of the room, narrowed eyes filling with tears as she tried to move away. The boy had one hand under her sweater, the other wrapped around Brooke's, holding it in place against his jeans.

Brooke stumbled back, her eyes rounded in surprise as Savannah grabbed the kid by the shirt collar and jerked him back. She spun him around, her hand fisting in his shirt, and started shaking him.

"What the hell do you think you're doing? She's *thirteen*! You don't touch a thirteen-year-old girl. Do you understand me?" She shook him again, harder, her hand tightening in his shirt as he tried to pull away. His hands scrabbled against her wrists, her arms. Grabbing, pulling, his mouth opening and closing soundlessly as she pushed him toward the door. She wanted to hit him, use her knee to double him over, to incapacitate him so he'd never be able to touch another girl again.

"Van! Savannah, stop!" Hands pulled at her, holding her back when she would have knocked the kid's head against the wall. "Savannah, enough."

No, not enough. Not even close.

It was the deep sobs coming from behind her that finally made her stop. She released her hold on the kid's shirt, pushed him away from her. "I don't ever want to see you around her again. Is that clear?"

The boy's face paled. His head jerked in a quick nod and he turned around, scrambling for the door and slamming it behind him.

"Savannah. Jesus."

She ignored Tessa, pushing past her to reach Brooke. The young girl was leaning against the wall, tears streaking her red face. Savannah pulled her into a hug, tried to catch her breath, tried to calm the rage still clawing at her.

"Are you okay? Did he hurt you?"

"N-no." The word was muffled against Savannah's shoulder as Brooke held on, crying and sniffling and shaking. "I—I didn't mean to…I just thought he'd kiss me. I-I didn't think—"

"Shh. It's okay. You're okay. You didn't do anything wrong."

"But I—I invited him over—"

"Brooke, listen to me." Savannah pulled away, brushed Brooke's hair from her sweaty face. "You didn't do anything wrong. Inviting someone over doesn't mean you invite them to do anything else."

Brooke sniffled again, her shoulders heaving with each shaky breath. "But…I wanted him to kiss me."

Savannah took a deep breath, wincing at the odor of alcohol, and tried to calm her nerves. Every part of her was shaking, her body still tight with tension. With anger. With blood-chilling fear. What would have happened if she hadn't been home? If Tessa hadn't noticed Brooke sneaking into the house?

Her stomach twisted as images flashed through her mind, none of them good.

"Brooke, sweetheart, that doesn't matter. Okay? Wanting someone to kiss you doesn't give that person permission to touch you." And oh, God, how could she even begin to explain this to a thirteen-year-old? How could she make Brooke understand that none of this was her fault?

She gazed down at the girl, finally noticing the glazed eyes—not from tears, but from alcohol. She smoothed her hand over Brooke's hair and gentled her voice, not wanting the girl to think she was in trouble. "Brooke, how much have you had to drink?"

"I—" She looked away and for a second, Savannah thought she was going to deny it. But she didn't, although she wouldn't meet Savannah's gaze when she spoke. "I had two beers. And…and a shot of something. Kevin…he—he said it would relax me. But I think there was something wrong with them because my stomach doesn't feel good."

Brooke stumbled against Savannah, would have fallen if she hadn't already had one arm around the young girl's shoulders.

Indecision warred inside her as she tried to figure out what she should do. Put Brooke to bed and let her sleep it off? Yes, definitely. But where? If Aaron found her like this, before Savannah had a chance to explain…

She tightened her hold on Brooke and looked over at Tessa, saw that her friend was thinking the same thing. "Let's get her back to my house, let her sleep it off while I figure out what to tell Aaron." No, not *what*…while she figured out *how* to tell him. Because he needed to know. She couldn't—wouldn't—keep this from him.

"Are you sure that's the best thing to do, Van?"

"No, but I don't have a better idea. Do you?"

"What are you going to tell Aaron?"

Brooke lifted her head, her eyes widening in fear. She tried to push away from Savannah, stumbled and almost fell. "No, please. Don't tell Dad. You can't tell him. Please."

"Brooke, sweetheart, it's okay. I'm not—I won't tell him anything yet. Okay? But he needs to know—"

"No, please. Promise you won't tell Dad. You can't tell Dad. Please."

"Tell Dad what?"

Savannah jumped at the clipped voice, whirled around to see Aaron standing just inside the doorway. She hadn't heard him pull up, hadn't heard the door open. And oh God, how long had he been standing there? How much had he heard?

Probably too much, judging from the stormy look on his face.

He dropped the small duffel bag to the floor, reached behind him and very quietly, very deliberately, closed the door.

Brooke whimpered, fell against Savannah and buried her face against her shoulder, begging her in a loud whisper not to say anything. Aaron moved closer, brows lowered in an angry slash over cold eyes, the muscle in his clenched jaw twitching.

"What the hell is going on?" His voice was low and controlled, each word precisely spoken between clenched teeth. Savannah wondered how long it would be before the anger she felt rolling off him in crashing waves erupted. Minutes? Not minutes—seconds.

She glanced at Tessa, made a small motion with

her head, silently asking her to leave. Tessa frowned, started to shake her head. But she must have seen the urgent plea in Savannah's eyes because she slowly, reluctantly, moved back through the kitchen and outside.

Savannah turned back to Aaron, infusing her voice with as much calm as she could find. It wasn't enough. Not nearly enough. "Aaron, don't. Let me explain—"

"Explain?" He stepped closer, stopping a foot away. He looked down at Brooke, studying her glassy eyes and sweaty, tear-streaked face. Noticing how she weaved and stumbled even though Savannah was trying to hold her upright.

Then he turned to Savannah, his eyes so cold, so flat, so...so *empty*, that she took a step back in surprise. "Aaron—"

"She's drunk."

"It's not—" Savannah stopped, the rest of the words stuck in her throat. *It's not what you think.* That's what she had been ready to say.

Except it was exactly what he thought. Only worse, so much worse.

"She's. Drunk." The volume of his voice rose, not a shout, but hovering on the verge. And then the explosion she'd been fearing finally erupted. Anger colored his face a deep red, flashing in eyes that she no longer recognized. He stepped back, ran an angry hand through his hair, stepped closer and stopped. "Are you going to explain why the *fuck* my daughter is drunk?"

"Aaron—"

"No!" He turned to Brooke, flung his arm to the side, pointing to the stairs. "Upstairs. Now!"

"Daddy—"

"*Now!*"

Brooke pulled away from Savannah, stumbled and nearly fell before hurrying to the stairs. She braced a hand against the wall, almost fell again.

"Aaron, I don't think that's a good idea. She needs—"

"Don't tell me what she needs! You're not her mother. You don't know anything about being a parent."

The words hit her with the force of a physical blow. Savannah jerked back, her shoulder hitting the kitchen door frame. Aaron was angry, furious. She knew that. She even understood it. But the words…oh, God, they hurt.

They hurt more than she could have ever imagined.

She stood there, her gaze locked with his, his anger washing over her. It was a living thing, burning her, drowning her. "Aaron—"

"No." He shook his head, stepped away from her. "Don't say anything. Just…get out."

Savannah stared at him, shock rooting her in place. It wasn't the words, not entirely. It was the expression on his face. In his eyes. Like he'd found her guilty of a crime she didn't even know she'd been accused of.

Like he was already turning his back on her.

She stepped back, collided with the doorframe, stepped to the side and kept walking, her eyes never leaving his. She closed her mouth against the words she wanted to say, forced herself to keep moving backward.

Moving away from him.

She felt the sliding door behind her, reached for

the handle with shaking hands, then turned and walked out.

    And kept walking.

CHAPTER TWENTY-SEVEN

Aaron sat at the table, his eyes burning from strain as he tried to concentrate on the small print of the classifieds spread out before him. Seeing, but not reading. He couldn't focus, couldn't make sense of the blurred words.

The house was quiet. *Too* quiet. The kind of quiet that clung to a room where death had occurred, dark and oppressive, suffocating.

The kind of quiet that made a man think too much, think too hard.

He shoved the paper away then ran his hands over his face, over and over, scrubbing the skin with his palms. Trying to scrub away every single doubt and fear. Every single regret.

But there were too many. A lifetime of regrets.

The crashing of a pan against the stove broke the deathly silence. Aaron didn't jump in surprise, didn't bother to turn his head in the direction of the noises that followed.

The refrigerator door opening then banging shut.

A pot slamming against the counter.

Water running, followed by the hollow clank of the plumbing when it was abruptly—forcefully—

turned off.

His mother's voice, clipped and impatient. "You owe that woman an apology."

And fuck, there it was. Again. How many times over the last few days had she said those exact same words? A dozen? A hundred? More?

He didn't know, had lost track. And he answered her now the same way he had answered her every other time: with silence.

He pushed away from the table, headed to the refrigerator and yanked the door open. His hand reached in, automatically going to the shelf where he always kept a few beers.

Only the beer was gone, along with every other ounce of alcohol in the house. The contents poured down the drain, the empty bottles tossed into the trash.

Because Brooke had been drunk. Falling down drunk, in the middle of the afternoon, while he'd been at practice.

When she should have been at school.

He slammed the refrigerator door closed then leaned his forehead against it, welcoming the cool smoothness of stainless steel against his skin. What the hell was he going to do? He had thought things were getting better with Brooke, that she was finally adjusting to her new life here.

That he was finally figuring out how to be a father.

It had been nothing more than an illusion, a false calm that only emphasized his failure.

"Did you hear me?"

Aaron sighed, turned and leaned against the refrigerator, crossed his arms in front of him. "Yeah, Mom. I heard you."

"Then what are you going to do about it?"

"The same thing I did the last twenty times you said it: nothing."

Silence, followed by the hollow ring of another pot being slammed against the stovetop. "You are the most stubborn, infuriating, maddening…*man*…I have ever known."

Aaron winced at the way she said *man*, like it was the worst kind of crime there was. He glanced at his mother, ready to apologize, then promptly snapped his mouth closed. She stood next to him, her petite frame stiff and tense, her brown eyes shining with anger.

"You need to make things right, Aaron."

"I'm trying."

"Really? How? By moping? By demanding everyone walk on eggshells, afraid to so much as sneeze?"

"I told you, I'm looking for a nanny—"

His mother snorted, the sound filled with the weight of her disdain. "The girls don't need a nanny. They need *you*."

"Yeah, except I haven't done a very good job, have I?"

"There's nothing wrong with what you've been doing. Are you perfect? No. But I don't know of any parent who is."

"Brooke was drunk, Mom. In the middle of the day. When she was supposed to be in school. I obviously screwed up somewhere for that to happen."

"I guess you're forgetting the first time you got drunk. If I remember correctly, you were about her age. You skipped school and—"

"That's not the same thing."

"Isn't it?" She looked away, reached over and turned the burner on low, then looked back. "Don't be a hypocrite, son. I raised you better than that. You should just be glad Savannah was here."

It wasn't the first time his mother had said that, and every time she did, he couldn't help feeling like he was missing something. "I don't even know what she was doing here."

"Maybe you should ask her."

"I'm asking you. You obviously know something I don't."

"It's not my place to say."

What the hell did that even mean? He started to ask her, changed his mind at the last minute. She wouldn't tell him, no matter how many times he asked.

He wasn't even sure if he wanted to know.

"You need to apologize to her, Aaron. Make things right."

"Make things right?"

"Yes. Before things go too far and it's too late."

He wanted to tell her it was already too late—he had seen the expression on Savannah's face. The surprise. The hurt his words had caused. He closed his eyes against the memory and kept his mouth shut, knowing there was nothing he could say.

Another pot slammed against the stovetop, harder this time. He jumped, opened his eyes and took a step back at the disappointment in his mother's eyes.

"Just once, I would like to see you fight for something besides hockey. To see you go after something with the same passion you show for the game instead of sitting on the bench, playing it safe."

He blinked, his mind struggling to make sense of the words. "What are you talking about?"

"You heard me."

"I heard you, but I have no idea what you mean."

"I know you don't. That's what worries me."

He pushed away from the refrigerator, started to move back to the table. "Mom, I don't have time—"

"How long were you married to Amy?"

He stumbled to a halt, swirled around as dread washed over him. This was a taboo subject, his mother knew that. "I'm not talking about this now."

"Did you ever stop to think that might be your problem?"

"Mom—"

"Answer the question, Aaron. How long?"

"You know the answer to that."

"Tell me."

"Twelve years."

"And how long were you married before you first talked about getting a divorce?"

"Mom—"

"A year. Not even a year. But you never did, did you?"

"Because Brooke came along. You know that."

"What about later? When Brooke was older?"

"There was Isabelle—"

"And after that? When you were both so miserable? What about then?"

"It wasn't that simple—"

"No. Divorce never is, especially when children are involved. But that wasn't the reason why, was it?"

Aaron looked away, no longer able to meet his mother's knowing gaze. "I don't know what you're talking about."

"You know exactly what I'm talking about. It was easier for you to just stay. To be miserable. To settle. To play it safe and just accept the way things were instead of fighting for an ounce of happiness. You did the same thing when Amy moved the kids away."

Aaron swallowed the burst of anger. "That's not true. Don't even say that."

"It is true, Aaron. You just let her move them across the country—"

"Because that's what was best! I couldn't be home with them, you know that. What kind of life would they have had, with me on the road all the time? Being bounced from team to team, city to city? Being left with a babysitter or a nanny. I couldn't have—"

"Then how is now any different?"

"It is."

"Tell me how. You're still playing hockey. Still on the road. Still playing nights and weekends. What's different now, when you could have just left them with Amy's parents?"

Aaron ran a shaking hand over his face, swallowed against the thickness filling his throat. "Mom, don't. I can't—"

"Tell me, Aaron. Why is now any different?"

He slammed a hand against the counter. "Because they're my daughters, dammit! Because I love them and they belong with me!"

A slow smile crossed his mother's face. She moved toward him and placed her hand on his arm, squeezing. "Exactly. They're *your* daughters. And because you decided to fight for them instead of just sitting back and letting life unfold around you."

"Yeah, for all the good it's doing. I'm making a mess of things, Mom. I don't know what I'm doing."

"You're not making a mess, Aaron. The girls love you, and you love them. Will you make mistakes? Of course you will. It's part of being a parent. But you're not making a mess."

Aaron glanced down at his mother's hand, placed his own over it and squeezed. "Thanks. I think I needed to hear that—"

"Don't thank me yet. I'm not done."

"But—"

"You're not making a mess of things with the girls. But with Savannah?" His mother stepped back and shook her head. "That's a different story."

"Mom—"

"No. Don't settle, Aaron. Don't sit back and let life happen like you've done in the past. Because this time? Life isn't going to wait for you to catch up—it's going to run right over you and leave you behind."

"Mom, it's not—"

"Grammy's right, Dad."

He spun around, surprised to see Brooke standing in the doorway, Isabelle standing behind her. Both of them looked miserable, uncertain, like they weren't sure they should be there.

But it was Brooke who looked like she wanted to cry. She took a tentative step closer, stopped and twisted her hands in front of her. She glanced at his mother, some kind of silent message passing between them.

His mother turned off the stove and walked out of the kitchen, stopping to give Brooke a quick hug before taking Isabelle's hand. "Come on, Isabelle. You can show me that new game you were talking about."

Aaron almost called out, almost begged his mother to stay. Something was going on, something he was positive he didn't want to know.

Especially when Brooke took another step into the kitchen and looked at him, tears in her eyes.

"Daddy, I need to tell you something."

CHAPTER TWENTY-EIGHT

Daddy, I need to tell you something.

The words slammed into him, robbing him of breath. He reached out, closed his hand around the back of the chair, forced air into his lungs. He tried to smile but he couldn't, he was paralyzed with fear.

Brooke kept standing there, looking up at him with tear-filled eyes, her hands twisting together. Around and around, her fingers almost white.

He didn't want to hear whatever she was going to say, he knew that. Knew it with a bone-chilling certainty that frightened him.

He pulled the chair out, dropped into it, then pointed to the chair next to him. Trying to sound calm and encouraging, even as his voice shook with fear. With doubt. "Um, okay. What, uh, what did you want to tell me?"

Brooke hesitated, finally moved closer. But she didn't sit down, didn't even look at the chair. Her gaze was focused on her hands, still twisting. Always twisting.

"Brookie? What is it?"

"Dad, I—" She looked up at him, quickly looked away. "Please don't be mad at Miss Savannah. It's—it's not her fault."

He released the breath he'd been holding, relief flowing over him. Is that what Brooke had been worried about? Did she think he blamed Savannah for what happened? That he thought Savannah had given her the alcohol? "I know it's not her fault, Brooke."

"Then why are you mad at her?"

"I'm not mad at her, Brookie. It's just—" Christ how was he supposed to explain that? To his *daughter*? He couldn't. Hell, he didn't even understand it himself. Even if he did, he wouldn't discuss it with a young girl.

"It's my fault, isn't it?"

"What? No. No, it's not your fault, Brooke. This has nothing to do—"

"If I hadn't brought Kevin home, if he hadn't tried—" Her voice broke, the words ending in a strangled sob. Aaron froze, terror gripping him, choking him. He couldn't breathe, couldn't see past the dots flashing behind his eyes.

He closed his eyes, squeezed them shut, forced himself to inhale. Slow, deep. To breathe. Just breathe. But Christ, he wasn't sure if he could, wasn't sure if he'd ever be able to breathe again, not when he opened his eyes and saw Brooke watching him, fat tears streaming from blue-green eyes that suddenly looked too old.

Whatever she was going to tell him, whatever that look in her eyes meant—he didn't want to know. Didn't want to hear. He felt like he was standing in front of a closed door, his hand turning the knob against his will. Because if he opened that door, if he looked at what was inside—his world would change and there would be no going back.

He ran his hand along Brooke's arm, surprised at

the chill pebbling her skin. He closed his hand over hers, felt her fingers trembling. Small, so small. He wanted to do nothing more than shelter her. Protect her. Keep her safe from whatever was behind that door.

But he couldn't because the door had already been opened, and there was no going back.

"Brookie, what happened? Who's Kevin?"

"He—he's Katie's brother. He's sixteen and goes to the high school."

Aaron forced himself to take another deep breath, struggled to find a calm that no longer existed. "And?"

"I—I had a crush on him. And he—he picked me up at the school and..." The words ended in another choked sob. The sound ripped through him, shredding his soul. He pulled Brooke into his arms, held her tight, squeezed his eyes closed.

"Shh. It's okay, Brooke. It's okay."

"I just wanted him to like me Dad but...but—"

"Brooke, it's okay." But fuck, it wasn't okay, it would never be okay again. And he didn't want to hear this, any of it. All he wanted was to go back in time, to protect Brooke, lock her in a bubble.

Then go find the little fucker and rip him apart with his bare hands.

Brooke was still talking, the words mixed with deep sobs. "Miss Savannah came in and she...she made him stop and...she was so mad and...I thought she was going to kill him and...I'm sorry, Daddy. I'm sorry."

"Shh. It's okay, Brooke. It's not your fault."

"That's what Miss Savannah said but—"

"And she was right. It's not your fault." He tightened his arms around her, reached up and pressed the heel of one hand against his eyes, swallowed against the thickness in his throat. Then he leaned back, searching his daughter's face through the fear that gripped him.

"Did—did he hurt you, Brookie?" He forced the strangled words through his raw throat, felt the bile rise in his gut at the need to ask, at the thought of someone—anyone—touching his daughter. Hurting her.

Brooke brushed her face against her shoulder, wiping away some of the tears, and shook her head. "N-no. Nothing happened. Miss Savannah made him leave."

Aaron took another deep breath, felt himself nodding. "And…and you're okay?"

Brooke nodded then quickly shook her head. "Please don't be mad, Dad. I didn't mean—"

"I'm not mad. Not at you." He ran his hand along her arm, tried to smile, to reassure her. No, he wasn't mad—he was furious. Beyond furious. But not at Brooke. Never at Brooke.

"But you're mad at Miss Savannah."

"No, Brookie, I'm not."

"You are. And it's all my fault. If I hadn't—"

"Brooke, listen to me. It's not your fault. None of this is."

"But it is. Because you're not talking to her anymore and it's because of what I did."

Aaron placed his hands on her shoulders, caught her gaze with his. "Brooke, listen to me. None of this is your fault. And it has nothing to do with what happened. I'm the one who messed things up with Savannah. Not you. Okay?"

Brooke stared at him for a long minute, tears

welling in her eyes again. Then she nodded and threw her arms around his neck, her shoulders shaking as she cried. Her shoulders shook with the force of her sobs, her tears scalding his neck. Aaron folded his arms around her, holding her, whispering words of reassurance as he squeezed his eyes closed against his own tears.

Knowing he had failed his daughter.

He hadn't been there for Brooke. Her own father, and he hadn't been there.

But Savannah had.

The same woman he accused of not knowing what his daughter needed. Accused of not knowing anything about being a parent.

Right before he told her to get out.

The harsh truth of how wrong he had been stayed with him the rest of the evening, throughout dinner, when his mother kept sending him knowing glances. After dinner, when the girls helped him clean up then sat down to finish their homework. Later, when they sat curled against him on the sofa as they watched an animated movie that made the girls laugh and giggle.

Even now, as he stood at the back door, staring out at the night as the girls finally slept.

He spun on his heel, walked out to the living room and grabbed the sweat jacket hanging over the back of the chair. His mother looked up from the book she was reading, and damn if he didn't see her mouth quiver in a knowing smile.

"Going somewhere?"

"Yeah. I won't be long."

She made a little humming sound, the corner of her mouth twitching again. "Don't worry about hurrying back. I'll be here."

His only response was a small grunt as he pulled the door closed behind him. The night had turned cold, the beginning of a front moving through, promising a return of winter weather. He shrugged into the jacket and turned the corner, heading toward the back of Savannah's house. Light splashed across her front lawn and he backtracked, moving around the front of the house as the door opened. She stepped onto the porch, her head down as she dug through her purse and pulled the door closed behind her.

"Hey."

Savannah jumped, then placed a hand against her chest as she narrowed her eyes at him. He almost laughed, choked it back when he realized she wasn't smiling.

When he realized she was dressed to go out.

He jammed his hands into the jacket pockets and moved across the yard, the frost-covered grass crunching beneath his feet. Savannah walked down the three steps, stopped on the sidewalk and simply stared at him.

"You, um, you look nice."

She glanced down at herself, looked back up, her face showing no hint of emotion, not even a brief smile. "Thank you."

They stood there, both watching the other, for a long minute. Savannah shifted, looked toward her car, turned back to him. "Did you need something? Because I was just leaving…"

You. I need you.

He swallowed the words back, shook his head. Shrugged and glanced over his shoulder then looked back at her. "Brooke told me what happened. About the other day, I mean."

"Did she?" He heard the doubt in her voice, knew she was wondering if Brooke had told him everything.

"Yeah. About the boy. About you coming over."

"Good. I'm glad." She moved toward the car, stopped and frowned. "You know it's not her fault, right?"

"Yeah, I know that." Was his voice just a little defensive? Maybe—but no more than hers had been.

"Good."

"I just...I wanted to say thank you. For, um, for being there. For helping her."

"Yes. Of course. No problem."

He took a step toward her, stopped, wanting to say the rest. *For being a better parent than I was.* But the words wouldn't come, stuck in his throat as she walked toward her car, her heels clicking against the concrete.

"Savannah?"

She paused, her hand wrapped around the edge of the open door, her face hidden by the shadows.

"I'm sorry."

She was silent for a long moment. Too long. Then she nodded, her voice nothing more than a whisper when she spoke.

"Me too."

Then she was behind the wheel, the engine whirring as she started the car and backed out of the driveway.

Aaron just stood there, numb to the cold, numb to everything as he watched the taillights of her car disappear around the corner.

CHAPTER TWENTY-NINE

Savannah slammed the lid closed on the laptop and pushed it to the side. She couldn't focus, couldn't even think straight enough to match the graphics with the right bullet points.

She couldn't think of anything except the look that had been on Aaron's face last night when he stood in her yard.

Lost. Lonely.

The memory tugged at her, making her think stupid thoughts. She pushed them away, forced herself to remember the expression that had been in his eyes the other day, when he had hurled that hurtful comment at her and told her to leave.

No, not leave. *Get out.*

Was there a difference? Maybe. Or maybe she was just splitting hairs. It didn't matter, because it hadn't been the words as much as it had been the expression in his eyes.

Cold. Flat.

And beneath that, the glimpse of betrayal. That's what hurt the most, that he could think...

She didn't know what he thought, had no idea what had been going through his mind. He had been upset, rightfully so. To come home and see Brooke—

No. No, no, no. She was *not* going to make excuses for him. It didn't matter how angry or upset he'd been, it wasn't fair to take it out on her. To assume the worst and act like she had been at fault.

She pushed the hair out of her face and uncrossed her legs, tugging the hem of her flannel pajama bottoms up as she slid off the sofa. It wasn't even seven o'clock on a Friday night, and she was already in her pajamas. How sad was that?

Sad. Beyond sad.

She grabbed her empty mug and moved to the kitchen, staring at the stove as she tried to decide if she wanted another cup of tea. Instead of tea, she should call Tessa. Tell her she changed her mind and wanted to go out instead. They could meet, have a few drinks, maybe hit a few nightclubs—

Savannah groaned. No, she didn't want to do that. Just the thought of getting dressed up, of being around people, gave her a headache. She didn't want to stand around with a fake smile on her face, listening to strangers she had no interest in talking to. Tessa had talked her into going out last night, and that had been bad enough.

She couldn't make herself go through that again.

So tea it would be.

She reached for the kettle, her hand pausing mid-air. Forget the tea. Wine would be better. There was a fresh bottle of Moscato in the refrigerator, barely touched. No sense in letting it go to waste. She'd have a glass of wine and curl up on the sofa with a book. A mystery, maybe. Or even a nice, gory horror.

She moved back to the living room, wine glass in one hand and a book in the other. She moved the laptop to the coffee table and settled into the corner of the sofa, ready to lose herself in the pages of the book.

Except she couldn't focus on the words in front of her any better than she had been able to focus on her presentation.

Dammit. What was wrong with her?

She tossed the book down and reached for the remote, ready to click the television on when a loud knock on the back door made her jump. Savannah froze, her heart lodged in her throat. Nobody knocked on her back door.

Nobody except Aaron.

Or the girls.

It must be the girls. Aaron had a game tonight. Didn't he? She frowned, trying to remember, but her mind went blank. He had games every weekend, sometimes here, sometimes away. Some weeknights, some Fridays. Was tonight one of those Fridays?

She didn't know, couldn't remember.

The knock came again, louder this time. More insistent. Then she heard someone calling her name.

Not Aaron.

Brooke.

She moved to the door, pushed the curtain aside, surprised to see Brooke and Isabelle standing on the patio, motioning to her with urgent waves. She unlocked the door, pulled it open.

"What—"

Isabelle grabbed her hand, pulling her outside so fast that she stumbled. "Miss Savannah, hurry. Please."

Panic pushed against her. Had something happened to Carol? If Aaron was playing tonight, Carol would be watching the girls.

She pulled the door closed, barely registering the

cold ground against her bare feet as the younger girl tugged her across the patio. "What is it? What happened? Is it your Grammy?"

"No, it's Dad. You have to hurry."

Savannah nearly stumbled, caught herself as she tried to look over her shoulder at Brooke. Icy fear raced through her. "Aaron? What's wrong? What happened?"

"I don't know. He was in the basement, working out and...just hurry, please."

No, it couldn't be. Nothing could have happened to Aaron. He'd been cleared to go back to playing, he was fine.

But what if he wasn't? What if the doctors and trainers and everyone else had been wrong? She kept trying to turn, to ask Brooke for details, but the older girl was pushing her from behind as Isabelle tugged, leading her across the yard and into the house.

"You have to hurry, Miss Savannah."

Her bare feet slid on the tile floor as she skidded to a stop, her heart pounding in her chest. "Where is he?"

"He's in the basement. Hurry." Isabelle tugged again, pulling her toward the open door just off the large kitchen. Music drifted up the stairs, the steady thump of rock-and-roll. She stepped onto the small landing, her hand on the railing, one foot poised mid-air to descend the stairs. There was another sound, barely audible over the music—the steady clank of metal against metal, like someone was lifting weights. Savannah hesitated and looked back at the girls, wondered why they no longer seemed as panicked, as determined.

No, they were still determined—but not because

something was wrong.

She reached for the door just as it slammed closed in her face. A second later, she heard the sound of a lock clicking into place.

Followed by the sound of two girls giggling.

She was going to throttle them. Both of them.

Savannah twisted the knob, but it didn't move. She pressed her ear against the door, banging it with the flat of her hand. "Brooke! Isabelle! Open this door right now!"

"No. Not until you two make up."

"Brooke, this isn't funny. Open the door."

"What is going on up there?"

Savannah whirled around, her mouth drying as Aaron walked out of the weight room, blotting his face with a towel. The tank shirt he wore was damp with sweat, the thin material clinging to his chest, his abs. The muscles of his bare arms stretched and flexed with each swipe of the towel. He stopped at the bottom of the stairs, his face going carefully blank as he looked up at her.

He blinked, blinked again. Then he frowned, his brows pulling low over his eyes. "Savannah? What are you doing here?"

She glanced at the door, heard the giggling from the other side, then met his frown with her own. "The girls think they're being funny."

"Being funny?"

"They came over to get me, told me something happened to you. Then they, uh, they locked the door."

Something flashed across Aaron's face. Annoyance? Surprise? Then he started up the stairs, his steps heavy. He reached past her, his arm brushing against hers, and tried turning the knob.

"I told you: they locked it."

He gave her a funny look then turned away and banged his fist against the door. "Brooke. Isabelle. Open the door."

"No."

His eyes narrowed for a brief second then he banged the door again, a little harder this time. "I don't know what you two think you're up to, but it's not funny. Open the door. Now."

"Not until you stop being stupid." Brooke's voice, stubborn and determined. "Both of you."

"Brooke, I swear, if I have to break this door down, you'll be punished for a year."

"I wouldn't do that, dear."

Savannah's eyes widened in surprise, but not as much as Aaron's. He exchanged a quick glance with her then looked away, the muscle in his jaw twitching. "Mother. What do you think you're doing?"

"The girls and I are going out for ice cream. Then I think we might go to the Galleria and do a little shopping."

"Mom, this isn't funny." He wiggled the knob again. "Open the door."

"Not just yet. Not until you two work things out."

"I'll just break the door down—"

"I wouldn't do that if I were you." There was the sound of something sliding across the floor, then the door shook a little as something was wedged against it. "I put a chair under the doorknob."

"That's not going to stop me—"

"Do you remember that trophy you won all those years ago? The nice crystal one?"

Even in the dim light, Savannah could see the color drain from Aaron's face. The muscles of his throat worked as he swallowed. "Mom—"

"It's sitting on the chair. Just thought you should know that. You know, in case you get any ideas about breaking the door down."

"Mom—"

"We'll be back later."

Savannah leaned closer to the door, listening to the sound of retreating footsteps and fading laughter. She straightened, her shoulder brushing against Aaron's chest, then took a step back. At least, she tried to—there wasn't much room to move.

"What trophy is she talking about?"

Aaron shook his head, still frowning at the door. "Nothing. It's not important."

"Do you think she was serious?"

He kept frowning at the door, and Savannah got the impression he was trying to figure out the answer to that. A few seconds went by before he muttered something under his breath and headed down the stairs. "Knowing my mother, yeah."

Savannah stared at his retreating back then turned back to the door. Then she sighed and sat down on the top step, wrapped her arms around her legs, and dropped her head against her knees.

Wondering how long she'd have to wait until someone let them out.

CHAPTER THIRTY

Aaron reached the bottom of the steps and ripped the towel from his neck. Of all the stupid, asinine, well-meaning stunts...he didn't know whether to laugh or bang his head against the wall.

Both.

Neither.

He stared at the empty bar, wishing he hadn't been so hasty in dumping everything, then went behind it and pulled a bottle of water from the small refrigerator. He uncapped it and took a long swallow, then looked back at the steps. Savannah was still sitting at the top, hugging her knees.

"You might as well come down and make yourself comfortable. We're going to be here a while."

His jaw clenched at the sound of her sigh drifting down the stairs. Shit. Was being stuck down here with him that bad?

Yeah, probably. Especially after the way he had messed things up.

She reached the bottom step and jammed her hands into the front pocket of her sweatshirt. He stared at the Bombers' logo on the front, told himself not to read into it. It was just a stupid damn sweatshirt. It didn't mean anything. She was probably wearing it because it was big and warm, the kind of shirt you lounged around in. Just like those flannel bottoms she had on—

He did a double-take then slammed the bottle down. "Where are your shoes?"

"My what?" She glanced down at her bare feet then looked up with a shrug, like it was no big deal that she was running around in bare feet when it was twenty degrees outside. "Probably next to my sofa."

"And why are they there instead of on your feet?"

"Because the girls dragged me out of the house before I could put them on, that's why."

"Why would you do something so stupid? Don't you know how cold it is outside?"

"Yeah, I do know. And it's not like I had any choice in the matter."

"You couldn't have told them to wait?"

"No, I couldn't. Not when they were freaking out because something happened to you."

"But nothing happened to me."

"Yeah, I can see that now. Do you think I would have rushed over here if I had known that?"

Aaron lifted the bottle to his mouth, hiding the grin that wanted to curl his mouth. She looked pissed. She'd probably be more pissed if she caught him smiling. "So, uh, you were worried about me?"

She shot him a dirty look. "Don't read into it. I would have done the same thing for anyone."

He hesitated, lowered the bottle "Like Brooke."

She looked away, her teeth pulling on her lower lip. "Yeah, like Brooke." Her shoulders moved up and down with a small sigh. She glanced at him over her shoulder, then leaned against the arm of the leather sofa. "Is she okay?"

"Yeah, she is." And she was, the incident mostly forgotten. Maybe she simply didn't realize the enormity of what had happened, of what could have happened. Maybe she was still too young, still too innocent. Maybe she really didn't know how quickly things could have changed.

Or maybe she was just dealing with it a hell of a lot better than he was, because he couldn't say the same for himself.

"How about you? Are you okay?"

Could Savannah read his mind? Maybe. Or maybe it was just a natural question to ask, and he shouldn't read anything into it.

He capped the bottle then walked around to the front of the bar and leaned against one of the stools. "Honestly? No. Every time I think—I want to kill him. And I'm not just saying that. I mean it. I've never felt like that before."

"Aaron…" She understood. He could hear it in her voice, in the way she said his name. She straightened, like she was going to move toward him, then she stopped and leaned against the sofa again. "I know how you feel. I may have, um, may have lost control a little."

"I heard."

Her head snapped around, surprise lighting her hazel eyes. "From Brooke? I didn't realize she had been paying attention."

"She was."

Savannah nodded then looked away, her hands still shoved into the front pocket of her sweatshirt, her gaze focused on her bare feet. God, he wanted nothing more than to pull her into his arms. To apologize. To beg her forgiveness and ask what he could do to make it up to her.

So why didn't he? Why was he sitting over here, not doing a damn thing?

Because his mother had been right. It was easier to just settle. To play it safe instead of taking risks. That's what he did. That's what he had done his entire life, in everything except hockey.

He didn't want to be that way anymore, didn't want to sit back as life passed him by. Didn't want to let this woman walk away, not after finally finding her.

"Savannah, what I said the other day..." He hesitated, cleared his throat and dropped his gaze to the floor. "I was out of line."

"Yeah, you were." She blew out a quick breath, the sound a little sharp. "But you were upset so...I get it."

"It doesn't matter how upset I was. It was wrong, and I'm sorry."

"I know. You told me that last night."

Yeah, he had. And she had simply said *Me, too* and drove away.

If she had the chance, would she do the same thing now? If she wasn't locked down here with him, would she simply climb the stairs and walk away?

He pushed off the stool, closed the distance between them in three long strides. Her head tilted back, surprise flashing in her eyes when he stopped in front of her.

"Savannah, I'm not perfect. Far from it. I've made mistakes. So many mistakes. Too damn many. But I'm trying. I'm learning." He reached out, ran a hand along her arm, across her throat, finally cupping her cheek. Her body stiffened—in surprise, maybe, or maybe something else—but she didn't pull away.

"I meant what I said, the day you went to Philly. I love you. Those weren't just words uttered in the heat of passion. And I hope to hell they mean something to you, even if it's nothing more than that you won't give up on whatever we might have going and walk away."

"Aaron—"

He shook his head, silencing her. Then he leaned forward, pressed a kiss against her forehead, and reached into the pocket of his gym shorts. She glanced down at the phone in his hand, frowning like she wasn't sure what it was.

"What's that?"

"It's my phone."

"You've had it with you this entire time?"

"Well, yeah—"

"And you're giving it to me *now*?"

"Yeah."

She looked up at him, her clear hazel eyes unreadable. "Why?"

"Why? I thought—I know you don't want to be stuck down here with me. I thought maybe you'd want to call Tessa to come let you out or something."

"You're giving me the phone *now*?" She pushed away from the sofa so fast that she knocked into him. He took one step back, then another as she moved toward him. "You're giving me the phone *now*? After everything you just said?"

"I'm not—I don't—" What the hell? Had he done something wrong? He glanced around, wondering what he was missing, took another step back as Savannah moved even closer, then another, not stopping until he collided with one of the stools.

"Do you want me to leave?"

Aaron hesitated, almost afraid to answer. He

couldn't read the expression on Savannah's face, didn't understand why she was looking at him the way she was. He finally shook his head. "No. I don't."

She dropped her head to his chest and for a horrifying second, he thought she was crying. No, it wasn't that, because she kept dropping her head against his chest, over and over.

Not dropping…*banging*. And she was muttering under her breath, something that sounded like—

"Stupid. Stupid, stupid, stupid." She finally stopped banging her head against his chest and looked up at him. Her body was wedged against his, braced between his legs as he leaned against the stool. It took every ounce of willpower not to wrap his arms around her, not to touch her.

And then, God, he didn't need to touch her because she was cupping his face in her hands, watching him with those clear hazel eyes. "Aaron, you don't tell someone you love them and then expect them to walk away."

"But—I didn't want…I wasn't sure—"

"Aaron?"

"Yeah?"

"I love you. Now shut up and kiss me."

He blinked, wondering if he was hearing things, wondering if he was hallucinating. No, he wasn't. Savannah was looking up at him, those beautiful hazel eyes filled with love.

She loved him.

He captured her mouth with his in a searing kiss, reveling in her taste. Her touch.

Her love.

Upstairs, Carol Malone pressed her ear to the door, listening as the voices faded into soft whispers before disappearing altogether. She smiled and slid the chair away from the door then quietly turned the lock.

Two young girls looked at her, their faces both excited and anxious.

"Did it work?"

"It most certainly did."

Brooke nudged Isabelle in the side. "Told you it would."

Carol placed her hands on their shoulders and led them away from the door. "Sh. Both of you. Get your coats on, and we'll go get that ice cream now."

"What about Daddy and Miss Savannah?"

"I don't think we have to worry about them for a while." Carol smiled. No, she didn't think they'd have to worry about them at all.

EPILOGUE

Two Years Later

"Nervous?"

Aaron glanced over at his wife, wondering again at how easy she could read him. Although, to be fair, a complete stranger would be able to see how nervous he was right now.

He wasn't the only one who was nervous. Brooke and Isabelle sat across from them in the hallway. Brooke's legs were curled under her in a way that made Aaron's knee wince in pain just looking at her. She was doing her best to look calm, like she didn't have a worry in the world—it wouldn't be cool for a fifteen-year-old to act otherwise. But Aaron saw the way her foot kept wiggling, and the way she kept twisting her fingers together when she thought nobody was looking.

Isabelle was kneeling, bouncing up and down as she stared at the timer on her phone. She was nervous and excited, and not afraid to let everyone know it. She looked up, blew the hair from her eyes, and gave everyone an update.

"One more minute."

Savannah made a soft little noise in the back of

her throat, not quite a whimper, not quite a sigh. Even she looked nervous, her face a little pale despite the color high on her cheeks. He squeezed her hand then pressed a kiss against her temple.

"You okay?"

She nodded. "I will be. Soon."

He brushed another kiss against her temple, ignoring the groan from Brooke and Isabelle. This was just a formality anyway. He already knew what the result was going to be, had known for a few weeks.

And so did Savannah.

"Okay, time's up." Isabelle jumped to her feet then froze. "Who's going to get it?"

Nobody moved, which struck him as oddly funny. He started laughing, choked it back when three identical expressions of indignation were leveled at him. He pushed to his feet, ignoring the pull in his knee, and moved toward the closed door. "I'll get it."

"But no peeking, Dad."

"I won't peek."

"Seriously, Dad, no peeking. That's cheating."

"He won't peek." Savannah looked up at him, a gentle smile on her face. No, he wouldn't peek. He didn't need to.

He went into the bathroom, grabbed the test stick off the counter, and walked out with it behind his back. Brooke and Isabelle jumped to their feet, excitement dancing in their eyes.

"Well? What does it say?"

"I don't know, you told me not to look."

"Then let us see!"

Brooke nudged Isabelle to the side, trying to look behind his back. "Come on, Dad, let us see."

He studied the two excited faces, biting back his

smile as Savannah moved to stand beside him. "What do you think? Should we let them see?"

"Guess we kind of have to, don't we?"

"Guys!" Isabelle drew the word out into three long syllables, sounding just like her sister had at that age. "This isn't fair. Stop teasing, let us see."

"On the count of three."

Brooke and Isabelle leaned closer, counting along with Savannah.

"One...two..."

"Three!" Aaron held the stick out. A second later, two excited screams filled the hallway, shattering his eardrums as Brooke and Isabelle grabbed each other and started jumping up and down.

"We're having a baby! We're having a baby!"

Aaron laughed then pulled Savannah into a hug and twirled her around. She grabbed onto his shoulders, her mouth clamping shut as she shook her head. He quickly put her down, his arms still around her, ready to carry her to the bathroom if she needed it. She shook her head again, smiled, and leaned against him.

"You peeked."

"No, I didn't."

"You already knew?"

He pressed his hand against the flat of her stomach and smiled. "Yeah. For a couple of weeks, the same as you."

Savannah closed her hand over his, her fingers trembling. "Are you okay with it?"

"I'm better than okay. I'm ecstatic."

"Not scared?"

"Scared? Me?" He kissed her, hard, then leaned back. "I'm beyond scared. I'm terrified. And I've never been happier."

Savannah laughed and reached up to cup his cheek with one hand. "I love you."

"I love you, too."

He kissed her again, long and deep, slow and warm.

Safe in the knowledge that he'd never have to worry about life passing him by again, not when he had his family with him.

Not when he had Savannah by his side.

###

Lisa B. Kamps

About the Author

Lisa B. Kamps is the author of the best-selling series *The Baltimore Banners*, featuring "…hard-hitting, heart-melting hockey players…" [USA Today], on and off the ice. Her *Firehouse Fourteen* series features hot and heroic firefighters who put more than their lives on the line and she's introduced a whole new team of hot hockey players who play hard and love even harder in her newest series, *The York Bombers*. *The Chesapeake Blades*—a romance series featuring women's hockey—recently launched with WINNING HARD.

Lisa currently lives in Maryland with her husband and two sons (who are mostly sorta-kinda out of the house), one very spoiled Border Collie, two cats with major attitude, several head of cattle, and entirely too many chickens to count. When she's not busy writing or chasing animals, she's cheering loudly for her favorite hockey team, the Washington Capitals—or going through withdrawal and waiting for October to roll back around!

Interested in reaching out to Lisa? She'd love to hear from you:

Website: www.LisaBKamps.com

Newsletter: http://www.lisabkamps.com/signup/

Email: LisaBKamps@gmail.com

Facebook: https://www.facebook.com/authorLisaBKamps

Kamps Korner Facebook Group: https://www.facebook.com/groups/1160217000707067/

BookBub: https://www.bookbub.com/authors/lisa-b-kamps

Goodreads: https://www.goodreads.com/LBKamps

Instagram: https://www.instagram.com/lbkamps/
Twitter: https://twitter.com/LBKamps

Amazon Author Page: http://www.amazon.com/author/lisabkamps

CROSSING THE LINE
The Baltimore Banners Book 1

Amber "AJ" Johnson is a freelance writer who has one chance of winning her dream-job as a full-time staffer: capture an interview with the very private goalie of Baltimore's hockey team, Alec Kolchak. But he's the one man who tries her patience, even as he brings to life a quiet passion she doesn't want to admit exists.

Alec has no desire to be interviewed--he never has, never will. But he finds himself a reluctant admirer of AJ's determination to get what she wants...and he certainly never counted on his attraction to her. In a fit of frustration, he accepts AJ's bet: if she can score just one goal on him in a practice shoot-out, he would not only agree to the interview, he would let her have full access to him for a month, 24/7.

It's a bet neither one of them wants to lose...and a bet neither one can afford to win. But when it comes time to take the shot, can either one of them cross the line?

Turn the page for an exciting peek at CROSSING THE LINE, available now.

"Oh my God, what have I done?" AJ muttered the phrase under her breath for the hundredth time. She wanted to rub her chest but she couldn't reach it under the thick pads now covering her. She wanted to go home and curl up in a dark corner and forget about the whole thing.

Me and my bright ideas.

"Are you going to be okay?"

AJ snapped her head up and looked at Ian. The poor guy had been given the job of helping her get dressed in the pads, and she almost felt sorry for him. Almost. Between her nervousness and the threat of an impending migraine, she was too preoccupied to muster much sympathy for anyone else right now.

"Yeah, I'm fine." She took a deep breath and stood, wobbling for only a second on the skates. This was not how she had imagined the bet going. When she cooked up the stupid idea, she had figured on having a few days to at least practice.

Well, not really. If she was honest with herself, she never even imagined that Alec would agree to it. But if he had, then she would have had a few days to practice.

So much for her imagination.

She took another deep breath then followed Ian from the locker room. It didn't take too long for her gait to even out and she muttered a thankful prayer. She only hoped that she didn't sprawl face-first as soon as she stepped on the ice.

Her right hand clenched around the stick, getting used to the feel of it, getting used to the fit of the bulky glove—which was too big to begin with. This would have been so much easier if all she had to do was put on a pair of skates. She had never considered the possibility of having to put all the gear on, right down to the helmet that was a heavy weight bearing down on her head.

She really needed to do something with her imagination and its lack of thinking things all the way through.

AJ took another deep breath when they finally reached the ice. She reached out to open the door but was stopped by Ian.

"Listen, AJ, I'm not even going to pretend I know what's going on or why you think you can do this, but I'll give you some advice. Shoot fast and low, and aim for the five and two holes—those are Alec's weak spots. The five hole is—"

"Between the legs, I know." AJ winced at the sharpness of her voice. Ian was only trying to help her. He had no reason to realize she knew anything about ice hockey, and not just because she liked to write about it. She offered him a smile to take the bite from her words then slammed the butt of the stick down against the door latch so it would swing open. Two steps later and she was standing on a solid sheet of thick ice.

AJ breathed deeply several times then slowly made her way to the other side of the rink, where Alec was nonchalantly leaning against the top post of the net talking to Nathan. They both watched as she skated up to them and came to a smooth stop. Alec's face was expressionless as he studied her, and she wondered what thoughts were going through his mind. Probably nothing she really wanted to know.

Nathan nodded at her, offering a small smile. She had to give the guy some credit for not laughing in her face when she asked his opinion on her idea. "Well, at least it looks like you've been on skates before. That's a plus."

AJ didn't say anything, just absently nodded in his direction. The carefree attitude she had been aiming for was destroyed by the helmet sliding down over her forehead. She pushed it back on her head then glanced at the five pucks lined neatly on the goal line. All she had to do was get one of them across. Just one.

She didn't have a chance.

She pushed the pessimistic thought to the back of her mind. "So, do I get a chance to warm up or take a practice shot?"

Alec sized her up then briskly shook his head. "No."

AJ swallowed and glanced at the pucks, then back at Alec. "Alrighty then. A man of few words. That's what I like about you, Kolchak." AJ though he might have cracked a smile behind his mask but she couldn't be sure. She sighed and leaned on her stick, trying to look casual and hoping it didn't slip out from under her and send her sprawling. "So, what are the rules?"

"Simple. You get five chances to shoot. If you score, you win. If you don't, I win." Alec swept the pucks to the side with the blade of his stick so Nathan could pick them up. She followed the moves with her eyes and tried to ignore the pounding in her chest.

She had so much riding on this. Something told her that Alec was dead serious about being left alone if she lost. It had been a stupid idea, and she wondered if she would have had better luck at trying to wear him down the old-fashioned way.

She studied his posture and decided probably not. He had been mostly patient with her up to this point, but even she knew he would have reached his limit soon.

"All or nothing, then. Fair enough. So, are you ready?"

AJ didn't hear his response but thought it was probably something sarcastic. She sighed then turned to follow Nathan to the center line, her heart beating too fast as her feet glided across the ice. She shrugged her shoulders, trying to readjust the bulk of the pads, and watched as Nathan lined the pucks up.

He finished then straightened and faced her, an unreadable expression on his face. He finally grinned and shook his head.

"I have no idea if you know what you're doing or not, but good luck. You're going to need it."

"Gee, thanks."

Nathan walked across the ice to the bench and leaned against the outer boards, joining a few of the other players gathered there. AJ wished they were gone, that they had something better to do than stand around and watch her make a fool of herself.

Well, she had brought it on herself.

She closed her eyes and inhaled deeply, pushing everything from her mind except what she was about to do. When she opened her eyes again, her gaze was on the first puck. Heavy, solid...nothing more than a slab of black rubber...

Okay, so she wasn't going to have any luck becoming one with the puck. Stupid idea. AJ had never understood that whole Zen thing anyway.

She swallowed and began skating in small circles, testing her ankles as she turned first one way then another, testing the stick as she swept it back and forth across the ice in front of her. Not too bad. Maybe she hadn't forgotten—

"Sometime today would be nice!"

AJ winced at the sarcasm in Alec's voice and wished she had some kind of comeback for him. Instead she mumbled to herself and got into position behind the first puck. She didn't even look up to see if he was ready. Didn't ask if it was okay to start, she just pushed off hard and skated, the stick out in front of her.

This was her one shot, she couldn't blow it.

WINNING HARD
The Chesapeake Blades Book 1

Taylor LeBlanc has hockey in her blood and the trophies and medals to prove it. Her dreams of playing pro come to an end when the only place for her to go is the newly-formed not-really-pro women's team, the Chesapeake Blades. It's not quite what she had in mind, but it's a start—except half the team is convinced she's receiving special treatment because her step-dad used to be the head coach for the Baltimore Banners and the team's PR Director wants to use her in his marketing campaign. To make matters worse, the PR Director is none other than her childhood nemesis, Chuckie-the-fart--who happens to be all grown-up and too gorgeous for his own good.

Charles Dawson never had the drive or the heart to follow hockey out of childhood. What he does have is ambition and passion—two things he needs in abundance to successfully market the brand-new women's hockey team to a less-than-enthusiastic demographic. He also needs patience—something that's in short supply when he's forced to deal with the one woman who has the uncanny ability to make him feel like the bumbling, uncoordinated, and socially awkward thirteen-year-old boy he used to be. Taylor isn't the mouthy little tomboy he remembers and sparks fly between the two, igniting an attraction that makes both of their lives unbearable when it becomes harder to ignore.

Taylor and Charles both want to win, but at what cost? Are they willing to trample every obstacle in their way--especially when the biggest obstacle could be the one thing they both need more than any trophy or medal?

Turn the page for a preview of WINNING HARD, the launch title of The Chesapeake Blades, now available.

PLAYING IT SAFE

Winners never quit and quitters never win.

The old adage ran through Charles Dawson's mind, over and over, picking up speed and threatening to split his skull wide open. Would anyone notice?

Considering six sets of eyes were trained on him—yeah, probably.

Not for the first time, he asked himself what the hell he'd gotten into this time. Yes, he was good at marketing. *Damn* good. But he wasn't a miracle worker and he was pretty sure that's what the Chesapeake Blades needed: a miracle worker.

Not just the Blades—the whole damn league. But the league wasn't his problem. Thank God. He was going to have enough of a problem marketing the fledgling team. Let someone else worry about the league, that one wasn't on him.

Not yet, anyway.

And not that it mattered. The two went hand-in-hand, no matter how many times he tried to convince himself otherwise.

Quitters never win.

No, they didn't. But was running for the lifeboats to escape a sinking ship really the same as quitting? Some would say it was simply a question of semantics.

And he wasn't about to split hairs with the group gathered in front of him, watching him like he was their last hope. Like *he* was their lifeboat.

God help them all.

James Murphy, the majority owner of the Chesapeake Blades, glanced down at the colorful presentation folder resting on the shiny desk in front of him. Bushy gray brows pulled low over steely eyes and the thin chest puffed out in importance. Charles knew he was judging the man harshly—Murphy really did have good intentions as far as the team was concerned. Although why in the hell he thought buying into the Blades was a sound investment was anyone's guess.

Money to burn, maybe? A tax write-off? Or maybe the man wanted to be part of something bigger. Hell, maybe he was just living out a childhood fantasy and nurturing dreams of the imagined glitz and glamor of owning a sports team. Charles didn't know and he didn't really care. He didn't deal with dreams and fantasies. He was here to do a job, nothing more.

Damn shame that this job was turning into a major headache that just might signal the end of an otherwise prosperous career.

"Did you have any of the girls in mind, Chuck?"

Charles inwardly winced at the nickname. Christ, he hated that name. It brought back memories of his awkward childhood, reminding him of those times when he'd been a young bumbling teenager who was a little too round and a little too clumsy to really fit in. A late-bloomer, his mother always said—usually as she was ushering him from one sport or activity to another, anxious for him to find a place to fit in and make friends.

Charles had finally grown out of the baby fat *and* the awkwardness and found his own footing, one that had nothing to do with sports. At least, not the way his mother had hoped.

The irony of his new position as Director of Marketing and Public Relations for the Chesapeake Blades wasn't lost on him. He would have laughed if anyone had told him a year ago that he'd be trying to market a women's hockey team.

A *women's* hockey team. It boggled the mind. But

here he was, trying to do the impossible in a market that had a real hockey team —the Baltimore Banners— playing fifteen minutes away. It was doomed for failure before it even started.

But if he could make it successful? Well now, wouldn't that be something? And that's what excited him—the challenge. *That* was why he'd agreed to this job, in spite of the lower salary and its dismal chance of success.

Because sometimes the challenge was everything.

Charles grabbed the last few remaining sheets and placed them in a tidy pile before putting them back in the worn leather bag he always carried. His gaze wandered around the table, knowing the faces looking back at him were still waiting for an answer.

Knowing they were all looking to him for a miracle.

He hoisted the bag over his shoulder then reached up to straighten the silk tie before turning back to Murphy. "No, I don't have any of the women in mind. I'd like to see them on the ice first. Get a feel for their presence and personality."

"I'd think that reading their bios would have helped with that."

"I didn't read their bios."

Stark silence greeted his announcement, just as he knew it would. Murphy glanced around the table then pinned Charles with his steely gaze, his eyebrows lowering even more. "You haven't read their bios?"

"No. I don't want to be swayed by words on paper. There's too much riding on this."

"I'm sorry, Chuck, but I'm a little confused. And I know I'm not alone. We made sure you had those bios two weeks ago so you could come up with a comprehensive plan. We've already lost valuable time. Do you mean to tell me you don't have any idea of which of the girls you even want to use for this marketing plan of yours?"

"You lost valuable time by bringing in someone who had no idea what they were doing. And while I might be late to the party, I can assure you—I know what I'm doing." Charles shifted the strap against his shoulder then leaned forward, meeting Murphy's stare with an intent one of his own.

"These women can have the most spectacular bio in the world. They could have a list of world cups and trophies and medals and awards by their name. None of it means anything if they don't have that spark and enthusiasm that's going to draw in the crowds you want and need. I don't want the words, James. I want the excitement. The enthusiasm. The spark."

Had he pushed too far? Charles held his breath, waiting for Murphy's reaction. The man wasn't a fool, even if his investment in a women's hockey team was questionable at best. Would he bluster at being questioned? Or would he let Charles do the job he had hired him to do?

Murphy pulled his gaze away and sat back in the leather chair, a thoughtful frown on his face. A tense minute stretched into two, then three and four, before the older man finally nodded. "Fair enough. We brought you in to do the job because you're damn good at it. We'll let you do things your way."

Charles didn't miss the silent *for now* tacked at the end of the sentence. Fair enough, just like Murphy had said. They both had jobs to do, jobs with the same end goal: winning.

"It's my understanding that the team is still

downstairs practicing?"

Murphy glanced at his watch then nodded. "For another half hour, yes."

"I'd like to watch, if you don't mind."

"I'm sure that won't be a problem." Murphy pushed out of the chair, signaling an end to the meeting. He clapped his hand around Charles' shoulder then motioned toward the door. "Let's go introduce you to the girls, Chuck."

"James, do yourself a favor—stop calling them *girls*."

"But that's what they are. Every single one of them is young enough to be my granddaughter."

"That may be, but you need to stop. They're *women*. And it's a *women's* hockey team and a *women's* hockey league. I'm going to have a hard enough time getting the market to take them seriously—I don't need you making my job harder."

Charles thought maybe he had gone too far this time because Murphy straightened his lean form and leveled another stare at him. In the end, he said nothing, just clamped his mouth into a thin line and nodded before leading Charles out into the carpeted hallway.

The superficial opulence of the conference room and office came to an abrupt halt as soon as they entered the hallway leading back to the rink. The front office had been designed to impress. To scream *success* and assure visitors—what few there were—that the team was much more than a passing fancy. But it was nothing more than an image, one that disappeared as soon as you pushed through the second set of doors leading to the ice.

The smell of sweat and stagnant water hit him as

soon as they pushed through doors. The air was damp and cold, from both the inside temperature and the large sheet of ice encased by the faded boards and scratched sheets of plexiglass. Charles halted, his eyes adjusting to the dim light as childhood memories assaulted him.

He'd played hockey for three years, mostly because his mother had been convinced he needed to play sports. Football, basketball. Soccer. Baseball. He'd done them all. But none of them had been his *thing*, not when he had been more interested in analyzing and studying. In trying to figure out ways to create something better out of something that was already there. In dreaming of ways to make things bigger and better. It was something his mother had never understood, not until his first job out of college.

Maybe not even then.

But out of all the sports he'd been forced to play, hockey held the most memories. The scratch of blades against ice. The burn of muscles rarely used. The rush of wind as he raced for a puck that he was never quite fast enough to get. The smell—God, just the smell was enough to send him hurtling back in time.

He brushed off the memories and followed Murphy along the boards, the leather bag slapping against his hip with each step. Shouts and grunts echoed in the chilled air around them. Two players crashed against the boards with a hollow thud, each fighting for the puck. Charles paused, watching them. The masks of their helmets hid most of their faces, but they couldn't hide the intensity, the *desire*, that burned through them.

It was the same intensity and desire he'd seen on the face of every professional player in every professional game he'd ever watched, no matter what the sport. That had to be a good sign, right?

"Fuck."

One of the girls—no, *women*, he was just as bad as Murphy—muttered the curse as the puck shot free. Both women tore off after it, sweaty ponytails swinging against their backs. Charles bit back a grin then wondered if he'd have to give a lecture on appropriate language before the season started. Hopefully it wouldn't come to that. And if it did...well, then he'd let the coach handle it.

Murphy paused at the end of the bleachers. "Did you want Coach Reynolds to call them over?"

"No, not yet. I just want to watch. Make a few notes." Charles headed to the top of the bleachers then took a seat and grabbed a pen and small notebook from his bag. No decisions would be made today—it was too early. But he wanted this time just to watch. To study. To see if any of the women stood out. To see if any of them had that certain spark, that little bit of magic that would *pop* and make them stand out.

That little extra something that he could build on and use to promote the team.

He knew exactly what he was looking for: charisma. Charm. And yes, even a little bit of sex appeal. It was sexist—he'd be the first to admit it. But physical looks would go a long way in helping to market the team, at least to start. Attractive and athletic, attributes that would entice the market's demographic. Something to hook their initial interest then keep the crowd coming back.

He hoped. A lot of it would depend on the team itself, as a whole, and whether or not they were any good.

He had a few backup plans, just in case. But he could worry about that later. Right now, he needed to get the crowd in the door. This would have been so much easier if he had been called in right from the beginning, instead of joining the front office two months before the season started.

That just made it more of a challenge, and a challenge is what he hungered for. As long as he kept reminding himself of that, he'd be fine.

Maybe.

A shrill whistle split the chilled air, startling him from the hasty notes he was scribbling. The women skated toward the door, removing helmets and juggling sticks as they headed toward the coach. He noticed the sweaty faces, red from exertion, tired but still excited from what they were doing. Would the excitement last, once the season started? God, he hoped so. It would make his job that much easier.

He jotted down a few final notes then flipped to another page and jotted down five different numbers. He tore the sheet from the notebook then made his way down the bleachers over to where Murphy was standing.

The older man glanced down at the small sheet of paper then back at Charles. "What's this?"

"A start. I'd like to see these players once the coach is finished with them."

"We can take care of that now." Murphy grabbed him by the elbow and led him over to the crowd of players huddled around Coach Reynolds. Charles winced when the older man interrupted the coach, saying something to her in a low tone as he pushed the sheet of paper into her hand. The coach frowned, looked down at the paper, then nodded.

"Wiley, Riegler, Woodhouse, Baldwin, and LeBlanc. Mr. Murphy would like to see you. Everyone else, hit the showers."

Five women looked over with varying expressions of curiosity, their voices low and muted as they made their way over to where he and Murphy were standing. Charles casually studied them, his gaze moving from one to the other to the other, analyzing his initial gut reactions to each.

A tall blonde with dimples.

A petite woman with a short mop of black curls and smiling brown eyes.

Another blonde, her platinum-streaked hair pulled back into a ponytail that didn't quite contain the thick waves.

A red-head, with a full pouty mouth and sculpted brows arched over clear green eyes.

But it was the fifth player that drew his attention. Number 67. Long hair, a mix of light brown and honey blonde, hung down her back, with darker strands clinging to her flushed and damp face. Wide eyes the color of whiskey. A crooked smile that made her look like she knew a secret that you'd pay anything to learn—or that she was up to no good. There was something about her—

"Girls, this is our new PR Director, Chuck Dawson. I want you to pay attention to what he says and help him out." Murphy stepped back then waved his hand, turning things over to him.

Charles stepped forward, his gaze darting back to Number 67. Why was she studying him that way? With her head tilted to the side and those clear amber eyes so intently focused on him? He forced himself to look away, told himself it was nothing more than curiosity, and pasted a smile to his face.

"Actually, you can call me *Charles*, not *Chuck*—"

Number 67 laughed, the sound clear and musical, then stepped forward. For a split-second, Charles thought she was ready to wrap him in a big hug—one he instinctively knew he wouldn't step away from.

And then she spoke and all thoughts of hugs—and every other inappropriate thought that had been swimming around in his muddled brain—vanished.

"OhmyGod, it really *is* you. Chuckie-the-fart!"

Made in the USA
Middletown, DE
07 September 2019